Hidden Song

Sister Blue Thread Series
Linda J. Reinhardt

* * *

Hidden Song
Book One
Silenced Song
Book Two
Lost Song
Book Three

Other Books to Treasure

* * *

Christmas Classics
Always Home for Christmas
Once Upon a Christmas
20 short stories to bring delight,
reverence, and meaning to the season
Sharon Bernash Smith, Rosanne Croft, Linda J. Reinhardt

Starry, Starry, Christmas Night
15 stories to prepare your heart for the King
Sharon Bernash Smith & Linda J. Reinhardt

The McLeod Family Saga
Like a Bird Wanders
Book One
Sharon Bernash Smith, Rosanne Croft, Linda J. Reinhardt

SISTER BLUE THREAD
1

Hidden Song

LINDA J. REINHARDT

Waterford, Virginia

Hidden Song

Published in the U.S. by:
OakTara Publishers, P.O. Box 8, Waterford, VA 20197
www.oaktara.com

Cover design by Yvonne Parks at www.pearcreative.ca
Cover image © thinkstockphotos.ca: little girl looking at apple/Dainis Eglavs
Author photo © 2011 Paul, Stephen Paul Photography

Copyright © 2012 by Linda J. Reinhardt. All rights reserved.

Scripture quotations are taken from the King James Version of the Bible. Public domain.

ISBN: 978-1-60290-357-9

Hidden Song is a work of fiction. References to real people, events, establishments, organizations, or locales are intended only to provide a sense of authenticity and are used fictitiously. All other characters, incidents, and dialogue are drawn from the author's imagination.

Printed in the U.S.A.

* * *

Dedicated to those
up against the choice,
have made the choice,
and had no choice

Acknowledgments

I'd first like to thank Jesus for blessing me with the passion to tell, read, and watch a story, and for circling me with support through my friends and family.

Ben, within the relationship of marriage, you bring a servant leadership, friendship, loyalty, and sacrifices beyond what I ever could have dreamed. In our relationship I live out the Bible verse proclaiming God answers our prayers exceedingly, abundantly, above all we could ever ask or think. Thank you for all of the years of sacrifice so I can follow a dream, a call. I love you and am so blessed to have you as my forever friend.

Sarrah, you are such a powerful prayer warrior, listening to the leading of the Holy Spirit, I am so grateful for your prayers for the Sister Blue Thread project. Thank you for all the times you keep busy so I can write. You are a great helper. I love you, Sunshine.

Cal and Margaret (Dad and Mom), thank you for all the times you picked up Sarrah from school. (She had so much fun during those times.) And for the times you listen and encourage me along the path, especially when I get discouraged. And thank you, my special mom, for all the hard work you did with me on the final proofing. I had fun working and chatting with you.

Wanda, you're the original Sister Blue Thread, my sister in family, in the Lord, and sister of the heart. Your support of my family and my dreams is beyond incredible. You've been a beacon of light to us in stormy weather. I love the memory of those long *hard* walks and all that God works out in our lives. You've listened and read my stories for years, and I've always known you're available so I can bounce things off of you. Thank you.

Now to all my other Sister Blue Threads: Brenda, not only were you at the birth of my darling Sarrah, you were at the birth of this book, praying this project through step by step just like you did during labor, for years. You listened, encouraged, and fought for my dream in prayer. Thank you, thank you, thank you for your faithfulness to pray, listen, and encourage me.

My brothers, Wayne and Gary Swanson, who are Blue Threads to me, too. I have the best brothers ever!

For the Blue Threads who were on the book prayer team, Chris White, Joan Alfsen, Linda Litke, Lorinda Lords, Michelle Apodacha, Anna Lund,

Shelby Bailey, and Heidi Timm, faithful warriors going into the presence of the Holy One to pray this project through so many battles. Thank you.

Thank you, Elizabeth Blankenship, for proofreading. Thank you, Sharon Bernash Smith and Sylvia Stewart, and my cousin, Sue Hotelling, for your critiquing. You all need to buy stock in the red pen market. I love you!

Sharon, since our first phone call almost seven years ago, I have been blessed by our relationship. Truly you have helped guide me in the craft of honing the gift of writing. It has paid off to listen to you. We've had such fun times and experienced some wonderful steps together. I'm so blessed to have a Sister Blue Thread like you.

Rosanne, I still remember the first time you read this story and you wanted to get to know Trudy better and in a deeper level. I'd skimmed right over letting the reader into her heart, and you helped me to understand why it was easier for me to write in that way. Thank you for your honesty and the years of friendship and Sister Blue Thread moments.

Thank you, Katrina Baxter, for the play date arrangement in order to have time to write during the day, instead of the wee hours of the morning or late at night.

Thanks to the sisters who heard, or read, or just supported me—Darlene Holt, Anna Lund, Bilinda Taylor, Angie Taylor, Connie Freeman, Lorinda Cheek, AJ Lane, Sally Freeze, Carol Wilson, Nancy Garrett. Your friendship and support is incredible in my life. To any Sister Blue Threads I may have left out, it is not intentional. Thank you for being there, along the road, to encourage me. I pray you will be blessed.

Foreword

As the Head Editor of *Today's Christian Woman* magazine for seven years, and also the Executive Editor of *Virtue* magazine, I was privileged to be able to hear the hearts of millions of women who have gone through the struggles of surprise pregnancy, unwed pregnancy, and post-abortion trauma. So many have made "choices" they now wished every day they could change. That woman may be you; it may be your friend; it may be your neighbor; it may be the person sitting next to you right now.

None of us are beyond the grace of God, and we all need it immeasurably. I'm grateful for women like Linda J. Reinhardt, who have a passion to minister to hurting women with *Hidden Songs,* and for their sensitive ability to reach out, comfort, encourage, and provide loving guidance to those who are in the midst of the choice and those who are living with the aftermath of that choice.

As an adoptive mom myself, I will be eternally grateful for the woman who courageously chose to carry my daughter to term and to make the choice to give her the opportunity to live and become the difference maker she already is in the world.

May we women truly become Sister Blue Threads to each other—never judging, but always understanding, supporting, and kindly asking the question that tends to put all of life in perspective: "What will matter most in the long-term?"

RAMONA CRAMER TUCKER
Former Editor, *Today's Christian Woman,* Executive Editor, *Virtue*
(Christianity Today, International)

1

Trudy shivered, clutching a thin blanket tight around her shoulders, rocking in a back-and-forth motion for comfort. The cold penetrated deep to her very soul. A careful glance around showed a sterile impersonal room. The machine positioned at the end of the bed sent a creepy feeling crawling up her spine.

I wonder how many other girls have sat here staring at this thing?

The slow ticking of the clock grated on her nerves. *How much longer do I have to wait?* She brought the cover up to hide part of her face, then peeked cautiously toward the door, fearing someone might actually walked through it.

Emotions threatened to overwhelm her. Frustrated, she pushed her long strawberry-blond hair back when tears started to roll down her cheeks. *I'm so scared! I wish Randy was here with me instead of staying in the waiting room.*

Faint sounds caught her attention. *What's that noise? It must be from outside. I can't see out the window from here.* Grabbing the blanket, she climbed down from the bed. The cold floor against her bare feet matched the chill in her heart.

Unlatching the lock on the window, she pushed up on it. *Ugh—when's the last time this thing was opened?* It moved just enough to fill the room with the excited screams and laughter of children. It knocked the breath right out of her. Gulping for air, her heart pounding in her ears, she desired to slam the window back down but was frozen in place. It was almost more than she could bear as the happy scene of the park unfolded.

Boys and girls ran, chased dogs, and pushed one another on swings. Two little girls held hands, their long ponytails blowing in the wind, and hopped onto the swings.

"I bet I can jump farther than you," one of them called out.

"Oh no, you can't," the other replied. Together they kicked and pushed, higher and higher, until one jumped out of her seat from midair with a squeal of delight. The other followed, landing close by.

"I won!" the first girl said, claiming victory.

Over and over the two played the game.

Sweet memories drifted through Trudy's mind of childhood days spent enjoying the same thing with her best friend, Brenda. The two had been inseparable. What fun they used to have playing together and dreaming.

One afternoon was spent hidden away in Trudy's grandma's attic, making plans to marry best friends when they grew up.

"We'll live on the same street," Brenda said.

"Next-door neighbors," Trudy added.

We were so silly. We hardly talk now.

She leaned her head against the window frame. Everything had happened so fast once she found out she was pregnant. Heat rose in her face, recalling what led her to take a test....

* * *

Her mom was heading out the door when Trudy bumped into her in the hallway.

"Trudy, I'm on my way to get some groceries. Is there anything you need? I checked the bathroom to see if you needed sanitary napkins, but you already had some in the cupboard. Did you pick some up?"

Trudy had only shaken her head, rapidly calculating the days since her last period. *I should have had my period a week ago. No...had it been over a month, two?*

Her mom continued to talk, while Trudy, stomach fluttering, felt hot all over and headed for her room.

I'm LATE!

Quietly shutting her bedroom door, she slid to the floor.

Am I pregnant? No. I can't be. How stupid is that thought? Leaning her head on her knees, she wrapped both hands around her head. *Of course I could be pregnant. Randy and I had sex. Ohhh...this cannot be happening! What am I going to do? I need to talk to someone...Brenda?*

No! All bridges had been burned with her best friend soon after she started dating Randy. She knew Brenda didn't approve, so Trudy had made a choice between the two of them. Randy had won. She couldn't imagine life without him.

Grandma? Never—it would break her heart! She would be so disappointed in me. Besides, I've been avoiding her too.

After dinner she borrowed her parents' car. She couldn't stand to wait and wonder. She had to get a pregnancy test. It was just her luck that some girls from school had walked up to chitchat while she was standing in the checkout line. Grabbing a towel from a nearby display, she covered the test packet. Sweat dripped down her arms as the girls continued to talk. She was next to be waited on. *Please leave...leave...please. What am I going to say if they see the test?*

Soon it was her turn to pay.

"So, I guess I'll see you tomorrow at school," Trudy said with a smile and a short wave before turning toward the cashier.

"Uh, yeah, okay, see you tomorrow, Trudy."

Breathing a sigh of relief, she didn't bother to look back over her shoulder to see where the girls had gone.

When she got home her parents were sitting in the living room.

"Hi, honey! Did you get what you needed at the store?"

"Yeah, Mom." Trudy stretched and did a big yawn, walking toward the stairs. "I'm really tired. I think I'll go to bed. 'Night."

"Hey, where's a hug?"

"Sorry." Trudy put her bag down before going over to hug both parents, then slipped up the stairs as quick as she could to the safety of her room.

The package came with two tests; she read the directions. The best time to take it was in the morning. *Well, I can't wait that long. I'll do one now and the other one in the morning.*

It was the longest three minutes she'd ever experienced. According to the directions the test strip had to face down on a flat surface. She was tempted to push the test to the edge of the counter to peek at it but was afraid of causing it to fall onto the floor. The secondhand slowly skipped the final seconds before she reached over to look at the results—two dark pink lines.

Pregnant.

That night was the darkest, loneliest, and most scary she'd ever experienced. Most of it was spent staring out the bedroom window. Sleep finally took over as the birds sang their wake-up songs.

The morning test had the same result. Furious, she threw it into the garbage can. She fell across her bed, pounding her fist against the mattress until she fell asleep again, exhausted.

Her mom woke her up holding the phone in her hand. It was Randy.

"Randy, you have to come over, now. We need to talk!"

"What's going on, Tru? Why not talk to me now?"

"No, I need you to come here right away. I'll meet you outside."

"What's the big deal?"

"Randy, I need you here now," she said firmly, then hung up the phone before he could respond.

She waited in front for him to arrive. When she saw his car coming down the road, she ran to the end of the driveway, grabbed at the door handle, and hopped in as the car skidded to a stop.

"Hey, what's the matter with you, Tru?" Randy reached over and tickled her arm.

Hands shaking, she unclasped her fist and revealed the test. "Look!" She gulped, watching for his reaction.

"This is a joke…right?" He smiled at her tentatively.

She shook her head, frowning. She jumped when his hand pounded the steering wheel.

"How could you let this happen?" he yelled, hitting the steering wheel again.

"Me?" Trudy asked, astonished that he would put the blame all on her.

"You should've been on birth control or something! Now what are we going to do? I'm going to college. I am not giving up my scholarship! My dad would flip," he said between clenched teeth. "Trudy, you've got to take care of this!"

"Uh, Randy, I am still back at the *me* question. When did this become all about *me?* And that *I* have to take care of this? Excuse me! But you were just as involved in this as I was. As a matter of fact, if fingers are to be pointed, then I'd point them at you, Mr. Experienced. You're the one with the list of women in your past. I don't have a list. You're the only one I've ever loved, so don't be putting all of this on me. You could've helped me figure some of this stuff out!" Trudy spewed, furious.

He has a lot of nerve. I've just shown him a positive pregnancy test and all he cares about is getting in trouble with his dad and keeping his scholarship. I'd like to spit in his face.

"Okay, fine. You're right. I'm just as responsible as you, but it doesn't change the fact that we have to take care of this problem. I have some savings. Just call around and make an appointment to have an abortion. Then we can go on with our lives, and no one will have to know anything about it." Randy put his arm around her and pulled her close. "I'm sorry, I was only thinking of myself, but honestly, Trudy, think of what it would do to your mom and dad…worse yet, how your grandma would feel. We can't do that to our families," he said in a consoling whisper next to her ear.

Although it didn't feel right, she'd agreed to make the appointment….

* * *

That had been a week ago and now here she was, still in shock and with a numb heart. *How could Randy be so indifferent?*

She turned back to the room and glanced around. *What's that weird contraption at the foot of the bed? Is that what the doctor uses to do the abortion?* Backing up closer to the wall and away from it, she stole another peek outside. *I wonder if people in the park know what happens on the other side of the wall? What would the children think? What if someone had aborted those children?*

"Abort them." The words came out slow. Something stirred in her heart. *They wouldn't be playing in the park. Their laughter wouldn't be echoing in this room.*

A sudden desire hit hard. *I wish I could be the way I was before Randy...innocent, walking in my faith, close to my family and friends.* The old Trudy wouldn't even consider being in a place like this. *What has happened to me? How did I get here?*

* * *

Before she started to date Randy, Trudy had been very involved with her church, especially the youth group. She had given her life to the Lord at a very young age and loved Jesus with all her heart and soul. Then Randy came into her life, and day-by-day she stopped looking to the Lord and lived only for Randy. She still went to church, but her mind wasn't there half the time. It was busy thinking of moments they had spent together.

She'd used to take time to pray and read her Bible at night. Now, if she wasn't with Randy, she would daydream about him and write letters. There was no time to spend with the Lord like before.

That wasn't the only thing. One day she'd stopped listening to the still small voice in her heart. She'd actually allowed Randy to make love to her one afternoon when his parents weren't at home. She had purposely ignored the tugging from the Holy Spirit that day and didn't put a stop to what they were doing. Randy was everything to her. Although he hadn't asked her yet, she planned to marry him someday, so she wanted to give him all...body and soul.

For sure, ignoring the Holy Spirit didn't happen overnight. The first time they kissed with passion, tingling sensations went throughout her body while a clear warning went through her mind. She knew better. Her body was the temple of the Holy Spirit. She was quick to draw away from Randy. He didn't understand when she explained why, but he respected her decision.

After that, he refrained from touching her at all, not even holding her hand. It drove her crazy. She at least wanted him to show some signs of affection.

Then one night, a couple weeks later, he brought her home and kissed her good-bye. She wrapped her arms around his neck, drawing him close. His kisses heated up, and she thoroughly enjoyed them. Then his hand started to move all over her body. Startled, she'd backed away.

Randy was frustrated she had stopped him, but she'd heard God and held her ground.

Randy was distant for a few days at school and didn't call her at night. *Is he going to break up with me? Why did I freak out like that and stop him? It wasn't as though we were having sex. We had our clothes on, and he didn't even try to go under my clothes. Maybe I'm paranoid! Did I really hear the voice of the Holy Spirit? Maybe I was just afraid!*

Finally, he called and asked her to come over to watch a movie. When she arrived and discovered they were alone, she took the initiative and kissed him with passion. She could feel him holding back for a moment; then he joined in.

It was so confusing. Trudy had felt her body respond to his touch, yet her heart and mind were telling her it was wrong. *This is so wonderful. How can it be wrong?* She ignored the restraining thoughts and gave into his caresses.

But she couldn't ignore the clear voice telling her to stop when she realized they were about to actually make love. *How did we get this far? When did our clothes come off?*

She pushed at Randy. He didn't understand at first, so she started to struggle. "Randy, stop! We can't do this! Randy!" Trudy yelled.

Randy sat up. Trudy rolled off the couch and grabbed her shirt, clutching it in front of her. She was standing naked in front of Randy. *How did this happen?*

"Randy, I don't know how this happened, but it shouldn't have. I…" Trudy grabbed her clothes out of the pile on the floor. Her hands trembled. Awkwardly, she fumbled, using the clothing for cover while trying to put them on at the same time.

Randy walked over to her.

She shut her eyes. *How can he do that? He's naked! Oh, Lord, what have I done?*

When he reached out, she turned and ran to the bathroom down the hall, afraid he would follow. *What if his parents came home!*

She looked in the mirror after she'd dressed. *I have to go back and face him before I leave.* Fear gripped her heart. *Will this be the final straw? Will he leave me and never come back? I can't blame him. I led him on, only to stop at the last minute. Oh, I'm such an idiot!*

Cautiously opening the bathroom door, she inched down the hallway until she stood at the doorway to the family room. He was dressed, busy putting pillows on the couch, and didn't look up when she entered the room.

"I'm sorry, Randy. I never intended for things to...," she started.

He cut her off. "Trudy, I don't have time for the games you like to play. We need to get things straight between us. I've never been with someone as innocent as you, so a decision needs to be made. Are we, or are we not going to have sex?"

Her heart shattered into a bunch of little pieces. He didn't sound like he thought she was very special. It sounded more like they were deciding whether or not to go to a movie.

Trudy turned to leave, embarrassed and hurt. Tears spilled over when she closed the door to her car. *Why didn't he try to stop me and apologize? I thought he loved me!*

Butterflies were making a ruckus in her stomach when she gained the courage to call Randy the next evening. *I can't imagine being without him.* The conversation was brief. He was on his way out to a party with guys from the gang he used to hang out with before they started dating. Fear gripped her throat—his old girlfriends were in that gang. Desperate, she tried to get him to come over and spend some time together, but he said he "needed space."

After a week of being ignored, Trudy had had enough. She asked him for a ride home after school.

"I have plans, Tru. Sorry, but I don't have time to stop over at your house." He turned away and slammed the car door.

He drove out of the parking lot while she was getting on the bus. She could only imagine what other kids were saying when they saw Randy get in his car alone.

That afternoon she went to his house. With trembling hands she knocked on the door, determined to know whether he loved her or not. She didn't want to lose him and would do anything to stay with him. Her heart leapt when the door opened. He gave her his only-for-her smile.

"Can we talk things over?" she asked. She discovered he'd been wrestling with the same emotions she had been.

"I figured we'd break up after what happened the other day. I mean...you left without saying good-bye," Randy said quietly.

"You never stopped me! I didn't know what to do. You acted like you didn't even care."

"*I* acted like I didn't care? What about you? Do you really care about me?" Randy asked.

"What would make you ask me that?"

"Every time I start to show how much I love you, you stop me...us. Don't you love me that way? You're the only one for me, Trudy. I want us to be together forever." He put his arm around her shoulder, drawing her near. "I've never felt this way before."

Trudy smiled. *Why didn't I just talk to him the other day instead of running out the door?* "I'm still confused, Randy. Why didn't you talk to me this week if you love me so much?"

"I figured I'd get hurt, so I stayed away." He gave her hair a gentle tug. "It was *so* hard to stay away from you."

How could I have hurt him that way? Laying her head on his chest, she sighed. He loved her as much as she loved him. He wanted to be with her forever. This time when she felt the familiar caress of his hand, she didn't panic but enjoyed the tender touch. She lifted her face and was met with one of his tender kisses.

Lifting Trudy up into his arms, he carried her to his room and gently placed her on the bed. Staring intently into her eyes, he removed his shirt. Her heart pounded as he slowly leaned down to kiss her once again.

There was no stopping this time. *We'll be together forever. Someday I will marry him. This is only the beginning for the two of us as one.*

Afterward, she lay wrapped in his arms as he slept. She felt uncomfortable. Slipping out of bed, careful to not wake him, she grabbed the pile of clothes from the floor and headed for the bathroom to clean herself as best as she could without taking a shower.

She panicked when she saw blood. Reality hit her. *I'm not a virgin!* She stared at the stain on the towel. Her mom had told her about the special gift a wife could give her husband—the one God had made just for her. On their wedding night, she'd be able to give him a gift that could only be given once.

My gift is gone!

Did Randy know the value of what she'd given him today? Did he realize how special he was to her? So special that she'd given up her virginity?

Thoughts of how Eve must have felt after she'd taken the bite from the apple filled her mind. There was no turning back. The choice was permanent—a choice against God's plan for her life. Had Eve felt this lost? Did the world suddenly look like a cold, dark, lonely place to her, too?

How would she face her parents, her grandma, and Brenda? Would they know what she'd done? Would she be able to pretend to be the innocent girl they loved? Suddenly she was angry. *Who are they to put so much pressure on me about how I should or shouldn't act? I love Randy. No matter what others think, I'll do anything so we can be together. It's none of their business what we do in private.* She closed her eyes tight for a moment. *This is my life.*

Determined, she ran out of the bathroom back to Randy's room. Ignoring the convicting, gentle voice in her heart that was all too familiar, she climbed into the bed and snuggled up close to the man of her dreams....

* * *

Trudy was unable to pull away from watching the children play. *Why did I run from the Holy Spirit? Why did I keep going down a path that was so lonely and miserable?*

Her stomach churned, recalling the lie she had been living since that day. She had spent countless hours alone at Randy's house while his parents were gone. Her parents believed she was spending time with him in group functions. She had gotten pretty good at telling them about the wonderful activities the two of them had been busy doing. They had no reason to doubt her; she was their Trudy. They were so proud of her and had always trusted her. She sighed.

Little did they know how miserable their daughter was. She hated lying to them but told herself it was because of their narrow-minded thinking. She put aside what the Bible said about sex outside of marriage. They would never understand the beautiful gift of love God had given to Randy and her.

She frowned. *I've felt so insecure lately, I can't even stand it when Randy says hello to another girl.* When Randy would tell her to chill out, Trudy would cry—Randy hated that. Soon they would be back in each other's arms, and Trudy would once again convince herself that it was okay with God since she planned on marrying Randy someday.

Once again the voice of the children playing next door drifted back inside. *What would my child sound like?* Trudy stepped back. *I'm not going there. I'd only be torturing myself. Besides I made a choice, and I have a right to make it. Or do I? Have I really thought about what I'm doing? Or am I covering up this pregnancy, like everything else in my life?*

She needed Brenda. *What good would it do to talk with her? It's not going to change anything. Besides, I was rude to Brenda earlier today. She probably wouldn't want to talk to me.*

But somewhere deep within Trudy knew that wasn't true. Brenda was a very forgiving person.

She leaned back against the wall as the giggles and laughter echoed off the walls, settling into her heart. "One potato, two potato, three potato, four…," she could hear them chant. She finished it with her own words: "Your mommy chose to have you no more."

"What other choice do I have, Lord?" she cried out, putting her hand to her mouth in astonishment. *It's been a long time since I asked Your opinion about anything.* She crossed her arms tightly together in front of her with a pout. *It's unfair I'm in this predicament. No matter how much I desire to go back, I can't. This is my choice!*

* * *

Brenda slammed the screen door as hard as possible, but it wasn't loud enough to satisfy how frustrated she felt as she threw her books on the couch. What a lousy day.

"Brenda!"

Oh no. Her mom didn't like it when Brenda slammed things around.

"What's all the racket?" her mom asked as she entered the living room.

"I had a lousy day." Brenda sighed.

"There are other ways to handle things. Slamming doors isn't going to solve your problems."

"I know. I'm sorry." *It sure feels good, though.*

Lorinda, Brenda's mother, put an arm around her daughter's shoulder. "Come out to the kitchen and tell me what made you have such a bad day."

Brenda got some pop and an apple from the refrigerator and sank into a chair. "It's Trudy again."

"Oh." Lorinda sat down with her. "I've been hoping the two of you would straighten out your problems by now. You used to be so close. I really miss seeing you two together."

"Yeah, me too," Brenda said sadly. "At first, I thought I was just jealous because Randy took so much of her time. The real problem, though, is the more Trudy became involved with Randy, the more involved she got with his group of friends."

"Which is perfectly normal," her mother interjected, "but not necessarily good."

"It hasn't been good for Trudy. She's not only hanging out with kids we used to pray for because they were making bad decision, but now it seems Trudy has chosen to go in their direction." Her heart felt as though it would burst. It hurt to have lost her best friend. She missed her.

"'Hi' has been about the only thing I've been able to get out of her lately, even at youth group, if she's there." Brenda shook her head. "Today I didn't even get that. She turned her back on me and walked away while her buddies Karen and Jodee had a good laugh at my expense."

Brenda's mother clasped her hand across the table.

"I'm sorry, honey. I'm sorry she embarrassed you like that."

"What was worse, though, was the look on her face. I know her well enough to tell when something's wrong." Sniffing, she said, "That in itself bothers me, because she's my friend. But it's clear she doesn't want to share her problems with me, and that hurts!"

Lorinda got up to hold Brenda while she cried over the loss of her friend. When Brenda settled down, her mother kneeled on the floor next to her, smoothing a wet, curly hair behind her ear. "Honey, whether Trudy realizes it or not, she needs you. You can still be her friend."

"Mom, she doesn't want me around!" Exasperated, Brenda pushed her hair back.

"I know. But you can be her friend by praying for her. I believe she needs your prayers right now more than ever to get through whatever is going on in her life."

"You're right, Mom, but I want to be directly involved with her."

"Honey, you will be directly involved by being faithful in praying," Lorinda explained.

"Trudy and I used to do that all the time. We always prayed for people together." Brenda sighed. A slow smile formed on her face. "Thanks, Mom. You're a great listener. I'm going to pray for her right now."

* * *

The door opened a crack. Voices drifted in from the hallway. Trudy rubbed her face with both hands to wipe away the tears and grabbed a Kleenex from the box on the counter to blow her nose.

She climbed back onto the table as the nurse closed the door, giving a brief smile. Trudy felt self-conscious, not knowing what to do with her hands.

"I'm Doris. I'll be your nurse during the procedure. Dr. Whiting will be here in a few minutes. I'm sorry you've been kept waiting so long, but we've had quite an afternoon. Let's have you lay down on the table."

Trudy lay back, gripping the sheet close to her chest. She wanted to hide underneath it.

"Who's here to give you a ride home?" Doris asked.

"My boyfriend." Her lip stuck to her teeth. She needed some water.

"His name? I need it for the records, in case there are any complications."

"Um, complications? What does that mean exactly?" Trudy was shaking.

Doris stared at her, looking as though she was probably counting to ten. "Sometimes women experience excessive bleeding, fainting…didn't you read the form before you signed it?"

"Uh, not really. I only wanted to get the paperwork done so I could get this over with," Trudy admitted.

"Do you have your copy with you?"

Nodding, she pointed in the direction of her purse. Doris handed the paperwork to her and then busied herself at the counter while Trudy read it over.

Her heart pounded in her ears. *What if I bleed to death or faint? I can't go to the hospital. Mom, Dad, and Grandma will find out I was pregnant—that I had an abortion.*

The children's chant returned: "One potato, two potato, three potato four…" and her mind added, *Your mama chose to have you no more....*

Doris turned to her. "Did you finish reading everything?"

Trudy nodded. Something was happening—the numbness of her heart was wearing off, and it hurt.

I'm pregnant...I'm going to have a baby.

She looked up at the clock. In a matter of minutes her decision would silence her child's voice forever. *Is this really the choice I want to make?*

Doris interrupted. "Did you hear me? I still need your boyfriend's name."

"Oh, I'm sorry. I was…thinking about something. His name is…uh…Randy, Randy Hunter," Trudy stammered.

While the nurse wrote the information, the doctor came in. He spoke quietly to Doris, and she handed him the clipboard.

Trudy raised a hand and dared to touch her stomach. Glancing up, she caught the doctor's eye. His bland expression was terrifying, like she was merely an object lying in front of him. She covered her stomach with both hands as if to protect the baby.

"So…," he started as he put down the clipboard and directed the nurse with a nod, "your name is Trudy. I'm Dr Whiting. While performing the procedure I'll tell you what I'm doing. I'll explain the sounds and what you may feel, such as pricking, etc. If you should feel or experience anything different, I need to know right away. To start, here's a sedative; then we can begin. It'll be done in no time, and you can get on with life and put this behind you." He patted her shoulder. "After the procedure, you'll need to lie here for about half an hour to make sure there aren't any complications; then we can release you. I suggest using birth control. I'll get some samples for you to bring home, along with a prescription."

Trudy tried to concentrate on what the doctor was saying about birth control. She agreed to take the samples and prescription. She doubted he would believe her determination to not have sex again until the day she was married, and she didn't have the energy for explanations.

Her stomach cramped and nausea gripped her as the doctor filled her in on everything that would follow. He explained exactly what would happen to the "tissue." She stared at the tubes and followed them with her eyes to the jars where her baby would end up; it was worse than a horror flick.

She remembered the protectiveness of the mothers in the park outside. *I'm giving this stranger permission to end my baby's life.*

As the doctor's mouth continued to move, Trudy heard only noise…and incomprehensible gibberish.

Lord! she screamed silently. *I can't do this. How can I live the rest of my life knowing I ended the life of a child? My child! I don't know how You can help me, but forgive me for even being in this place. I beg You to help me. Please!*

She looked at the nurse and the doctor. Had they heard her?

When the nurse handed her a cup of water and some pills, Trudy stared at the doctor in terror. He was talking to her with a huge needle in one hand. He was telling her to do something, but she couldn't grasp what. She was going to throw up. *I can't do this! I can't!* She was consumed with determination.

"STOP!" she yelled, pulling away from the doctor, knocking the pills out of her hand. "Stop everything! I'm not going through with it." She threw her legs over the side of the bed and hunted for her clothes. "I'm leaving—now!"

The doctor simply looked tired, dropped the needle on the tray, and left the room.

Turning back to the nurse to say something, Trudy began to vomit instead. Doris came over and held her hair back until she was done, then handed Trudy a towel to wipe her face.

"Thanks!" Trudy managed. With shaky hands she began to put on the rest of her clothes, tears flowing down her cheeks. *I have no idea how I'm going to do this. Randy's probably going to leave me. I can't even begin to imagine what my mom and dad will say, but this isn't the answer…Jesus, I believe You helped me. If others leave me, will You stay like it says in the Bible?*

For the first time in a long while, that was all that mattered. She picked up her purse and headed for the door.

* * *

Upstairs, a fresh breeze drifted through the open window of Brenda's room as she knelt by her bed in fervent prayer for her friend. Suddenly, a great burden lifted from her shoulders. And, in its place, came peace.

2

With determination, Trudy hurried down the hallway to get away from the horrible experience. Catching a glimpse of Randy sitting in the waiting room reading a magazine, her steps faltered. *How can he just sit there like that? He has no idea what I've been through!*

"Trudy," the nurse called from the doorway, "stop by the front desk to get your money back since we didn't do the procedure."

Trudy clutched her waist tightly and stole another glance at Randy. *He is going to freak out on me! Oh…I'm not ready yet to tell him I'm keeping the baby.* Swiftly she searched the hallway for a place to hide, but the closed office doors made a shiver run up her spine. *I'm not going back there.* Having no choice but to go in Randy's direction, she took a hesitant step. Her feet dragged, feeling heavier with each step she took.

Still, it was only too soon before she found herself standing in front of him. He hadn't noticed her checking out at the front desk.

When he did look up, concern flooded his face. *I can't tell him now.* He stood and gathered her into a hug. "Are you okay?" he whispered.

Trudy nodded, then pulled away.

"Finished?" he asked gently.

"Yeah, we can go now." She started toward the door.

"Hey, wait up," Randy called, catching up in time to grab the door before she could open it. "Let me get this. I want you to take it easy."

She rolled her eyes, feeling tired. *I want to go home, curl up in bed, and stay there.*

While he unlocked the car door, she looked across the street, noticing the picketers for the first time. Their signs read: *Save the unborn* and *Choose life.* Some had graphic pictures that caused her stomach to turn.

"Come on, get in the car. You don't need to see that right now," he said. "What a bunch of freaks!" Closing Trudy's door, he hurried to the driver's side.

When Trudy rolled down the window, a lady pushed a brochure in. It shouted, *A baby is a person, too.*

"I didn't do it," Trudy murmured to the woman.

"Oh, praise God! I'll be praying."

"Get away from the car," Randy yelled as he climbed into the driver's seat. He roared the engine, and the tires squealed as the car peeled out of the parking lot.

The lady had to jump back to prevent from being knocked over.

* * *

Jodee, one of Trudy's friends, watched from across the street, in the line of picketers, unable to believe her eyes—Randy and Trudy coming out of the abortion clinic! She didn't believe in that religious garbage, but she did believe in saving the lives of the unborn. *I thought religious people like Trudy did, too. How many times has Trudy and her do-gooder friend Brenda wasted my time talking about loving Jesus?*

Hmmm...I wonder what Brenda thinks about this? Come to think of it, Trudy hasn't had much to do with Brenda lately. In fact, this afternoon she had snubbed Brenda. Jodee and her best friend, Karen, had successfully embarrassed Brenda, razzing her about Trudy giving her the cold shoulder.

Jodee hated goody-goodies. Usually they turned out just like everyone else; they were only better at hiding it. Jodee cocked an eyebrow and smiled. *I wonder what do-gooder Brenda would think about this. Maybe I'll just have to see!*

* * *

As Trudy and Randy drove away, Trudy couldn't get the nerve to tell him. All she wanted was to get away from everything. Trudy thought of Grandma Kay. *I wonder if Grandma would let me stay at her place for the weekend?* The more Trudy thought of her grandma and how they used to talk, the more she wanted to be with her.

"Randy, do you mind taking me to my house?" Trudy asked. "I want to see if I can go stay at my grandma's for the weekend."

Randy eyed her with surprise. "You want to go home? I'd think that was the last place you'd want to go. I thought we could spend some time alone together."

Trudy sighed. She dreaded being alone with him right now. "I need to be by myself. At Grandma's I can have some time to think."

Randy put his hand on Trudy's knee. "I think it's important to have some time together, to talk, after all we've just been through."

Trudy pushed his hand off her knee. "After what *we've* been through? I don't think so! I believe it was *me* in that room—not us." She glared out the window.

"You're upset. I know today's been hard, but getting in a fight isn't going to make it better."

Trudy shook her head. "Randy, I want to be alone. Would you please drive me home?"

"Fine!" Randy accelerated with a lurch. "If that's the way you want it!"

The rest of the ride was silent. As they pulled up to her house, Trudy breathed a sigh of relief, but then she felt his hand on hers.

"Don't leave mad," he said. "Why don't I come in with you? If your mom says it's okay to go to your grandma's, I'll drive you out there."

Great, Trudy thought sarcastically, *more time to have a chance to tell him.*

"Come on, Trudy. We can talk on the way out. You can even yell if you want to," he said generously.

Trudy rolled her eyes. "Whatever, Randy. If that's what you want to do."

"You don't have to sound so enthused about it," he said sarcastically.

Before she could reply, Randy opened his car door. Trudy tried to get out before he could get to her side of the car. She didn't want him to treat her like she needed to be taken care of.

Her mom opened the door when they reached the porch steps.

"Hi, Mrs. Thomas! How are you today? Your flowers sure are looking nice." Randy was always the perfect gentleman to her parents.

"I'm fine, Randy, and thank you. How many times do I have to say, just call me Sheryl?" Sheryl laughed, giving his shoulder a playful punch. "What have you two been up to this afternoon?"

"Not much really," Randy said.

Trudy couldn't believe how easily Randy avoided the truth.

"Well, anyone hungry? Bill called, and he's grabbing a bite at work. So there's plenty of food." Sheryl closed the door behind them.

"I'm not hungry, Mom," Trudy said.

"Tru...you feeling okay?" her mom asked with concern. "I've never known you to pass up a meal."

"I'm fine. Hey, I was wondering. Can I call and see if Grandma minds me coming out for the weekend?"

Her mom's brow creased. "Is something going on? I can't remember the last time you wanted to stay with Grandma."

Trudy swallowed. *I'm going to break down right here, right now. Please don't ask me anymore questions, Mom, please! I'm not ready to tell either you*

17

or Randy.

"Mom, I'm fine...only I miss Grandma," Trudy lied.

Sheryl glanced back and forth between the two of them. Trudy could tell she knew there was more going on than what she was being told.

Trudy had always been very close to her dad's parents. After Grandpa Elwood passed away, Trudy and her grandma had grown even closer. There was a very special bond between the two—until recently. Her mom had voiced concerns about the change more than once. But Grandma Kay had such a strong faith in Jesus, it made Trudy uncomfortable to be around her, considering the decisions she'd been making lately. Still, Grandma was the one person she wanted to be with right now.

"If it's okay with Kay, then I see no reason why not. But you'll have to wait until Dad gets home to ride out to the farm with us. I need the car this weekend and I don't feel like making the drive back alone," her mom said.

"That's okay. I'll drive her, Mrs. Thomas...I mean Sheryl," Randy offered.

"If you're sure, then go ahead," She smiled.

Trudy went to call her grandma.

"Are you okay?" Grandma Kay asked. "You don't sound like your usual happy self."

"Grandma, I just want to spend some time with you."

"Okay, honey, I'd love to see you. I'll get your room ready."

It will be so embarrassing to tell her I'm pregnant. As Trudy finished packing and went down to the living room, she could hear Randy and her mom laughing in the kitchen—probably over something Randy said; he could be a real charmer.

"So you're finally done packing?" her mom teased. "Randy almost ate us out of house and home waiting for you." She messed Randy's hair a bit as she got up and went to the counter.

"Here, take Grandma some of this cake. Your dad and I won't eat it all ourselves. You two can enjoy it."

"Randy, are you ready?" Trudy asked, taking the cake.

"Sure." Randy got up from the table, carrying his plate over to the sink. "That sure was good!"

"Glad you liked it." Sheryl followed Trudy to the front door. "Now, Trudy, be sure to call me when you get to Grandma's, so I know you got there okay. See you Sunday at church." After kissing Trudy's forehead, she gazed into her eyes.

Trudy looked down at her feet to avoid any eye contact.

Sheryl squeezed Trudy. "Have fun, honey."

"I will. Love you." Trudy hugged her mom and walked out the door while Randy picked up her suitcase and carried it to the car.

"Good-bye, and thanks, Randy, for driving her," her mom called after them.

"Bye, Mom!" Trudy called.

Randy responded with a smile and a wave.

* * *

Sheryl watched until they turned the corner and drove out of sight. Closing the door, she went to her room to pray for her daughter.

* * *

Trudy and Randy rode in silence, which was okay with Trudy. It gave her a chance to think. *How on earth am I going to tell my family I'm pregnant? They'll be so disappointed in me.* Her stomach did a flip. *I hope they don't stop talking to me or kick me out of the house. Would they do something like that?* Inhaling deeply, she blew her bangs off of her forehead. *Where would I live? Grandma Kay's? No, she's not going to be any happier about this than Mom and Dad. Well, I'll have to deal with this somehow. I'm not going back to have an abortion!* A shiver ran up her spine remembering the experience at the clinic. *Anything's better than that creepy place.*

Trudy peeked at Randy. When she first told him she was pregnant, they didn't even consider keeping the baby. *Will he try to convince me once again to have an abortion? Will he leave me all alone?* Trudy swallowed hard to get rid of the lump in her throat. *I hope not! I love him so much!*

Randy was the most adorable guy she'd ever seen—curly, blond hair, skin that was lightly tanned year round, and big, blue eyes with long lashes.

Still, no matter what he says...even if he leaves me...I won't do it!

I can't imagine life without him, though. He's the most important person in my entire world. She covered her chest with her hand when pain pierced through her heart. *I feel so trapped. I wish I could do everything over again. I wouldn't have sex. Why did I do that? I'm too young for this. I want OUT!! Why can't I wake up and find this is a bad dream? Lord, why is this happening to me? I'll change, I promise, just please make this all stop. It's not fair!*

They passed the sign for a park where she used to hang out on summer nights with the youth group from church. Glancing at Randy, she knew she had to tell him—now—get it over with.

"Do you think we could stop at the park?" she asked.

"Huh?" He looked in the direction she was pointing. "Sure." Randy pulled into a parking spot that overlooked the river.

Butterflies beat their wings at such breathtaking speed in her stomach that it was hard to swallow. She opened the car door barely in time to empty what was left in her stomach on the ground outside.

"Ewww!" Randy exclaimed. "Are you okay? Did it get in the car?"

Closing her eyes, she pressed her head back against the seat, not caring and unable to answer.

"There are some napkins in the glove compartment," he offered.

She gave a slight nod.

"Tru?"

Groaning, she reached for a napkin. A bunch of them fell on the floor.

"Whoa! Hey, I'll get those." He grabbed the stray napkins. "Want some water?" He handed her a bottle.

Gratefully she brought it to her lips, sipping. It felt good on her throat.

"Why don't we walk around? It might help you feel better," he suggested.

Trudy nodded, stepped out of the car, and started walking toward the river. Randy came up next to her, putting his arm around her shoulder. They walked silently to the river's edge.

"I guess you threw up from all the stuff you've been through today. I'm sorry that it was so tough on you." Randy leaned his head on hers.

Lord, help me!

"Randy, I..." With a shaking hand, she pulled the money to be used at the clinic out of her jeans pocket and placed it in Randy's hand.

"Hey, what's this for?"

"It *was* for the abortion."

"What do you mean?"

"I want to give your money back. It isn't right for me to keep it."

"What? You didn't do it?" He slapped his hands on his thighs and pivoted away from her. "Tell me you did it," he said, turning back.

Tears welled in her eyes, and she looked away.

"Please tell me you went through with it," he pleaded, staring at her.

She didn't respond.

"What were you thinking? What *are* you thinking is more the question."

She couldn't reply; her stomach was churning again.

"Trudy, answer me! What are you thinking? You're pregnant! Do you know what that means?" he yelled.

I'm pregnant. Then Trudy found her voice. "Of course I know what it means. What I'd like to know is, do you?" she shouted.

"Of course. It means a huge responsibility—one I can't handle right now!" His face was red as he yelled louder than Trudy. She took a quick look around to see if there was anyone else in the park who could hear him. When she touched his arm, he stiffened. "Randy, let's both calm down, okay?"

He stood looking down. She could only see the side of his face and how tight his lips were.

"Would you please listen to me, for just a minute?"

He met her gaze. She could see in his eyes she was losing him.

"Randy, please try to understand," she begged, but his expression never changed. "When I was waiting for the doctor today, I had a chance to think about what *my* feelings were about this whole thing. When I first took the test, I was scared! I worried about telling you and everyone else. I had a bunch of wrong reasons for making that appointment. Today I had to face the fact that the people I used for an excuse would never, in their entire life, want me to have an abortion. Except…you."

His expression still didn't change.

"There was a window in the office, and I saw children playing. Their moms were watching over them. I thought of the baby inside of me and what was about to happen to it. Then the doctor came in and explained this horrendous procedure. He called it 'tissue,' but I know better. It's a baby." She looked earnestly at him. "Our baby," she ended in a whisper.

His face remained set, stone-like.

Then Trudy did the thing she hated most when she was upset—she started blubbering. "I…I…" Her lips quivered, making it hard to talk, but, determined, she went on. "I couldn't live with that. Women have a choice about what to do with their bodies. I made my choice. I want my baby to have life." She pushed the words out firmly, her confidence growing as each one came out.

Turning toward the river, she murmured, "I wish with all my heart you'd feel the way I do about the baby. I'm scared, but I know we can face this together. I know we can."

Footsteps interrupted her thoughts, and she swiveled. He was walking to the car.

"Randy!" she yelled. She hurried after him, afraid he'd leave her there. She caught up with him at the car. "Randy, what are you doing?"

He pivoted toward her with disgust. "Well, since I can't leave you here in the park, I'm driving you to your grandmother's house like I told your mother I would."

"Just like that? Don't you want to talk about this? I mean, this is pretty important!"

"What's there to talk about? You've made your decision. I can't say I have much *choice* in the matter. You're pregnant! You're not going to take care of it. So, what's there to talk about?" Randy got in, slammed the car door, and started the engine.

She could feel the wall between them. Tears streamed down her face. He hated it when she cried. Normally he'd hold her. But this time he didn't even glance her way as she sniffled and got in the car.

I can't stand this wall between us. I want him to be the charmer I know and love. Staring out the window, she saw nothing. *How can I reach him? I can't bear Randy not being here for me.*

The car stopped, and Randy got out. He pulled her suitcase from the back. She hadn't even realized they'd made it to Grandma Kay's. She watched him carry her bag up to the porch. When he got back in the car, he stared straight ahead. *What am I to do now?*

His silence spoke volumes to her.

"Do you still have my grandma's phone number in case you want to call me this weekend?" she ventured.

"Yeah, but I'll be too busy to call," he answered without looking her way. "Listen, I really have to go. I have a lot of stuff to do tonight."

Like what? This is the same guy who, a few hours ago, thought we needed to spend some time together, alone. I don't believe it. Well, I guess we're breaking up. This is going to be hard, very hard.

"Trudy!" Randy interrupted her thoughts. "Do you mind? I need to go. Now!"

Fine. Without a word she started getting out of the car.

"Trudy!" Hope jumped up in her heart. She turned back around, but he was only holding out her mom's cake. "Don't forget the cake."

Grabbing it, she got out of the car, slamming the door as hard as she could. The crunching of the loose gravel under her feet tore at her heart as, step by slow step, she walked away from her first and only love.

The roar of the motor grew fainter. Reaching the porch, she slid down on the steps, put her head in her arms, and cried.

* * *

Grandma Kay heard a commotion outside—the roar of an engine and the sound of gravel spraying out from car tires. Moving as fast as her body would allow, she arrived at the front door in time to watch Trudy walk up to the house with her head hung low. Her heart broke as her precious granddaughter plopped down on the porch step and began to cry.

Oh, Lord, it's been so long since she's been to see me. She's hurting. Thank You for bringing her here. Equip me for what is ahead.

Kay wanted to rush outside and comfort Trudy while she cried but decided it would be better to let her have this time to herself. She lifted prayers to Jesus until the sobs subsided.

How can I help her, Lord? You know what's happening in her life. I ask for your wisdom and love. Thank You, Jesus.

* * *

Trudy sat deep in thought with the burden of her circumstances weighing heavily on her mind. She didn't notice when Grandma Kay came out on the porch and sat in her old rocker to wait. Eventually, the familiar creaking of the chair caught Trudy's attention. Glancing in that direction, she was met with a loving smile from Grandma Kay.

"What kind of troubles are you carrying on those shoulders? Anything you'd like to share?" Grandma's voice came out in a gentle whisper while she rocked back and forth in a slow rhythm.

Trudy smiled sadly, turning to lean against the porch railing. They'd had many conversations together like this.

"I messed up bad, Grandma."

"Okay. Everyone messes up sometimes."

"Yeah, but I can't fix it. My life…it's over," Trudy said quietly. "No one can help me." She put her face in her hands.

"Hmmm, I don't know about that. There isn't anything the Lord can't handle."

Looking down at her shoe, Trudy shook her head. "I don't think this is something I can hand over to Jesus, Grandma. It's definitely something He won't be too happy about."

"I understand how you'd feel that way. I've been there before too, but I've learned to believe what He said. If I confess my sins, He is faithful to forgive me, no matter what!"

A long sigh escaped Trudy. *Did I expect anything less? The only answer in life to Grandma is Jesus.*

"Grandma, that's nice and all. I know He forgives, but what then? After I'm forgiven, what am I supposed to do with the problem? It'll still be here!"

Trudy grumbled.

"Yes, it will," Grandma agreed. "That's when you ask Him for help. Believe me, I've cried for help plenty of times. He always gives me wisdom."

Okay, why did I want to stay with Grandma? To be preached at wasn't one of the reasons. But then isn't this how Grandma has been all my life?

"Honey, remember the day you went before the church and confessed Him as your Savior?"

Trudy rolled her eyes. "Of course I remember."

"He's still your Savior, Trudy."

"I know." Trudy stared out at the yard.

"He knew on the cross you'd end up where you're at, and He died for whatever it is you've done wrong. Doesn't that make you think that possibly He may know how to handle it?" Kay stopped rocking and leaned over toward Trudy. "Let me tell you a little story. One night I had a vision of me as a little baby all dressed in white. I was crawling down a hill, but at the end of this hill was a cliff. Now, God was standing there with His arms open to pick me up and carry me to the other side. I had a choice. I could crawl down that cliff, all by myself, and most likely fall, skin myself up a bit, and get my beautiful white dress dirty. I'd also get hurt and cry. Or I could ask God for help and let Him carry me to the other side."

Trudy recalled His help at the abortion clinic. *I was able to say no after I cried out to Him. There was no way I would have been able to stop the doctor, not on my own. I was too afraid.*

"Sometimes life can get going so fast, it's hard to listen to the voice of the Spirit. Instead, well, it's easier to make our own decisions, and then everything gets messed up."

Trudy laughed shortly. "Ain't that the truth."

Grandma sat by Trudy. "I love you, and oh, how I've missed you. I know without a shadow of a doubt you believe what I'm saying. You wouldn't have come to see me this weekend if you didn't. We've had enough conversations in our lifetime for you to know what to expect when we talk." She stroked Trudy's hair.

In the light of the setting sun, Trudy cautiously met her grandma's eyes. "I'm scared."

Kay pulled her into a loving hug. "Why don't we pray? Lord, I lift up these burdens that Trudy is carrying. I ask in the name of Jesus Christ, our Savior and Lord, that You would give her faith to trust that You can take care of anything that comes her way. Give her wisdom and, Lord, prepare those of us who love her. Make us available to do Your work and use us to guide her, in Jesus' name, Amen."

Grandma Kay held her while they sat together listening to crickets and the other sounds of early evening. "Trudy," she spoke softly, "remember when Peter denied Jesus?"

"Yeah."

"Well, after he had a good cry, he didn't run from Jesus. He ran to Jesus." Kay squeezed her tight. "It's okay to have a good cry and then run to Him and not away from Him."

They watched the sun go down until it dipped below the horizon.

"That was beautiful, thank You, Lord," Grandma Kay said. "I'm tired. I had a busy day." She yawned, emphasizing the point. "But I'd stay up a bit longer if you want to come in and eat. Then we can sit around and talk for a while."

"Do you mind if I pass and just sit out here for awhile?"

"Not at all. I'll see you in the morning. There's food in the fridge if you get hungry. I set up your bed, and there are towels in the bathroom."

Trudy listened to her grandma's footsteps across the porch and the creak of the screen door. The familiarity brought comfort.

"It's good to have you here, sweetie. Good night."

Trudy swiped her face to catch the tears. *Will I ever stop crying?*

What a day. A glance at her watch showed it was nine o'clock. Friday evenings she'd normally watch a movie, curled up with Randy, while his parents were on their date night. His little sister was usually at his grandparents.

I wonder what he's doing? Does he miss me? How am I going to go on without him? A lonely feeling, along with the cool breeze, chilled her. *I don't want to be without him!* She went into the house and grabbed a throw off of the couch, stopping for a moment when Grandpa Elwood's picture caught her eye. He used to love to sit and talk with her into the night, about almost anything. They just liked to spend time together.

It was still hard to believe he'd gone on to heaven. At first, it was difficult to come out to the farm without him here, but she didn't want Grandma to be alone. So she'd started coming as often as possible, and they became very close.

When Grandpa died, did she feel as lonely as I do now? Did the days look long and empty? Is life merely an endless road of losing loved ones? Trudy went back outside, curling up in the old rocker, drifting down memory lane. Her thoughts were interrupted.

"Do not fear. I will send a comforter." It had been a long time since she'd heard that voice so clearly. Words that had been pushed aside the last few

months came to the front of her mind, words that Jesus had said in the Bible: *"I will never leave you nor forsake you."*

Is it true? Was He still here? I've ignored Him and turned from all I believe to love someone else. Didn't His word say to love God with all of your heart, soul, and mind? That He is a jealous God? Certainly He wouldn't still be here.

But the words came through her mind clearer than before. *"I will never leave you nor forsake you."*

"What? Never? Why, God? I mean, I can hardly believe You're still here. I had sex, and I wasn't married. I almost took the life of my child. And, oh yeah, in case You haven't noticed, I'm pregnant and not married! I can't change the way things are. I'm a mess. What good would I be to You, or to anyone for that matter?" Trudy said aloud.

"If you confess your sins, I will be faithful and true and will forgive you your sins and cleanse you from all unrighteousness."

"Jesus, I blew it! It isn't like I can confess my sin and go on like a perfect Christian. I'm going to get big and fat." Shamefully she bowed her head. "Everyone will know I stepped away from You," she whispered. "Everyone."

"Thy word is a lamp unto my feet and a light onto my path." As she heard the words clearly, hope sprang up in her heart. *"Thy word is a lamp unto my feet and a light onto my path."*

Grandpa's old beat-up Bible lay on a small table next to the rocker. She picked it up, holding it close to her heart, remembering how it used to look clasped firmly in Grandpa's old worn hands.

"How can Your Word speak to me now, Lord?" Laying her head back against the rocker she gazed up at the stars twinkling above, and at the moon peeking out from behind a small cloud.

"Jesus was naked on the cross." She heard Grandpa Elwood's voice. It was one of their last talks.

"Grandpa, He was not! Everyone would have seen him," Trudy had protested.

"What? Do you think I would make up something like that? What would I do that for?" Grandpa asked.

"I don't know. It just…oh, how embarrassing!"

"Yep, they beat him, spit on him, hammered nails into him, and then took his clothes."

"But why are you even bringing this up, Grandpa?"

He leaned in close, his eyes gazing intently into hers. "A time may come in your life where you're going to feel naked. Like there's no place to hide."

"Grandpa!" She rolled her eyes.

He leaned back, nodding. "Jesus understands. He's been there. Don't forget that."

Oh, Grandpa, you were right. I feel so naked, and I have no place to hide. Everyone will know.

She stared at the Bible. *Will it really make any difference to read it?* Carefully she picked it up, flipping through the pages until she reached the story of Jesus on the cross. It had always been hard for her to read how cruelly they treated him. She read each word with care. *Jesus, I know You did this for me. I'm so ashamed. How do I start over? I don't even know how to begin.*

She got up from the chair and leaned against the porch post. "Jesus, You said You would cleanse me from my sins, if I confessed them, and that You would never leave me nor forsake me. So…" she released a long sigh, "the first thing I'm going to do is choose to believe in Your promises. I have no idea what to do after that, but for now…"

I've taken my first step.

Frogs croaked and crickets chirped an evening song while Trudy again gazed up at the stars. Little by little she relaxed into the peaceful Presence that surrounded her.

3

The light from the morning sun woke Trudy from a peaceful sleep. A quick look at the alarm clock caused a low groan. *Eight o'clock!* Rolling over, she pulled the covers up to catch some more sleep. Instead, thoughts of the day ahead danced through her mind.

I might as well get up. She threw the covers off and swung her legs out of the bed. *Maybe Grandma made some of her cinnamon rolls for me.* She grabbed her robe, then something stopped her. Turning around, she went back to the side of the bed. It had been a long time, but she did what her grandma had taught her to do years ago. "A day is easier when you've put it into the hands of the One who made it for you," Grandma had told her. Trudy knelt and prayed.

The smell of coffee and cinnamon rolls greeted Trudy as she came down the stairs after her shower. Grandma was at the sink washing dishes. Trudy hesitated, butterflies dancing in her stomach. *Lord, I know You are with me. I pray for Your strength. I pray for Your presence with my family.*

Taking a deep breath, she walked to her Grandma. "Good morning," she said, giving her a hug from behind.

"Good morning, dear. I didn't expect to see you until later this morning. I figured you were up pretty late last night." Grandma went to the stove and took some rolls out of the oven. "I've been keeping these warm for you. There's butter on the table and orange juice in the fridge. Would you like some coffee too?"

"Sure, do you have time to have a cup with me?" Trudy asked.

"I've got plenty of time to sit and talk with you." Grandma sat at the table in the breakfast nook while Trudy poured the coffee.

She grabbed a roll. Keeping herself busy, she dragged out buttering it. *What do I say? The only thing on my mind is my baby. Should I tell her now?* Trudy popped a bite in her mouth and chewed it slowly. "Yum, good, Grandma. You make the best rolls."

Grandma smiled lovingly. "Thanks, Trudy."

At that moment Trudy decided to just say what was on her mind. "Grandma, I've never been able to keep things from you. That's why I stopped coming around." She looked up to see sadness on her grandma's face. "I didn't want you to know what I was doing. Maybe this isn't the perfect time or maybe I should wait and tell my parents first, but I..." Trudy rubbed her forehead as she let out a groan. "I don't know what to do. I'm facing the biggest problem ever in my life...and, well, you've always been there for me."

Tears misted Trudy's eyes. She stared at the garden outside the dining room window, biting her lip until she felt Grandma take her hand and wrap her own hands around it. Hesitantly, she glanced at Grandma Kay and was greeted with kindness.

"Sweetie, why don't you stop torturing yourself and tell me what's bothering you." Grandma gripped her hand harder.

Here, here I go! "Grandma, I'm...I'm *pregnant*," she wailed.

Grandma Kay sat back in her chair, putting her hand over her mouth.

"Randy doesn't want the baby." Trudy sniffled. Grandma scooted close to Trudy and handed her a tissue. "Yesterday we went to an abortion clinic."

"Oh, my!"

"I couldn't go through with it. I left without getting an abortion. I told Randy on the way here, and he...left me." Trudy fell into Grandma's arms, sobbing on her shoulder. "My life is over."

Grandma Kay let her cry. "It's okay, honey. It's okay." She grabbed a towel.

Trudy wiped at her face. The sobs were getting slower now.

"Oh, honey, life may seem to be over," Grandma Kay whispered, "as *you* know it anyway. You're on a different road. It can be hard, but you did the right thing. It took a lot of courage to walk out of there."

"Oh, Grandma, it was awful! I was left waiting in a room, like, forever! I had time to think." Trudy sniffed. "I thought about everything that had happened this last year and choices that I had made. By the time the doctor came in, the only thing I wanted was out. I cried out to Jesus. God gave me courage, Grandma, because I was scared stiff."

"Oh, goodness child, I believe with all my heart you were kept waiting in that room because of God's intervention. I'm sure He had people praying specifically for you yesterday."

"Yeah, probably." The thought hadn't occurred to Trudy. "I don't want to have a baby, but I don't want to have an abortion either."

Grandma Kay patted Trudy's hand and gestured toward the garden her darling Elwood had designed. "Why don't we take a walk? There's something I'd like to show you." Grandma Kay stood to open the back door. The breeze was cool. "I think we'd better put on our sweaters. Can you run upstairs and get us each one, honey? I'll clean up the rest of our dishes real quick like."

Trudy came back with the sweaters as her grandma was finishing and wiping her hands on her jeans. She opened the back door and went outside.

"Let's go over here." Grandma Kay led the way on one of the rocky paths. "Do you remember how much Grandpa loved this garden?" She didn't wait for a reply. "His favorite spot was down by the oak tree, you know, where your old wooden swing is hanging. He put a bench there and planted beautiful rosebushes, but those pesky deer would come and eat them. He had quite a battle with them. We enjoyed watching the deer, but then we'd get so exasperated after discovering they ate our flowers. They seem to love Grandpa's favorite plant the most."

Trudy listened sadly. Everywhere she looked was a memory of Grandpa Elwood. Watering, weeding, always with his old dirty hat on his head, and a smile on his face while he hummed a song.

"It's so beautiful. Let's sit for a minute." Grandma motioned to the bench. "Sometimes in the early evening, I watch your swing sway in the breeze, and I remember you and Grandpa laughing as he pushed you higher and higher. Oh, you would squeal and giggle. What was that song? Up, Up, Up..." She started to sing. "Way up high, way up high, 'til you touch the sky," Trudy finished, blinking away the tears. "You must miss him so much."

"Yes, I do," Grandma Kay said quietly. "There's his favorite rosebush."

Trudy gasped. "What happened to it?" It was dried out, weeds surrounded it, one big thorny one twisted up in the middle of it. The rest of the garden was still beautiful. "It's dead. Grandma, didn't you water it?"

Grandma Kay shook her head.

"No? What?" Trudy didn't understand. She got up and pulled some of the weeds away from the bush. It was a lost cause. Grandpa's favorite! *How could she have let it go?* For the first time in her life, Trudy was angry with Grandma Kay.

"When your grandpa was dying, I told God I wasn't ready to let him go, but he died anyway. I thought God hadn't listened to me and simply went on with His plans." Trudy stopped pulling weeds since Grandma Kay spoke so softly she could barely hear her. "One night I missed Elwood so much. I wanted to find a way to be close to him. I came out to pluck some roses from this bush to put in a vase beside my bed. The deer had eaten the flowers—all of them. I was so angry, I kicked the bush and screamed at the deer."

Trudy plopped down in the dirt, her heart breaking for her grandma.

Grandma Kay sat lost in thought for a moment before she continued. "There were a few petals lying on the ground. I carefully picked them up and carried them into the house. I didn't know how to go on without Elwood. I slept in his shirts, sat in his chair, and smelled the petals that are now in my Bible. I felt like God had left me alone. I couldn't get myself to work on that plant again until just a few days ago when I decided to dig it out. It was a sore reminder every time I'd sit here.

"I put my garden gloves on, grabbed a shovel, and pushed the old wheelbarrow over. I started digging and pulling weeds, all the time reliving the pain of that night. Then I discovered the most amazing thing!" She got up from the bench and walked over to Trudy. Kneeling down, she pushed aside the weeds surrounding the bush. There, among the weeds, was a pink rosebud. "God gave me a rose!"

Trudy gasped. "But...how? This bush looks dead, choked by weeds!"

"My only answer is...God." Grandma put her arm around Trudy's shoulder, leaning her head on top of hers. "I watered it and I think I'm going to buy fencing to protect it from the deer."

"Wow, Grandma, that's incredible!"

"I wanted to show you this bush for a reason. See this?" Grandma Kay pointed to the big thorny weed growing up through the middle of the bush, twisting around the branches. "What if we say this is your pregnancy and your relationship with Randy?"

"O-kay," Trudy said slowly. "Where are you going with this, Grandma?"

"Well, it's like the burden you're carrying. It's eating you up inside and making you miserable."

"Yeah," she agreed.

"The old dried-out bush is how you feel about yourself right now, not worth much, and the weeds around the bush are the thoughts you believe people will have about you."

"Wow, Grandma, this is a perfect picture."

"Remember I told you I was going to dig it up and get rid of the ugly thing?"

Trudy nodded.

"I stopped when God showed me the rosebud. Even though it didn't look like it at first glance, it was still able to bloom, just like it was created to do."

Trudy drew her knees up close to her chest, resting her chin on them, staring at the rosebud that poked out through the weeds.

"If I water and fertilize this plant, it will get healthy and strong. Just like when we read His Word, pray, and fellowship, we grow healthy and strong spiritually. When I pull out the weeds, the plant isn't going to be choked anymore. Just like you won't be choked by all your cares as Jesus changes and renews your mind. The fencing is like spiritual armor put on to protect you."

Grandma placed her hand gently on Trudy's cheek. "There's one more thing." She pointed again to the bush. "The beautiful rosebud signifies life. When we make decisions to step out of God's will, we often face consequences even after we've been forgiven. You didn't get a disease or illness, but God gave you a life to care for and protect."

Trudy put her arms around Grandma Kay, resting her head on her shoulder.

"Grandma, I..." Trudy couldn't find words to say. *Now I know why I came to Grandma Kay.*

"Oh, honey, I love you so much." Grandma Kay squeezed Trudy's shoulder. "Listen, why don't I run into town for some fencing? Then you can have some time alone. When I get back, we can do some work on this *beautiful* bush." She winked at Trudy and tapped her nose.

Trudy nodded. "Do you mind if I don't walk back to the house with you?"

"Not at all, honey. I'll see you in a bit," Grandma Kay walked away, whistling a sweet melody that danced around the hope that sparked in Trudy's heart.

* * *

Brenda entered her room, peeling off sweaty clothes and grabbing a robe. She felt so good after a Saturday morning run, especially when there was time afterward to lay in a hot steamy bath filled with lavender bubble bath. During the week she usually had to get ready for school in a rush, but Saturdays she loved to indulge in this luxury.

The phone started ringing in the hallway. "Oh, brother, I better get that. It might be Mom or Dad," she said, turning off the bathroom faucet. Grabbing her robe, she ran for the phone.

"Hello?" Brenda answered.

"Hi, is this Brenda Sanders?" the voice on the other end asked.

"Yes, it is. Who's this?"

"This is Jodee, Jodee Myers from school. Do you remember me?"

How could I forget! You're the one who laughed in my face yesterday. "Yes, I remember."

"I thought you might, considering yesterday we had that embarrassing situation. I'm really sorry about that," Jodee said.

Brenda looked at the phone with surprise. *Jodee called to apologize to me for yesterday? Wow!* "That's all right, Jodee. Don't worry about it."

"Trudy said she could always count on you, that you never held a grudge.

She was right!"

Trudy talked about me like that to her new friends?

Jodee continued, "You know, since Trudy would mention that you're always there for her, I kind of thought..." Jodee grew silent.

"You kind of thought what?" Brenda asked.

"Well, Trudy might have talked to you about this trouble she's having."

Brenda tightened her lips. *What should I say? If I act like I know, then I could find out what's wrong with Trudy. No, I shouldn't do that. That's wrong; it's gossip.*

"You still there?"

"Yes, I'm here. Uh, I was just thinking."

"Oh." Silence. "Well, if you don't want to talk about it, that's okay. I understand. I mean, it's pretty personal. I've only known her for a little while, and she probably wouldn't feel comfortable coming to me about it anyway. So it's probably none of my business. I was only concerned."

"No. I mean, I don't know. Trudy hasn't talked to me about anything in quite awhile. She'll probably come to you, though, if she needs you."

"Humph, yeah, well, I wonder how Randy is taking all this?"

Brenda was beginning to feel uncomfortable. She didn't want to talk about this unless Trudy wanted her to know. "Listen, Jodee, I'm sorry I couldn't help you. Not to be rude, but I better get going."

"Oh, yeah, sure. I just thought since I saw Randy and Trudy drive off from the abortion clinic she'd probably need all of our support," Jodee added.

Brenda's breath was sucked right out of her. *What! No, not Trudy! Oh Lord!* "Jodee, I've got to go," Brenda felt sick.

"Oh, hey, I'm sorry, you said that before. Maybe I'll call Trudy myself. I mean, if I saw them drive off, I can only imagine how many other kids from school saw her. She's going to need support from her friends. But, hey, that's what friends are for, right?" Jodee asked with a sarcastic laugh.

"Uh, yeah, I've got to go. Bye, Jodee." Brenda hung up before Jodee could say anything else. She slid down the wall to the floor, laying her head down on her arms that were resting on her knees. *Oh God!* Visions of the scene at school yesterday floated through her mind. *I knew something was wrong, Lord. I saw it in her eyes before she turned away from me. She was scared! Why didn't I reach out to her? Who cares about what Jodee and Karen were saying to me? Trudy needed a friend. Thank You that my mom directed me to pray for her.*

A protective loyalty strengthened Brenda's heart. *Jodee's right. Trudy needs her friends. Lord, no matter how Trudy feels about me, I pray You'll help me to be there for her. I can't even begin to imagine what she's going through today. I pray she'll receive my friendship.*

Brenda stood from the floor and dialed Trudy's number, only to discover she was at her grandmother's house for the weekend. She started to punch in Grandma Kay's number but stopped.

I don't think I should handle this over the phone. No, I'll have to wait until Monday. Disappointed, Brenda headed for the bathroom to take a bath. *I can't wait until Monday! I need to talk with Trudy today.* Brenda turned on the faucet to take a quick shower. *So much for my lavender bubble bath. What's going on with Trudy is more important. Lord, I pray for wisdom for what may happen today.*

Brenda was on her way within the hour even though her mom came home before she left and insisted Brenda eat some breakfast. After practically stuffing the food down her throat, she ran to the car, praying the entire way to Grandma Kay's.

* * *

Trudy sat deep in thought, swaying back and forth on the old swing that hung from the ancient oak tree just off her grandma's garden. Grandpa Elwood put it up when she was a small child. Oh, how she loved it when he would push her up high toward the sky. When she grew older, the swing had become a place to come and gather her thoughts. Sometimes he would sneak up on her and give her a push, then duck under the swing as it passed by and sit down, leaning against the old tree.

Trudy held onto the ropes and leaned back with closed eyes. Birds chirped and the stream bubbled as it passed by. *I love this spot.*

"Do you think I can throw a rock, and it would land in the stream?" Grandpa Elwood asked her one time.

Trudy looked over at the stream, a mere few feet away. "Sure, but I'm kind of in your way," she teased.

Grandpa had stood and tossed the pebbles over her head. With each *plunk* he smiled at her. "Don't worry. I'd never do anything to hurt you. God is like that swing, you know."

Trudy shook her head. He always had a point to his silly antics.

"What?"

"Yep, you can rest in His hands, just like you're sitting in that swing." One of the pebbles bounced off the rope of the swing and hit Trudy's head. "Oops, sorry about that."

Trudy rubbed her head. "So I can be like a sitting duck, huh?"

"Even when life sneaks in and sends you some blows, it's better to be in His hands than standing on your own. If the pebble wouldn't have hit the rope, it would have hurt a bit more than it did. If you aren't resting in His hands, you can always jump right back in them, like this swing; it always invites you to come and sit for awhile."

Lord, if I would've stayed in Your hands, I wouldn't be experiencing this situation. Grandpa was right, though, you were right there for me, inviting me to come back and rest in you. Grandma was right, too. I didn't get a life-threatening disease. She gently touched her stomach. *You gave me a life to take care of, and that life is bringing me back to You.*

Trudy noticed a deer timidly watching her. "Come here, little buddy," she whispered, reaching her hand out. The startled deer sprinted into the trees and over the stream. Trudy looked around, puzzled. "What scared you?" The slam of a car door answered her question. *Grandma must be back.*

When Trudy opened the back door of the house she heard her grandma talking to someone. "It sure has been a long time since I've seen you! You're even prettier than the last time I saw you. I think Trudy's in the backyard," Grandma said. Trudy couldn't make out the voice of the other person.

"Trudy!" Grandma Kay called as the back door slammed.

"I'm in the kitchen."

"Someone's here to see you!" Grandma seemed excited.

Trudy started walking toward the front of the house when Grandma entered the kitchen with Brenda.

Brenda!? Trudy thought with happy surprise. "Brenda!? What are you doing here?"

Brenda smiled, looking a bit uncomfortable. "I, well, came to talk to you."

"Me? Well, of course 'me,' but what about? And how did you know I was out here?" Trudy realized that sounded rude. "I mean, I'm glad you're here!"

Grandma went to the refrigerator, took out some lemonade, and poured two glasses. "Here—why don't you take this lemonade outside and talk? It's so nice out there." She handed both Trudy and Brenda a glass.

"Do you want to go out back, Brenda?" Trudy asked.

"Yes, that would be nice." Brenda seemed relieved.

Trudy led the way out the back door and over to the chairs on the deck. *I can hardly believe Brenda's here. We haven't talked in ages! I owe her an apology. I wonder, could we ever be close again?*

Brenda took a deep breath. She appeared extremely nervous.

"Brenda, are you okay? I mean, what's going on? You could've called me on the phone." Trudy looked down, shamefaced. "Especially since I haven't been very nice to you lately. I'm not trying to be rude, really I'm not…"

"Listen," Brenda interrupted, "I have something I need to talk to you about and, yes, it's pretty serious. I got a phone call from Jodee Myers this morning."

"Jodee?" Trudy was surprised. *Everyone* knew that Jodee *did not* like Brenda.

"Yes, and as usual, it ended up not being a good thing when we talked. She said some insinuating things about you and implied that I needed to talk to you about them, no matter what has gone on between us." She wagged her finger back and forth between the two of them.

"Insinuating things? What kind of things?"

"First of all, I will completely understand if you tell me it's none of my business." Brenda bit at her lip.

"Listen, I know I've been a jerk to you, and I'm really sorry. I don't know how to explain, but I couldn't hang around with you anymore. I've changed. A lot. Not for the good, but still I've changed. It doesn't mean I don't care about you or trust you. If you have the courage to come and talk to me, then it's obviously important. So go ahead. Whatever you say is okay."

"All right…here goes. Jodee said she saw you and Randy leaving an abortion clinic yesterday," Brenda said quietly.

Trudy hung her head, embarrassed. *What do I say now? Hey, Miss Perfect, I know you won't understand, but I made a mistake. I'm pregnant. I'm going to be a mom at sixteen. She'd never understand. I can't look at her. I wish she'd leave.* Tears dropped one by one onto her lap. She was startled when Brenda placed a gentle hand on her shoulder.

"I'm here to be your friend, Trudy. I don't know how or what to do right now, but I want to be here for you if you'll let me." Brenda's voice was filled with compassion. "No matter how you feel, you're my best friend and always will be in my heart. I'd only hope if I were in the same position, you'd be there for me."

"You'd never be in this place," Trudy said softly, with a hint of bitterness.

"What?" Brenda sounded offended.

"You're 'perfect,' Brenda. You always get it right." Trudy kept her head down.

"Whatever! I could be here as easily as you. I've never been in love before, I've never been pregnant, so I have no idea how I'd handle it."

"Oh, Brenda." Trudy waved her statement away. "You'd never compromise your relationship with God. You got it. I compromised, I ignored

Him. I put Randy before God." Trudy struggled to not start weeping. "I want to be right with God, but I don't want to lose Randy."

"Is that why you stopped talking with me? Did you think I wouldn't understand?" Brenda asked.

Trudy nodded.

"Trudy…" Brenda sat in her chair, leaning her head back, looking up at the sky. "How can you judge me like that? Haven't I always loved and encouraged you? I don't know where you got the idea you had to be perfect to be friends with me, but…I'm so sorry that's how it was for you. I thought we were much closer than that."

"I don't know what I was thinking, I just know that Randy became everything, and I didn't want anything or anyone to get in the middle of it. Maybe I knew you'd tell me the truth, and I didn't want to hear it," Trudy admitted. "I'm sorry, really I am!"

"You could've given me a chance." Brenda said sadly.

"I didn't want to lose Randy."

"I see."

"Brenda, *I am sorry*. You know, deep down I knew my choices were wrong, and it wasn't just you. I stopped talking to my parents, Grandma Kay, and worst of all, God!" Trudy admitted. "I was making wrong decisions that I wanted to be right. But I need you to know I didn't have an abortion."

Brenda's face brightened.

"Don't get me wrong, I was there to have an abortion, but I was kept waiting for the longest time in a room and during that time God got ahold of my heart. I couldn't do it; I left without having one."

"So you were at the clinic yesterday afternoon then?" Brenda asked.

"Yes, right after school."

"Oh, my goodness! You've got to be kidding me?"

"No, why would I kid about something like that?"

"Well, after school I was upset. My mom suggested I be your friend by praying for you, so I spent the afternoon in prayer and after awhile a feeling of peace came over me."

"You were praying for me while I was there and you didn't even know what I was doing? How amazing is that?" Trudy was filled with wonder. "If you only knew all of the things that I thought about and how God showed me abortion wasn't the answer."

"I'm so glad you didn't go through with it. How did Randy respond? And what about your mom and dad?" Brenda asked.

"I haven't told my parents yet; just my Grandma. Randy, well, let's just

37

say he's not too happy about it. He dropped me off here yesterday and burned rubber on the way out. He said he'd be too busy to call me this weekend," Trudy said sadly.

"I'm so sorry."

"Yeah…now I have to face telling my parents. I'll probably tell them tomorrow night. I can imagine how hurt they're going to be."

"Boy, I don't envy you at all. That would be pretty scary to have to tell your parents news like that."

Trudy nodded. *"Scary* isn't the word for it. You can't even begin to know what my future looks like to me. It's pretty overwhelming."

"Wow, the biggest things I worry about is how to get along with people, what college to go to, you know, things like that. They seem so simple in comparison. But you, you have to think about not only your future, but your child's. And, along with that, you have to deal with everyone else's reaction. Not fun." Brenda whistled and shook her head as she finished.

"Uhh, thanks, Brenda. Thank you very much for painting a gloomier picture than I've been painting all afternoon. Things look much better than I thought," Trudy teased.

Brenda laughed. "Sorry. But I hope you know you're not alone."

"I do now, Brenda. Will you forgive me for how I treated you? And for walking away from the friendship we had? You're the most wonderful friend in the world, and I treated you terribly. I'm really sorry!"

Brenda shifted in her chair, shaking her head. "Friendship we had? You mean 'have,' don't you? Of course I forgive you. You are my best friend, my sister, really."

"I know we *were* as close as sisters, I hope someday we can be close like that again," Trudy finished sincerely.

"We will, we are, sisters. I forgive you. Please don't feel guilty." She smiled gently at Trudy.

Trudy smiled back. *Brenda is such a treasure.* "I really missed you!"

"I missed you, too!" she responded before Trudy caught her up in a big bear hug that set them laughing.

* * *

Grandma Kay watched the two girls hugging and laughing together. *Lord, I am so sad for how quickly Trudy will soon have to grow up. I pray for these moments of innocent childhood to not pass her swiftly by. Thank You, Lord, for this time she can enjoy her youth and that she has such a wonderful friend in Brenda, who I know will be a rock in the storm for Trudy. How my heart yearns for the Trudy of yesterday, but still I give thanks, Lord, for the Trudy of today. Please help us to allow You to lead us down this path. Help us not to take our own paths in this or any other situation.*

* * *

Randy threw the basketball as hard as he could over and over against the backboard. He had almost gotten it down to a rhythm. *Why? Why? Why didn't she do it?* Finally exhausted, he plopped down on the driveway, leaning his back against the house, rolling the ball between his stretched-out legs. *I can't believe she didn't have the abortion. What are we going to do now?*

Dad will hit the roof; Mom will cry. Dad will probably try to make us get married. I don't want to get married. I love Trudy more than anyone in the world, but I'm not ready for that. No way. I have dreams. Randy bounced the ball over his head. *Why couldn't I have talked rationally to her yesterday? Maybe she would have changed her mind. I hope she's okay.* He tapped his head against the wall. *How on earth am I going to tell my parents?*

His parents had been excited when he'd started dating Trudy, since she was different than the girls from the crowd he hung out with, girls who liked to go to parties and stay out late. Trudy went to church, her social events were with the youth group and she had a curfew. They liked that and thought they didn't have to worry about him.

He looked down, shaking his head. *I can only imagine how disappointed our parents are going to be. How could I be so stupid? I knew she was different, so why didn't I respect that? She was so innocent! It was one of the things I first liked about her.*

Randy stood, wiping dirt off his sweats. He'd better go in and give her a call. He needed to see whether she had told her parents yet. *Why didn't she have the abortion?* He threw the ball one more time at the backboard and let it go wherever it may as he entered the house, slamming the back door behind him.

4

Randy rubbed his forehead while hanging up the phone. *What was that all about? What happened to Trudy? I thought I could talk her into getting rid of the baby and all she could talk about was how she was going to trust God. She even asked me for forgiveness.* "Whatever," he mumbled. "I don't want to think about it anymore. I'll deal with it tomorrow."

Randy's family was downstairs, in the middle of watching a movie, so he decided to go to his room to have some time to himself. Picking up the hand controller he began playing a video basketball game. The conversation with Trudy echoed through his mind, breaking his concentration.

"So did you tell yet," Randy had said without any greeting.

"I've told my grandma and…Brenda. She came out to the farm this afternoon."

"Brenda? What did she want? I didn't think you hung around with her anymore?" he grumbled.

"Well, I do now. We've talked. Seems Jodee Myers saw us coming out of the clinic yesterday and called Brenda to tell her about it."

"What? Oh great! I wonder how many other people she's shared this piece of news with?" *I don't believe it. Now the whole school will know. Jodee's such a blabbermouth!*

"Who cares? Everyone will know soon anyhow. I won't be able to keep it a secret."

"So you're determined to keep the baby."

"Yes," Trudy said. He could hear the confidence in her voice.

Randy sighed.

"Randy, I really love you. I'm not trying to make you mad or ruin your life. I just…" He could hear her start to sniffle. "I hope someday you'll understand. Abortion goes against everything I've ever believed in."

"Oh, how convenient for you. So I suppose having sex when you aren't married is okay? I mean, as long as you don't get caught, right?"

"Randy!" Trudy gasped. "Okay, I don't blame you for saying that, especially with how I acted. But I have to admit, I had to convince myself it was okay, that God would understand. But it wasn't. Having sex outside of marriage isn't God's way. In fact, the Bible says it's a sin," she answered quietly.

Randy didn't know what to say.

"Randy, I'm so sorry. I made a big mistake in our relationship. I shouldn't have let it go in the direction it went. I've decided to do things God's way now. But, even though I'm forgiven, I'll still have to pay the consequences."

Does this mean we're finished? I'm not ready to be a dad, but I still want to be with Trudy.

"Trudy, I need to go. I only wanted to talk about us, not this other stuff," Randy interrupted. "I don't get it anyway; you're talking nonsense. How is Jesus going to change anything?"

"Well, for one thing, *things* aren't going to change, but I am, and so can you. If I would've followed him, I wouldn't be pregnant simply because I wouldn't have had sex until I was married," Trudy explained.

"Whatever. I've got to go. I didn't expect this phone call to be about God. Maybe I'll call you in a few days." He didn't wait for her to respond, but just hung up the phone.

How did life get so complicated? This sucks. I'm not ready. Unable to concentrate, Randy put the video game controller down and grabbed his coat. "Dad, Mom, I'm going out for a little while," he yelled down the stairs, hoping they would hear him in the movie room.

His mom's face appeared at the bottom of the stairwell. "Where are you going, and what time do you plan on being back?"

Randy shrugged.

"Randy," his mom said in an exasperated tone.

"I'm going over to The Cave to see if any of the guys are there," Randy said.

"Okay, take my cell phone, since you're out of minutes, and please use it for emergencies only. Don't forget we're going to Aunt Cissy's in the morning for a couple days, so don't stay out late."

"Mom!" Randy whined. "I told you I don't want to go. I'm staying home."

"And I told you it'll be one of the last times we go as a family to see her. After graduation you'll be busy with sports and then college."

"Whatever. I'll see you in the morning." Randy turned to leave.

"Randy," his mom called.

"Yeah." He turned back toward her.

She blew him a kiss. "Love you."

"Love you too, Mom," he called back, making his way out the door.

* * *

After Trudy hung up the phone, she walked wearily into the kitchen. Brenda and Grandma Kay were busy upstairs making a bed for Brenda, who had decided to stay overnight. Needing a moment before joining them she stepped outside, letting out a long breath of air, relieved that the day was over, yet filled with a greater sadness than when it started. She leaned her head against a porch post. *Why can't Randy understand? I hate being apart from him. I want to be with him.*

The window from above opened. "Trudy, are you outside on the porch?" Brenda called.

Trudy walked out from under the overhang so Brenda could see her. "Yeah, I'm out here."

Brenda stretched and yawned sleepily. "Well, your grandma went to bed and I'm going to sleep, too. I'm taking the bed by the window since I got here first."

"Go ahead. I'll be up in a bit, but if I knew you were going to steal the best bed location, I'd have been there already." Trudy swatted at a moth.

Brenda grinned and started to duck her head back in through the window, but stopped and looked down with concern at Trudy. "So, do you need some company?"

"Actually, I need to be alone right now."

"I understand. Remember, I'm here if you need me. 'Night."

"'Night," Trudy called back as Brenda's head disappeared. "'Night, Grandma," she whispered when Grandma's bedroom light went off.

* * *

Brenda wasn't sure what woke her. A sleepy glance around the room revealed Trudy's bed was empty. *Trudy must have gotten up for water or something.* Brenda started to lie down again, snuggling under the quilt. *Wait, what's that noise?* Brenda sat up to look out the open window. Something white moved back and forth in the yard. Brenda leaned out further and rubbed her eyes to wake up so she could focus better. *It's Trudy swinging! What's she still doing outside?*

Brenda scooted out of the bed and searched for something to wear over her T-shirt. She grabbed a sweatshirt, pulling it over her head as she stumbled down the stairs.

* * *

Trudy could hear Brenda calling her name softly. *I don't want her to see me crying.* She wiped at her tears.

"Trudy." Gentle disapproval tinged Brenda's voice. "Since when do you have to hide your tears from me?" Brenda leaned down and put her hand on Trudy's shoulder.

"How"—she tried to talk—"how did...did you know I was still out here."

"Something woke me. I looked out the window to figure out what the noise was and saw you." Brenda sat on the grass.

"I didn't think I'd wake anyone up out here. Sorry about that."

"It's all right, Trudy," Brenda said with tenderness. "I'm glad I woke up."

"I don't know if I can do this, Brenda." She closed her eyes. "Have a baby on my own. I can't..." Trudy got all choked up again.

"I'd probably be just as afraid as you are right now. But, Trudy, you made the right decision yesterday. This may be hard, but the other road would've been so much harder." Brenda leaned forward. "And there's one thing I know, for certain. You *can* do it. I *know* you can do it."

"That's easy for you to say," Trudy said bitterly.

"Yes, yes, it is. You know why?" Brenda didn't wait for an answer. "Because I know you. I know what kind of family and friends you have. I know Jesus is right here with you, and in times like right now, when you can't carry on, He will carry you to the next step. He's not ever going to leave you alone."

"I sure felt lonely earlier—like I was the only person in the world. The future looked pitch black."

"Do you feel lonely now?"

"No, not as much," Trudy said.

"I hope someday you'll know it's okay to talk about stuff and let me be your friend. You don't have to be alone."

Trudy gave a little smile. "Thanks." She abruptly stood, offering her hand to help Brenda up. "I think I'll be able to sleep now."

"You sure?" Brenda sounded worried. "You don't want to talk some more?"

"No." Trudy yawned. "I cried so much it wiped me out."

Brenda put her hand on Trudy's shoulder, holding the door open when they reached the porch. They crept up the stairs so as not to wake Grandma Kay. Crawling into bed, Brenda asked again, "Are you going to be all right?"

"Yeah," Trudy said in a sleepy whisper. "Thanks, Brenda, good night."

"Good night."

Trudy could hear Brenda fluffing her pillow as she drifted off to sleep.

* * *

Music blared in the dimly lit room where groups of teenagers tried to talk over the latest song playing. Some sat in pairs talking in low tones. It had been a long time since Randy had shown up alone at the popular "kids' bar" called The Cave. It gave him a strange feeling.

Several families had gotten together and set it up for those under twenty-one to play pool and foos-ball and to drink nonalcoholic beverages soon after a group of college kids died in a car accident. They all had over the legal amount of alcohol in their blood.

"Hey, Randy!"

Randy looked to see who was calling him. *Oh no! It's Tony.* Tony had been a good friend of Trudy's when she was involved in youth group. Tony was always very friendly at youth group and school.

"What are you doing here, bud? Where's Trudy?" Tony asked.

Randy shrugged with a small smile. "I'm going to get a drink. Be back in a minute." *What did I expect? Of course people will wonder where she is. What do I say? I don't even know what's going on with us right now.* Randy took his drink and went back over to the pool table.

"Want to play a game?" Tony asked, holding a pool stick out to him.

"Sure." Randy took the offered cue stick. Tony racked the balls and waved his hand for Randy to break.

"Is Trudy sick or something?" Tony asked.

"She's staying at her grandma's this weekend."

"Oh. It's weird to see you without her."

"Yeah, well, it's weird to be without her." They both laughed, and Randy concentrated on his shot.

"Hey there, Randy!"

He recognized the voice. *Jodee Myers!* "Hi, Jodee," he said cautiously.

"So, where's Miss Trudy? I sure hope she isn't sick or something," Jodee said in an overly sweet voice. She looked toward Karen and started giggling.

Randy expelled a long breath through gritted teeth. He put down his cue stick, preparing to leave before Jodee and Karen started to mouth off.

"Are you leaving us so soon?" Karen purred close to his ear. "Missing Trudy?"

"Leave me alone." Randy sneered.

"Ooh, a little touchy tonight. There isn't something bothering you, is there, Randy?" Karen asked, looking innocent. "Don't worry. I promise I won't slip and tell where my dear friend Jodee saw you yesterday." She gave him a sly smile with a small tilt to her head.

Randy could feel his face turn red, and he clenched his fists.

"What's the matter, Randy? Afraid everyone will find out the truth about precious Trudy?" Jodee took another turn at baiting him.

"Hey you two, why don't you leave the guy alone?" Tony interjected.

Jodee and Karen gave Tony a haughty look. Randy picked up his jacket and tried to walk past the two of them.

"Isn't it something how perfect little Trudy seems to be? She's not so perfect now, is she, Randy?" Jodee brought her face close to his. He could smell her mint gum.

"Jodee, back off!" Randy warned.

"What's going on?" Tony asked. "Why are you two messing with him?"

"No reason. We're just having some fun, giving him a bad time because we know something about him and Trudy." Jodee pushed away from Randy.

"Well, go bug someone else. It's not often I get to spend time with just Randy," Tony said.

Jodee shrugged. "Okay, no biggee to us. But wouldn't it make you wonder if you saw the two of them coming out of an abortion clinic?"

Randy started to lunge at her, but Tony grabbed his arm and held on.

"What? There's no way, right, Randy?" Tony asked.

"Now you boys should have lots to talk about." Jodee laughed raucously over her shoulder. She and Karen walked away arm-in-arm, to the other side of the club.

"Are they joking?" Tony asked.

Randy shook his head. *Those little...*

"I don't want to talk about it. I've got to go." Randy shook off Tony's grip and started to walk away, but Tony grabbed his arm again.

"Randy, talk to me," Tony insisted.

"What for? It isn't any of your business," Randy yelled, jerking his arm free of Tony's grasp.

Kids turned to see what the commotion was all about.

Randy walked toward the door, throwing a glare in Jodee and Karen's direction. The outside air felt good on his face. He let out a long breath.

"Randy!" Tony called from the door.

Randy's shoulders dropped. Without responding to him, Randy went to his car. He could hear Tony's footsteps pounding the pavement behind him. *Why doesn't he just leave me alone!* He stopped abruptly and pivoted. Tony crashed into him, sending them both sprawling to the ground.

"You idiot, what are you doing?" Randy searched for his keys that had flown out of his hand.

"Sorry, Randy." Tony found Randy's keys. "Here."

"I told you in the club. I don't want to talk to you about it. Now let it go, okay?"

"Hey, Trudy's my friend. I'm concerned about her."

"Okay." Randy sighed. "She didn't have an abortion. Happy now?"

"I'm so glad to hear that! But wait—why were you at the clinic?"

Should I tell him? I don't want a lecture.

"C'mon, Randy, did she go to have an abortion? Did she change her mind?" Tony asked.

"Yes. We went so she could have an abortion. She changed her mind and wants to keep the baby," Randy said dully.

"But you still want her to do it, right?"

"Of course I still want her to do it!" Randy said firmly. "We don't have any business having a baby. I don't want to get married yet. I have college."

Tony shook his head.

"What?" Randy asked exasperated.

"You didn't know? When you have sex, there's an off-chance you could make a baby," Tony said.

"Oh, aren't you funny. Ha, ha."

"I'm quite serious. If you didn't want a baby or to get married, then why have sex?"

"Are you telling me you've never had sex?" Randy asked incredulously.

"No, I haven't," Tony answered.

"Well, I'm sorry for you." Randy turned toward his car.

"Randy, wait. I have my reasons for not having sex."

"I figure it's because you're religious. Anyway, I don't care! It's just too bad for you." Randy was exasperated.

"Well, most of the reason is because of my love for God, but I also have other reasons. Could you give me a few minutes?"

"What for, Tony?" Randy asked impatiently.

"First, I want to say I'm sorry for how I responded," Tony said remorsefully.

"Hey, it's okay." Randy unlocked his door.

"I also have something I want to tell you. I promise I won't take much more of your time."

"Honestly Tony, do I have a choice? You chased after me, even when I told you I didn't want to talk to you about the whole thing. So…jump in."

Randy relented with a shake of his head.

"What I'm telling you is confidential. Please don't pass this around to your friends," Tony started as soon as they were seated in the car. Randy nodded his okay for him to continue. "My brother's girlfriend had an abortion," Tony said quietly.

"Really? But your brother doesn't seem like he would..."

"What? Have sex or an abortion? He's changed since..."

"What? Your brother was able to go on like nothing happened, right? See, I knew it was no big deal," Randy said.

"She died."

"What?" Randy felt like he'd been kicked in the gut.

"Her uterus ruptured during the abortion. She lost a lot of blood. My brother called an ambulance, but by the time we got her to the hospital, it was too late." Tony's voice shook with emotion. "I called her dad. He got there just as she died. He didn't even get to say good-bye. He laid his head down on her chest and screamed. The medics couldn't get him to let go of her."

Tony stared out the window, wiping at his face. His voice became so soft Randy had to strain to hear him speak. "It was the most horrible sound I've ever heard. He begged her to open her eyes. My brother couldn't take it, so he took off. He called my mom from his cell phone to say good-bye. Then he drove down to the train tracks. When a train approached, he floored it. He didn't judge it right, so the train hit the back end of his car and flipped it." Tony stared at his lap, sniffing loudly, tears dropping unchecked. "It's a miracle! I could have lost my brother that night, too."

"Oh man, Tony! I didn't know," Randy said with compassion.

"No one knows. We agreed with her family to keep it a secret to protect her reputation." Tony exhaled.

"My brother and I ended up going through quite a bit of counseling. We've discovered there are lots of girls who've been seriously injured or died from abortion."

I can hardly believe this. I never thought of Trudy dying. I only wanted us to get rid of the problem. What if Trudy had gone through with the abortion and died? Randy's heart jumped in his throat. "I'm sorry, Tony."

"I know this is heavy stuff, and you weren't expecting me to lay all of this on you, but I have to ask: Is it worth the price?"

Randy jerked back as though he was hit.

"Even if you don't care about the baby, at least think about what an abortion could do to Trudy," Tony pleaded.

I am, Tony, I am. I would never want to hurt Trudy. I love her.

"I've seen you two together, and I believe you really do love her. Your face lights up whenever she flashes you one of her special smiles."

"Yeah, I do love her," Randy whispered, the corners of his mouth curled.

"Then why don't you take some time to think about what you're wanting her to do? You don't have to go by my story alone. You can talk to someone at a PRC—that's a Pregnancy Resource Center—even look on the internet."

"Okay, okay, Tony. Maybe I'll think about it. My mom insists I go with my family to visit my aunt." Randy wiped the moisture off of the windows. There were only a few cars left in the parking lot. *Maybe I should take some time to think about it. What would several days matter?*

"Yeah, I guess I'll do that," Randy consented.

Tony gave a sigh of relief. "Could I ask you something?"

"I seem to be at your disposal. Go ahead." Randy gave a short laugh.

"Hey, I don't mean to be pushy."

"No, really, Tony, go ahead. I'm only giving you a bad time."

"When you came to youth group, was it because you wanted to be with Trudy, or because you believe in and love God?"

"I believe in God," Randy answered defensively.

"I didn't say you didn't. I just asked why you came to youth group."

"Yeah, you did. Sorry. Okay, I'll admit it was to be with Trudy. I'm not really into religion."

"Good, neither am I."

"What? Tony, you have Christian written all over you," Randy scoffed.

"I have Christian written all over me? I'll take that as a compliment." Tony chuckled.

"Now you're confusing me. I thought you said you weren't into religion."

"I'm not. I'm into following Jesus."

"What's the difference?"

"Do you really want to know?"

"Yeah, I guess so. Trudy was saying the same thing tonight. She said she'll change because she's listening to Him or something like that. I don't get it."

"Here—let me show you something." Tony pulled a little book no bigger than a matchbook, made of different colors, out of his wallet.

"What's that?" Randy was curious.

"It's called a wordless book. Here." Tony leaned toward Randy. "See this gold page? It stands for heaven. That's where God lives. The streets are made of gold, everything's perfect, and there are no tears in heaven. The problem is we can't live there because"—Tony turned to the dark page—"this dark page. It represents the wrong choices we make. It's called sin."

"Oh, no! You're not going to tell me I'm a sinner and I'm going to burn in hell, are you?"

"Well, sort of …" Tony laughed. "Not really, but anyway, God is perfect and heaven is a perfect place. No one can add up, so we can't live there because no sin can enter heaven."

"I'm not a bad person." Randy fiddled with his keys, dangling from the ignition.

"I know. I'm not perfect. I make mistakes all of the time. Are you perfect?" Tony asked.

"Everyone makes mistakes. No one's perfect."

"God is perfect. He doesn't make mistakes. When I get up in the morning, I start making mistakes. I'm human," Tony said.

"So God doesn't understand that?"

"He does. He loves us even though we're flawed. He wants us to live with Him in heaven, so that's why He sent His Son, Jesus, to earth to live with us and teach us His ways." Tony turned to a red page. "Jesus paid the price for every wrong thing we've done or ever will do. The Bible says He was beaten so bad you couldn't even recognize Him. Then they nailed Him to a cross, and He died."

"But I remember in youth group the pastor saying Jesus was God in the flesh. If He was God, then why didn't He just make them stop beating Him? How come they could overpower Him and nail Him to a cross?"

"Good question!" Tony responded with excitement. "Jesus could've called a bunch of angels to cream the guys who were beating Him, and He could've refused to go to the cross. Instead, Jesus prayed. He knew what was ahead of Him. The last words written about His prayer was that He wanted to do the Father's will, not His own. He got up and let himself be arrested. He chose to pay the price for every wrong ever committed. The Bible says if you believe, you will be saved. He will make you white as snow." The next page was white. "God washes you clean and forgives you of every sin you've ever done. He makes you perfect and welcomes you into heaven."

"So then the rules come in, right?" Randy asked.

"No, see this green page; it's for growing. Just like a parent teaches a little kid, God teaches His children. When you read the Bible, pray, and hang out with other believers, you grow. As you grow in knowledge of Him and learn to *love* Him, you change."

"Hmm, that's what Trudy said tonight."

"So let me ask you something. When you die, do you know where you're going?"

Randy shrugged and sat in thoughtful silence. Tony sat beside him in silent prayer.

Randy finally spoke, shifting in his seat. "You know, I never thought it was important to consider before. But it's important enough to Trudy that she'd risk all of her relationships by not having an abortion. Just because Jesus wouldn't want her to." Randy rested his arms on the steering wheel. "What you said to me about Jesus…I never knew that."

"Now that you do know, what do you think?" Tony waited.

"I'm not sure. I want to do something, but I'm not sure what."

"You can say to God, 'I choose to believe. I don't understand it all, but I choose to believe. I'm sorry for my sins. I want to follow you, give my life to you. I believe you forgive me.'" Tony gazed intently at Randy. "That's prayer—talking to God. Hey, I'll pray with you and you can follow along."

Randy felt a stirring in his heart, a longing. *What's going on here? I want this, but I'm scared. What will it be like following Jesus? I want to know.* He nodded, unable to speak.

Tony understood and started out in prayer. "Lord…"

* * *

"Tony's still in Randy's car. Do you suppose he's preaching at him?" Karen tossed her cigarette out the car window. "I can't believe you saw Randy and Trudy outside of an abortion clinic. What were you doing there anyway?"

Jodee rolled her eyes. "Hello! I was picketing. You know how I feel about abortion." She took a long draw on her cigarette.

"Yeah, I know, but I didn't realize you were still carrying signs around to try to stop girls from having one. Do you think you're accomplishing anything? Has anyone ever turned around and left the clinic?" Karen asked.

"I don't know. But what else am I supposed to do?" Jodee said angrily.

"Hey! Don't get all uppity. I wasn't putting you down. I honestly want to know."

"I'm sorry. It's just so frustrating. I don't know what else to do. And no, I don't see anyone turn around and run to their car deciding against abortion." Jodee looked down at her hands. "I wish I knew something else to do."

"Maybe you could tell them your story," Karen suggested.

"My story?" Jodee gulped hard, fighting the lump that threatened to rise in her throat.

"Yeah, it might stop someone from making that choice. I mean, if you feel so strongly about it."

Jodee rubbed her forehead nervously. Karen was the only person who knew what had happened to her. *I don't know if I could let anyone know the truth about me. But I wonder if Karen's right. Maybe someone would change their mind and make the right choice.*

"It's a good idea, but I don't know, Karen. I'll think about it."

"So...do you think Randy's going to turn into a do-gooder like Brenda and Tony? I mean, Tony's been talking to him for a *long* time." Karen laughed.

"Randy? A do-gooder? No way—he wouldn't nerd out like that." Jodee stared out at his car. *Is he becoming a do-gooder? Is he figuring out what is so different about them? Yeah, Randy could become a do-gooder, but not me. No way. I'm not good enough. Besides, if anyone found out what my life was really like, they'd know what a loser I am.*

5

"Are you sure you don't want to ride to church with us, Grandma?" Trudy called out as she was getting into Brenda's car.

"I'm sure, honey. I don't want Brenda to have to drive all the way back out here. It's such a bother, and besides, it takes a lot of gas. I'll see you after church. Would you like to go have some lunch?"

Trudy hesitated. *Mom and Dad will probably want to join us. Mom's pretty perceptive, and Dad can see right through me. It could be uncomfortable.* "Um, Grandma, why don't I check with you afterward?"

"Okay. I'll talk with you later. I love you, dears." Grandma Kay drove down the driveway with a wave.

"Are you afraid your parents will come to lunch?" Brenda asked.

Trudy felt color rise in her cheeks. "Am I that obvious?"

"Well, it's obvious they'd want to join you and your grandma, especially since you've been out here all weekend. They'll probably want to catch up with you."

"That's what I'm afraid of," Trudy admitted in a quiet voice.

"Do you have any idea when or how to tell them?" Brenda checked for cars before pulling onto the highway.

"Are you kidding? No. I just wish it would all go away." Guilt rose inside Trudy. "That sounds horrible. It's so confusing. I don't want the baby to go away. But I wish I wasn't in this position. It's hard to come to grips with it. I know I'm making the right choice, but the whole situation seems too big to handle."

"I can only imagine," Brenda answered with compassion.

"Yeah, I wish I could say that."

"What? What do you mean by that?"

"That I was *only imagining* this whole thing!" Trudy said with frustration. She received a tender look from Brenda. *I love being able to talk with her again. Why did I ever think she wouldn't be my friend? She's so supportive. Well, she wouldn't have supported the choices I was making. Lectured me a lot, but that would've been her loving me.* "Thanks, Brenda, for putting yourself out there and confronting me yesterday. It *really* means more than you will ever know. I love having you for a best friend."

Brenda gave an awkward smile. "I missed you, Trudy. I'm so grateful that God allowed us to be friends again. He answered my prayers."

"Your prayers?"

Brenda nodded.

"I'm sorry. You were hurt during all of this, weren't you? I've been pretty selfish for the past year. I honestly haven't been thinking about you or others. I convinced myself that you and my family wouldn't understand."

"We all fumble around sometimes. We're not perfect. The good thing is that we were able to work it out and be friends again. I can only hope that when I'm fumbling around, you'll be there to catch me."

"I can't imagine you fumbling around," Trudy mumbled with an edge to her voice.

"Trudy, you said something like that yesterday. I'm trying to understand what you mean. I'm not perfect! I simply haven't walked where you've walked. How would you, or anyone else for that matter, know how I would respond? I need to know people will be there if I fumble."

"That's just it! If you were in the same circumstance as I was with Randy, you *would* make all the right choices. You're different. You have a relationship with God that's like an adult."

"Yes…I do love the Lord," Brenda agreed slowly, "but we are all capable of falling. Everyone has a weak spot, Trudy. Don't put me up on a pedestal. There will be times in my life when I'll have to make choices that'll be hard."

I want to seek God as quickly as I watch her seek Him. I want to know Him in a deeper way. Trudy's heart jolted. They were pulling into their church parking lot. *I'm so nervous. Will everyone know? My parents! If my Mom sees me, she'll know I'm hiding something. She searched my eyes Friday. She knew something was up. I'm not ready. I want to go back to the farm.*

"Come on, Trudy! I can see that wild-eyed look you get when you're nervous. You're okay. I'm right here with you, and for crying out loud, Grandma Kay knows your secret. Don't you think she'll intercede for you? She knows you're not ready to tell your parents. Now come on, and relax. Just enjoy being with God."

* * *

"Randy!" Randy's mother, Cassie, knocked on his bedroom door. "Randy!" She called once again while opening it. She smiled down at Randy, who continued sleeping. He could sleep through anything. She went over to his bed and shook him. He turned onto his side groaning. "It's time to get up. We'll be leaving in about an hour to go to Aunt Cissy's." Gently, she brushed the hair from his forehead. "Come on now. You need to get up and get ready."

He squinted and gave her a slow smile. "Wake up, sweet baby," she said with tenderness.

Randy rubbed his eyes and stretched. "What time is it?"

"You don't want to know. I heard how late you got in last night. Were you with Trudy? What do her parents think of her being out until that time?"

"No, I wasn't with Trudy." He turned his face back into his pillow and then lifted his head to steal a look at the clock, only to plop it back into his pillow with a groan. "Six o'clock! Who wants to get up at six on a Sunday?"

"We're leaving in about an hour. You need to get up and get ready now."

"So soon?" Randy yawned and stretched, nearly kicking his mom off the bed. "Do I have to go? Can't I stay home? I've got too much going on."

"Well, so much for my sweet baby. Come on, Randy. Your aunt would be upset if you didn't. Besides, I didn't plan for you to stay home."

"Plan? What do you have to do? I can take care of myself," Randy retorted.

"Randy, you're going with us. That's final. Now hurry up and get in the bathroom, then get your stuff together so we can leave."

Randy fell back on his bed, frustrated. "I can't believe I can't just stay home. Why do we have to leave so early?"

"Randy," she said firmly, "we go through this every time we're going to do something as a family. Could you make things easy for once?" She headed toward the door.

Randy sat up, still sleepy. He grabbed his robe and followed her groggily to the bathroom, passing his dad on the way.

"Good morning!" his dad said with a big smile. "How's my boy this morning?"

"Morning," Randy groaned. *How can Dad be so cheery in the morning?* Randy closed the bathroom door and caught a vision of himself in the mirror. *Dad?* He got closer to the mirror and looked at himself. *Dad? Did Dad look this young when he first became a father? I doubt it.* He stared a bit longer. *I'm going to be some kid's dad! I can't even get myself up in the morning.* Randy's knees were weak. Nauseated, he sat on the side of the bathtub, burying his face in his hands. *How on earth am I going to tell my parents!?* Randy sat like that until his mom knocked on the door.

"Randy I haven't heard the shower yet. You need to hurry! We're leaving soon," she called from the other side of the bathroom door.

Yeah, yeah, yeah, who cares!? He turned the shower on as hot as he could stand, wishing the water could wash his mind clear of the mess he had made of his life.

∗ ∗ ∗

Randy leaned against the back of the car seat with his headphones on and his eyes closed. He was listening to his favorite CD. It brought him back to times he had spent with Trudy. He missed her. It would be a week before he could see her again! *I wish I hadn't acted the way I did when she told me about not having the abortion. It did make me mad, though. Scared, actually. I still can't believe it.* His stomach knotted up and he gritted his teeth. *Why did this have to happen?* He stared at the back of his parents' heads. His hands got clammy. *I have to tell them about the baby soon. They're not going to be happy.*

"Randy!" His little sister, Katey, pulled the headphone from his ear.

Randy pushed her away, using some of the frustration he felt about the baby on her in the push.

"Ow! You big bully!" Katey slugged his arm.

"Knock it off, Katey!" Randy pushed her again. He would never hit his sister. Even so, she always ended up crying when they fought. He thought it was so she wouldn't get in trouble. It usually worked.

"Randy!" his mom called over the back seat. "Quit acting so rough with your sister."

Katey eyed him with a triumphant smile. Randy shook his head. He had enough troubles; he didn't need this. Crossing his arms, he leaned his head back again on the seat.

Katey started to grab his headphone again, but this time he caught her before she yelled in his ear.

"What do you want?" he yelled at her.

"Mom! Randy is yelling at me! I was only trying to get his attention to see if he was hungry or not," Katey called to their mom.

"Well, Katey, maybe you shouldn't be grabbing his headphones," their mom answered. Randy grinned at his sister, but then his mom continued. "And Randy, you can be more patient with your sister. I'm not going to have this go on between the two of you the whole trip."

"Yes, Mom," Randy and Katey answered.

"So who's hungry?" their dad called.

Randy didn't feel like eating, but he knew his dad must be hungry or he wouldn't be saying anything. "We could stop now to eat," Randy answered.

"Yeah, let's stop now," Katey said.

Randy's dad pulled into a restaurant parking lot. Katey jumped out of the car first, trying to tempt someone to race her in. No one took her up on it. She waited at the door for them.

When they entered, the waitress showed them to a table and they ordered their meals. Randy stared out the window as his parents talked about the drive. Katey played with the kid's stuff on the table.

Randy surveyed the different buildings down the street, noticing they were pretty much the same stores as in their city. He didn't know why they'd be any different. *Whoa! Now that's different.* He smiled when a girl walking down the street in front of a church caught his eye. She wasn't as pretty as Trudy, though.

He recalled the first time he saw Trudy. She hung around a different crowd than he did, but her locker was across the hall from his.

One day at the beginning of the year, he was in a pretty bad mood. Everything was getting on his nerves that day. He opened up his locker and a couple of girls were giggling like girls do. It bugged him. He turned around to scowl at them. Instead his heart beat funny when his eyes met hers. The look on her face seemed to include him in whatever was happening to make her smile. He caught himself grinning back. The rest of the day he was in a great mood, and he couldn't quit thinking of the girl at the locker.

"Randy, Randy." He heard his mother calling his name. "Randy, are you all right?"

"Huh? Yeah, I was just thinking." Randy shook his head to come back to reality.

"Are you thinking of Tru-udy?" Katey laughed.

"Katey, stop teasing your brother," his mom said. "It's time to eat."

Randy couldn't believe it! He hadn't noticed the waitress put his food in front of him. It was a struggle to eat. He couldn't stop thinking about Trudy and the baby. Randy looked out the window in the direction he had noticed the girl. She wasn't there anymore. Instead, he saw a sign in front of a church: *Did you know God hears you Monday through Saturday too? Did you know He talks to you through His Word? The Bible? Come join us for WORSHIP and Fellowship with God on Sunday mornings.*

Randy recalled all that had transpired the night before. Tony had said the same thing. If Randy wanted to develop a relationship with God, he should spend time reading the Bible. Tony had given him one to use and a pad of paper with instructions to write down anything that stood out to him. He wrote some verses for Randy to look up during the long drive with his family.

Hmmm, maybe I should get the Bible out of my suitcase in the trunk.

As soon as breakfast was over, Randy got the keys to the car from his dad. He ignored his sister's comments as he opened the Bible to hear what God had to say to him.

* * *

Trudy's dad, Bill, was standing in front of the church talking to Grandma Kay. Trudy slowed her steps. "I can't do this, Brenda."

Brenda turned and took hold of Trudy's hands. "Yes, you can. Trudy, remember what we talked about in the car? The different thing you see in my relationship with God? I think it's this, right now. If I were in your shoes, I would be scared, but now is the time to call on God and allow Him to get you through. You, dear Trudy, are not alone. He's with you."

He is with me. He said He would never leave me nor forsake me. Okay, I'm going to lean on Him to get me through this, until the appropriate time to talk to my parents.

Trudy nodded at Brenda, and they walked arm-in-arm up the church steps. "Trudy!" Bill called out. He closed the gap between them, enclosing her in a big bear-hug. "How's my girl? I missed you this weekend. But I can't tell you how happy it made me that you were spending time with your grandma!"

"It was quite a blessing!" Grandma Kay interjected.

Bill included Brenda in the hug. The girls grinned at each other. He was known for his squishy hugs.

"Okay, Dad. I love you, but I think we've had enough hugging." Trudy pretended to complain.

"I agree!" Brenda squeaked in a high voice as he gave them a final squeeze before letting them go. The four of them laughed together.

"What's all the laughing about? Are you having a party without inviting me?" Sheryl joined the group, putting her arms around Trudy and Brenda. "Good morning, girls! How was your weekend?"

Mom's got to be curious about Brenda. We haven't hung out in over a year.

"It was great, Mom." Trudy smiled up at her.

"That's good. Is everyone up to going to lunch together after church? Brenda, can you join us?" Sheryl asked.

"I would love to, but let me check with my mom and dad."

"Why don't you ask them to join us?"

"Okay, I'll do that," Brenda answered.

"Well, we better get inside," Grandma interjected. "I suppose you two will want to go sit with your friends, so let's all meet out here afterward."

Whew! I'm glad that's done. Trudy walked with Brenda to their seats. The other kids made room for them.

"Hey, Trudy." A voice came from the pew behind her. She turned around to see who it was. *Tony!*

"Tony! How're you doing?" She reached over the pew for his hand, and he gave her shoulder a friendly squeeze before holding her hand. Tony was like one of the girls to her. They'd known each other since they were in diapers. He welcomed her with a hug.

"What have you been up to?" she asked.

"Not much. I did hang out with Randy last night." Tony sounded excited.

"What!?" *Why would Randy hang out with Tony? Does Tony know? No. Why would Randy tell him?* Trudy felt her face flush. Tony must have noticed. He put his other hand over hers and held on a bit tighter. *He knows! I've got to leave!*

"It's okay, Trudy," Tony said softly.

Trudy pulled her hand back over the pew while looking for her purse.

Brenda gave her a curious look. "What's up?" she whispered.

"I've got to go." Trudy started to leave, but Tony leaned over the pew while Brenda gripped her purse.

"I said it's okay. A wonderful thing happened last night with Randy."

"With Randy? You saw him last night?" Brenda asked awed.

"Yes, he came to The Cave. We played pool," Tony explained.

"What was so wonderful?" Trudy asked cautiously.

The worship leader started speaking, interrupting their conversation. *I'll have to talk to Tony later.* Tony waved before sitting back in his seat. Brenda gave an okay sign with her hand, her face filled with concern. Trudy shook her head. *What on earth is going on? Lord, what does Tony know? I can't focus on this music. Help me, Lord.*

Trudy glanced at Brenda again, who wore a questioning expression. Trudy gave a half-smile, mouthing, "I'm okay." Brenda nodded, turning her attention back to worship.

It's been so long, Lord, since I've been here to worship. Once again my thoughts are cluttered with other things. I want to learn to worship You, Lord, and put my life in your hands. Trudy tried to sing along with the rest of the church. *I pray to put my mind on You, to love You more than I love Randy.* She closed her eyes to focus on the words of the song. *Why couldn't I have heard about Randy after the service? It would be easier to concentrate.*

"When you draw near to Me, I will draw near to you."

Lord?

"I will never leave you nor forsake you."

Trudy's heart felt peace. *I want to trust and love You more than anything in my life. I believe my prayer will be answered because I want to draw near to You, Lord.* Trudy sat with a smile, not noticing when the music stopped playing.

* * *

Randy lost track of time while he read the Bible. It amazed him to read of the things that Jesus did for the people. He couldn't understand, and it upset him, when the people turned on Him and wanted Him to be killed. *Whoa! That's awful! Everyone turned on Him. Why did the soldiers beat Him?* He cringed when they put thorns on Jesus head. *Man, Jesus didn't do anything!*

He wrote down questions to ask Tony later: What is a prophecy? How did Jesus know what was going to happen to Him? Why didn't Jesus use His power to set himself free?

He was curious to know what happened to Jesus. *I think it has something to do with Easter. I'm not sure what, but I know Trudy's family makes a big deal over celebrating what Jesus did on that holiday.* He was amazed how Jesus acted when He was hanging on the cross. *Jesus prayed to His Father to forgive the people that were there. Man, I can't even imagine! He's pretty cool. I'd like to be like that.* Then Jesus died. *How disappointing.*

Sad, he looked out the car window. *Why did He have to die? Jesus was a really nice guy, so why'd they have to kill Him?* Randy didn't feel like reading the rest of the story, but he decided to at least finish the chapter. *What? Wait a minute. Did it really happen like this? Jesus came back to life?* Reading further he read the accounts of Jesus meeting with the disciples. *How did He do that? Well, how did he bring those other people back to life? Like the guy named Lazarus. Now he brought himself back to life? This is amazing.*

"Hey, Randy!" his dad called to him.

"Yeah."

"How would you like to drive for a while? Give your dad a break?"

Randy knew something was happening to him since he'd rather finish reading about Jesus than drive. But he agreed to drive.

His dad got settled in the back seat. "Is this what you've been so interested in while we've been driving?"

Randy looked over his shoulder, "Yeah. You wouldn't believe what it says in that. You should read it."

Randy's dad chuckled. "If it caught your attention and got you to read as much as you have, I think I will." So he sat back and opened the Bible.

* * *

When the service was over, Trudy walked down the aisle as quick as possible. She planned on hiding in the women's bathroom to avoid talking with Tony. Brenda, however, had different plans.

"Wait, Trudy, there's my mom and dad. Let's go see if they want to go to lunch with us." Brenda held her arm, turning them to her parents' direction. Instead, Trudy was face to face with Tony again.

"Trudy, I want to talk to you," Tony said.

"Tony, we're kind of in a hurry. We're going to lunch with our parents. Why don't I give you a call?" Trudy offered, brushing his arm.

"It looks like you may have a minute." Tony nodded toward the Sanders, Brenda's parents. They were in a circle praying over someone, and Brenda had joined them. Trudy's shoulders fell as she let out a sigh.

"Okay, I'm going to be honest here. I'm not feeling very comfortable right now. I don't know what Randy told you last night, but…" She looked him straight in the eye. Tony rubbed her arm with a gentle caress, his eyes filled with compassion. "Tru, you know my story, and I'm your friend."

"Still, can you tell me what you two talked about?" she asked nervously.

"I think it's okay for me to tell you. And yes, he did tell me what happened Friday. I'm proud of you, Trudy. Very proud. You made the right decision. It may not feel like it, but you have."

Trudy felt hot all over. "I'm ashamed," she whispered.

"Shame is not from God, Tru. Did you confess this to Jesus?"

"Yeah, for the first time in my life, I'm realizing what it's like to have a 'relationship'"—she put her fingers up to do a quotation sign—"with God."

"That's great! I'm happy for you."

"Thanks." She glowed from his encouragement.

"So, in this relationship, does shame fit? I think 'love'"—he did the quotation sign back to her—"is what fits in a relationship."

Trudy smiled at him. *He really is a great guy. Why is this guy single?*

"So, Trudy, ready to go?" Brenda and her parents walked up interrupting their conversation.

"I'll give you a call later this week." Tony gave her a salute. She didn't miss the wink he directed at Brenda before walking away, Trudy noticed for just a second Brenda looked a bit flustered, but she quickly recovered. *Hmmm, I wonder what's going on there? I need to file this away to ask Brenda about later.*

* * *

"Oh my goodness, Tru, your face is pretty red," Brenda exclaimed before she started backing the car out of the parking spot.

"What?" Trudy pulled the visor down to look in the mirror. Oh no, her face was red! "I'm in trouble now." After having lunch with their parents, they had spent the afternoon doing homework on a blanket at the park. With her fair skin she was in the habit of putting sunscreen on, but she must have needed to reapply it. Brenda, on the other hand, rarely burned but turned a beautiful brown.

"This is horrible. I hope I don't peel." With urgency she rubbed cream all over her face. She caught Brenda's look of sympathy. Suddenly, Trudy felt a smack to her head. Squealing tires was the last sound she heard before everything went blank....

* * *

Something white blocked her vision. Brenda pumped and pumped at the brake, but still the car rolled. *What happened? What did I hit?*

She then realized she was pressing the gas pedal instead of the brake. Moving her foot over to press the brake, the car stopped. The white ended up to be the air bag that had gone off on impact. Dazed and in pain, she turned her head toward Trudy. Her friend's eyes were closed.

"Trudy? Oh no! Trudy!" Brenda yelled. She opened her car door. "Somebody help! My friend is unconscious." She grabbed her cell phone and dialed 9-1-1.

The police said they were on their way, so she hung up and called her parents. "Mom! We've been in an accident. Trudy's unconscious," Brenda cried.

"What! Where are you?" Lorinda screamed back.

"Uhh...we're down by the river."

A paramedic approached her. "Miss, you okay?"

"My friend isn't. She's..."

Trudy moaned from inside the car. "Brenda..." Trudy slowly tried to get up.

"We need you to stay still, ladies. We'll get some carts over here immediately. You'll need to go to the hospital to get checked out." The paramedic signaled toward the other EMTs, and both girls were soon strapped down on carts and put in the back of a waiting ambulance. Their parents would meet them at the hospital.

* * *

Trudy could hear her parents. "Where's our daughter, Trudy Thomas?" and "How is she?" She took some deep breaths, trying not to panic. The paramedics had strapped her to the cart, and she couldn't move her head to the left or right.

"Trudy!" Her parent's faces appeared above her, blocking out the light glaring in her eyes.

"Mom, Dad." Trudy's voice whined just she had as a little girl. "I want out of this thing."

"I know, honey, but the doctors are going to do some X-rays and then they'll be able to unstrap you." Sheryl stroked her forehead and cheek.

"When? I'm scared."

"In a couple of minutes. I need to look you over and do a few quick tests." A friendly looking lady smiled down at her. "I'm Dr. Young. Do you know where you are?"

"The hospital," Trudy answered.

"Yes. Do you know what day today is?"

"Sunday." Trudy then went on to answer a series of questions.

"Good, good. Okay, we're going to bring you into the X-ray room." The doctor smiled at the two technicians who came to push the cart.

X-ray! Oh no! I'm not sure, but I think X-rays can hurt babies. What do I do? I haven't told my parents yet. They can't find out this way.

"Excuse me." Trudy tried to get their attention. "Excuse me."

"Yes, young lady, what can I do for you?" one of them answered.

"Are my parents with us?"

"Yes, Trudy, I'm right here. Your dad is waiting back in the room. He's calling Grandma Kay," her mom answered.

Oh, God, what am I going to do? Do I tell her here, now? I can't let them hurt the baby. Lord, help me.

"Okay, ma'am, it's a pretty small space in here. Let's have you wait just outside this door. As soon as we're finished, we'll bring her back out to you."

Trudy sighed in relief.

"Uhhh, excuse me. I have a slight problem," she said.

"What was that, Miss? Are you okay?" the nurse said with concern.

"No. Can my mom hear me?" Trudy asked.

"Your mom? She's outside, honey. As soon as we're done, we'll get you back to your mom. You'll be okay," she said in a soothing voice.

"No, no. I have to tell you something, but she doesn't know yet. I can't have an X-ray."

"What? Honey, we need to make sure you didn't break anything."

"But I'm *pregnant*," she whispered forcefully.

"What? You're…ohhh." The nurse signaled to the other tech. "Sid, come here." She waved him over. "She's pregnant."

"And you haven't told your mom yet?" Sid let out a low whistle. "We can take care of that."

"No, don't tell her. I don't want her to find out this way." Trudy panicked.

"Shh, I wouldn't do that. I have a lead cape to put over you to protect your baby." Sid grabbed it and laid it across Trudy's stomach. "There you go. Everything will be okay now."

Thank You, Lord! Thank You.

* * *

Sheryl watched through the small window of the door. She could barely make out what was happening because one of the nurses blocked her view until she assisted the other one in putting a lead cape over Trudy's stomach area. *That's funny. Now why would they be doing that? I've only had that done when I thought I was pregnant.* A knot formed in her stomach. *Maybe it's because of her age, to protect her from the radiation. That's it.*

* * *

"Okay, little Miss. We can unstrap you now. Nothing looks broken in your neck, but you will still need to lie on this cart for further tests."

"Thank you. I'm so relieved to be untied; I'm very claustrophobic." Trudy exhaled.

"I hear you on that one," the tech answered. "I don't like being tied down myself." She opened the door while Sid pushed the cart through. Trudy's mom came alongside the cart and held her hand as they went down the hall.

"Where are we going now?" Sheryl asked.

"There is quite a bit of bruising on her abdomen; the doctor called for an ultrasound," Sid answered.

"An ultrasound?" Trudy gulped. *That's what they use at the counseling center for pregnant women to see their baby! What am I going to do now?*

"Yes, it's a simple procedure to see your abdomen. It won't hurt you at all," Sid said in a consoling voice. "Well, good luck to you." He pushed her into the ultrasound room.

Good luck? Who needs luck? I need God's mercy right now.

"Can I come in with her, or do I need to wait outside?" Sheryl asked.

I want you to wait outside. Maybe the screen will be turned the other way.

"You can come in. There's plenty of room," the technician said in a friendly voice, going on to explain to Trudy what she would be doing to her. The jelly felt cold on her stomach. Soon she felt the wand moving in circles across her abdomen.

Trudy kept her eyes on her mom. Sheryl smiled down at her, gently caressing her forehead.

"Oh," the technician said quietly.

"Did you see something?" Sheryl turned to look at the monitor.

"Uh, well, I'm not allowed to report anything. The doctor will have to give you her report."

"If there's something wrong, I want to know." Sheryl said as she looked over at the monitor.

No! Don't let her see. Not this way, please, Lord! Trudy's heart raced.

"What's that flashing light? It looks like..." Sheryl stared at it with a questioning look, brows furrowed. Her eyes became large, her mouth dropped, and she looked down at Trudy. "Trudy?"

She knows! She knows! I didn't want her to find out this way!

The technician rubbed the jelly off of Trudy's stomach with a towel.

"Okay, the doctor will meet you in your room and give you a full report." Her steps were hurried as she called for assistance. Sid entered to push Trudy back out of the room.

Trudy glanced at her mom. Their eyes met. Her heart sank. She could see the clear disappointment in her mom's eyes.

* * *

Grandma Kay was sitting in her rocker listening to the radio. Sunday evenings were her favorite time to be alone, to read and pray. When a song played that touched her heart, she would sing along, ending the day praising Jesus. Tonight there were quite a few things to pray about. She didn't worry. She knew Jesus took care of everything. She had learned not to ever try to carry burdens around on her own shoulders. She trusted Him to know what to do far better than she ever would.

After her prayer time, she'd wait to hear His still small voice of wisdom. Oh, how she loved these times.

Glancing over at Grandpa Elwood's empty rocker caused her to remember how hard it had been the first time, after her dear husband had died, to spend this time with Jesus. Her heart felt so lost. Ever since they were first married, it was their special time together, clear to the end.

Most of that night was spent staring at his empty chair, missing her sweet husband, not hearing the music or looking at the Word.

"Why? Why, Jesus, did you take him to heaven before me? I wanted to go first." She sobbed. Then the Lord reminded her of the last words Elwood had whispered slowly in her ear.

"I did my living, sweet Kay. I've seen all Jesus wanted me to see. My job is done. You still have living to do, dear one. Miss me, but don't waste time grieving me. Remember our happy times and how much I loved you. Remember that Jesus will never leave you." Her ear was pressed close to his cheek to hear him. She clung to those last moments of feeling his breath on her face, the warmth of his hand, the smell of his skin.

"You made me a very happy man. I thank God He gave me you." She could feel his smile, their tears mingling as they rolled down his face.

"Elwood, you made me a very happy woman. I will always love you."

He nodded in response, tightening his grip on her hand. "I'll be waiting for you in heaven, dear." Then he simply went to sleep.

"Elwood? Elwood? No…I'm not ready. I want to talk some more! Let me hear you," Grandma cried out. "Come back."

Sitting alone in her living room, she started singing that night, realizing she didn't have to wait for someday. For when she was singing to Jesus, she believed Elwood was up in heaven singing along.

The ringing of the phone startled Kay as she tried to get her whereabouts. Her cheeks were wet with tears. *Oh, that startled me.* She got up and answered it, checking her caller I.D. *Bill.*

"Hello?" she answered.

"Mom." He sounded urgent.

"What's the matter, honey? Are you okay? Trudy? Sheryl?" she asked. *Did Trudy tell them she was pregnant?*

"Trudy was in an accident. We're at the hospital. They just took her in for X-rays," Bill stopped talking and took a deep breath. "I called for you to pray for her."

"I'll be there as soon as I can, Bill. I'll be praying the whole way."

"Thanks, Mom." Bill sounded relieved.

"Bill, Jesus is right there with her. He's watching over her."

"I know, Mama, I know."

Grandma Kay hung up the phone, grabbed her car keys, and ran out the door as fast as her old legs could carry her.

6

Silence rang loud. Trudy and her mom waited for the doctor. *Where do I begin?* Trudy took a peek over at her mom.

"Trudy, do you have something to tell me?" Sheryl asked warily.

Trudy nodded.

"Well?" Sheryl prodded gently.

"I didn't want you to find out this way, Mom. I'm so sorry," Trudy blubbered.

"Please, tell me it's not what I think I saw on the ultrasound." Sheryl covered her face.

"I wish I could say it wasn't, but Mom, I'm pregnant."

Sheryl blew out a long breath. "How did this happen? I mean, I know how it happened, but you…I thought your choice would be different. You were going to save that for marriage. I guess that doesn't matter now. What matters is making sure you and the baby are healthy."

Trudy's heart sank. "Mom, I'm sorry I disappointed you. This last year, I've been living a lie. When I went out to Grandma Kay's, I came face-to-face with that, and I'm making a clean start in my relationship with God, and everyone around me. I've been lying to you and Dad about what I've been doing," Trudy admitted.

"Lying?"

"Yes. I didn't go to youth group events with Randy; we went to his house. I believed we were going to get married, but he doesn't want the baby."

"He doesn't want the baby? What does he want? An abortion?"

"Yes, we went to a clinic," Trudy said softly.

"You went to a clinic? What? Not an abortion clinic?"

Trudy nodded.

"Trudy, I taught you…I…can't believe this." Sheryl paced the room. The door opened, almost hitting her when she passed it.

"Grandma Kay is on her way. I talked to Lorinda and Steve. Brenda's doing okay. They're getting ready to take her home. She has minor bruising and a sore neck," Bill said as he entered the room. He stopped in his tracks, looking from Trudy to Sheryl. "What? What's the matter? Did the doctor find something wrong?"

A knock on the door interrupted his questions.

"Hello? We have the report back. Seems like everything checked out fine. I recommend bed rest for a couple of days this week and warn you away from ibuprofen due to your condition. Ice every hour for ten minutes, and you will need physical therapy for your legs and arm. Here is a number for a Physical Therapist in case you don't know of one. Call your doctor this week to do a follow-up. Any questions?"

"Condition? What condition?" Bill asked with a puzzled expression.

The doctor looked from Trudy to Sheryl to Bill, assessing the situation. Trudy shook her head.

"I'll tell him. There's no need for you to explain," Trudy answered defeated.

"Tell me what? What's going on?" Bill said loudly, panic ringing in his voice.

"I'll leave you now. Report back here if you experience anything on this sheet of paper. Follow up with your doctor in two days." The doctor handed Sheryl the paperwork to sign and then left the room.

"Okay, what's going on?" Bill said firmly.

"Bill, sit down, so Trudy can explain," Sheryl offered.

"Explain what? Just tell me."

"Dad…" Trudy's voice shook.

"Trudy, honey, what's wrong with you?"

"I'm pregnant," she whispered.

The words caused Bill to fall back, mouth open. "You're…we're…finding this out here? Now? Great!"

"I didn't plan…"

"Obviously, why now?" Bill shouted. Sheryl touched his arm, shushing him. He stepped away from her. "Is that why you went out to the farm? Does Grandma Kay know?" He didn't give Trudy time to answer. "Let's get you out of here and deal with this at home." Bill moved about the room picking up Sheryl's and Trudy's purses.

"Hellooo!" A small petite nurse peeked her head in. "I have a wheelchair for you. Are you ready to go? Sir, could you bring your car around? I'll meet you at the emergency exit doors."

Bill grunted his answer and stormed out of the room. Sobs racked Trudy's body as the nurse helped her onto the chair.

"It's okay, honey, it's good to cry. Accidents are very stressful on the body and the emotions." Sheryl reached down to hold Trudy's hand while they walked out of the hospital.

* * *

Bill pulled the car up to the emergency exit door. Her whisper, "I'm pregnant," screamed in his ears. The same words he'd heard Sheryl say many years ago. *Now my daughter's pregnant! What did we do wrong? Sheryl and I made sure to teach her about God, and His ways, to prevent her from making the same mistake we did.* Scenes from the past he'd kept tucked away came to the forefront of his mind....

* * *

"Bill." Sheryl twisted her long hair around her finger, a sure sign she was nervous.

He captured her hand while landing a gentle kiss on her forehead. "What are you so nervous about, little flutterbug?" He laughed, pulling her close to him.

Sheryl pushed against his chest. "This is serious, Bill." She held his hand, her eyes scared.

"What's the matter, babe?" he worried.

"I'm pregnant."

"Pregnant!" A thousand emotions coursed through his body. He held her close. Both of them were scared. What were they going to do? Sheryl believed her parents would never talk to her again if they found out she was pregnant. Bill didn't want to disappoint his parents.

Sheryl heard about a girl who had been in the same situation. She'd had an abortion so nobody would know she'd ever been pregnant. It had just been legalized. It sounded like a good idea to Bill and Sheryl.

A few weeks later they skipped school and drove to another city where nobody knew them. They had no idea what would actually happen. Bill went in the room with Sheryl. Although they tried to have him sit in the waiting room, Bill wouldn't hear of it. He insisted on staying with her.

Bill had to use all of his restraint to not throw up when the tubes filled with blood. *It's our baby. I let them take our baby.* They both walked out shell-shocked.

That evening they ended up confessing to his parents what they'd done. The abortion was scarier than the initial news of Sheryl's pregnancy.

At first his parents were hurt and angry, but over the course of time they were a source of help to Sheryl and Bill. After the abortion Bill's faith in God became real and not something he had inherited from his folks.

The same was not true for Sheryl. She broke up with Bill. It was over two years before they got back together—a torturous two years for him, for he loved her and wanted to marry her. But she went down a dark, scary road emotionally, nearly taking her own life before receiving forgiveness and healing from God.

After they were back together, they still struggled physically. Fortunately one or both of them came to their senses. Bill's drive home, after an evening with Sheryl, was filled with guilt and shame. They started to meet in public places or in groups.

Bill begged her time and time again to please marry him. But Sheryl wasn't ready. Then one night, when Sheryl's parents were out of town, Bill dropped by for just a moment. Neither of them came to their senses. They woke up in the morning together.

Two weeks later Bill heard the words again, "I'm pregnant."

Sheryl asked him to go with her. Like last time, Bill agreed. How could they let people know what the two of them had been doing? They were Christians now. They should know better.

Neither spoke on the way to the appointment. Bill opened the door to the clinic for Sheryl. Scenes from their last visit ran through his mind. He almost vomited. This time he didn't win the argument. Sheryl had to go in alone. He gave her a slight kiss on the cheek with a quick squeeze. Sheryl wouldn't look at him. Her shoulders sagged and her head was down, eyes to the floor.

Sitting in the waiting room was torture. *God forgive us for what we are about to do. I'm so sorry.*

The words, *"Go get her and bring her home, trust me,"* raced through his mind over and over again. Bill's knees were shaky as he walked across the room and down the hallway to the door he believed she was in. He did a soft knock and then knocked with more resolve.

The door opened slightly. It was Sheryl.

"Put your clothes on. We're going home. I love you, and I will love our baby," he said with more courage than he felt.

"I know. We need to trust God. We don't belong here." Sheryl gave him a slow smile, nodding.

On the way home Bill convinced her to marry him. Finally! They would do it right away.

The time came to share the news of their impending marriage to his parents. His mom cocked her head a little, and kindness like he'd never seen before poured out of her eyes. "You're going to have a baby, aren't you?"

Sheryl stepped back. "How did you know?" Her voice shook.

"I didn't until just now. The words 'Grandma Kay' floated musically through my mind."

Sheryl stared shamefaced at the floor. Kay walked to her and squeezed her close. "I love you, Sheryl. You're already like a daughter to me. Now I can truly say you're my daughter. I'm very blessed. I love your baby too, honey."

"I almost had another abortion," she whispered.

Kay started to step back, shocked, but caught herself in time. She barely nodded. "Bill?"

"We were afraid. We wanted to hide," Bill admitted.

"You can hide from eyes you can see," his dad said softly. "But you cannot hide from the eyes you cannot see. God asks for confession, from *all* of His children, every day for their shortcomings. He would never ask you to hide."

"I know, Dad. He's the one who impressed on our hearts to go home and trust Him."

"When my parents find out, they'll never talk to me again. I don't want to lose them," Sheryl had whimpered.

Elwood responded, "I don't know what to say, except we'll need to pray about this. If that happens, and I say if, Kay and I will always be here for you. I know we can't replace them, but we'll be here."

Bill had always admired his dad, but never more than at that moment.

Sheryl was right. Her parents didn't come to the wedding. The last time she saw them was when they moved Sheryl out of their house. Sheryl still sent pictures of Trudy every Christmas, but they never replied.

Soon after having Trudy, Sheryl found herself pregnant again. Only this time she miscarried not once, but twice. She believed it was her punishment for having an abortion. Finally, she went through a study at church that gave her a foundation of truth. She walked in forgiveness and was able to mourn. Life changed forever for Sheryl. She was now free to be a mom. And she loved it more than anything in the world.

Now my Trudy's pregnant. God, these are such different shoes to wear. I need You, God, I need You. He got out of the car to help the nurse assist Trudy into the car.

* * *

I'm tired. Only one more mile until the exit. The clock read 6:00. *I could go to sleep right now.* Randy glanced in the rearview mirror. *Wow, my dad's still reading the Bible? That's something.*

"I guess I dozed off for awhile. Were you okay driving?" His mom gave him a smile as she stretched.

"Yeah, I was fine. I'm kind of tired, though," Randy answered honestly as he turned onto their exit. He could see the motel his dad had told him about earlier.

"Katey?" Cassie looked in the rearview mirror. "Al, could you wake up, Katey? We're about to pull into the motel."

"Huh?" His dad looked up from reading, glancing over at Katey. "Oh, sure." He nudged Katey gently. "Wake up, sleepyhead. We're at the motel."

Randy pulled in by the manager's office. He waited in the car as his dad went to register them and get the key for their room.

While they waited, Katey teased Randy. "You mean we made it here safely, with Randy driving? Wow!" Katey leaned over the back of the front seat and tugged on his hair. "How many cars did you run off the road, Randy, huh?" She giggled.

"Very funny. Go back to sleep so we can have peace again," Randy replied.

"Okay, you two. I'm putting an end to your teasing before it gets out of hand. Here's your dad," Cassie said firmly.

They walked over to a restaurant after getting situated in the motel. Randy couldn't stop thinking about Trudy while he was eating. *I miss her so much! I can't wait to get home and see her, but then...there's the baby. I'm still not ready to deal with that, I'd rather be here for now.* Lost in thought as they walked back to their room, it took him by surprise when he felt his dad's arm around his shoulder. Randy looked up and smiled.

"So Randy, got something you need to talk about?" his dad asked.

Butterflies started dancing in his stomach. Randy stared at his feet, wishing he could tell his dad, but he couldn't do it yet. "Not really. I mean, I don't really feel like talking about it right now."

His dad squeezed his shoulder, "Well, how about if you and I go for a little walk anyway. I have something I'd sure like to talk to you about."

"You do?" Randy worried. *What did I do now?*

"Don't look so worried. Can't a dad just want to talk with his son?" Al asked. He turned and called to Cassie and Katey, "Randy and I are going for a walk. We'll see you back in the room. Be sure to lock the door when you go in."

"Okay," Cassie called back. "Don't be long."

"We won't."

As Randy and his dad started to walk away, Randy could hear his sister whine. "Why can't I go for a walk? I want to go for a walk with Daddy. Why does Randy get to do everything?" Randy shook his head, glad she was going in the opposite direction than him.

They walked in silence for a few minutes. *I wish Dad would let me know what he wants to talk about. We haven't had that great of talks lately.* After a few more blocks his dad finally started speaking.

"So, Randy, I've been reading that Bible you brought along with you," he started.

"Yeah."

"What do you think of it? I mean, what made you bring it in the first place?"

"I don't know." Randy sighed. *Should I tell him now what's going on?* "Trudy said something the other night about following God and His will. I didn't get it, but then I went to The Cave and bumped into a good friend of hers from her church. He explained some stuff and I prayed a prayer with him. He gave me a Bible and some verses to look up while we were traveling."

"Huh. What kind of prayer?" Al asked.

Randy shoved his hands in his jeans pocket. *I don't know how to explain this.* "It's kind of complicated to explain. He told me how Jesus died for my sins and if I believed I would be saved. When I die I'll go to heaven, but while I'm here on earth I can live a life getting to know God and follow his purpose for my life."

"Interesting." Al stopped walking. "When I was about ten years old, my Grandma brought me to church and they did what is called 'an altar call.' I went forward and for a while after that I grew in my faith, but after my grandma died, I don't know, I…" His voice faded, and he stood lost in thought for a moment. "My grandma taught me to read the Bible every night, but for some reason I stopped. Today, I could actually hear her voice. She used to tell me about Jesus all the time."

"I didn't know that. Dad, we've never even stepped foot in a church."

"I know, son. Right now, I'm not proud of that fact at all." Al started walking again. "My mom died when I was really young, three or four years old. My grandma moved in to help my dad. Dad worked a lot. When she died, I felt lost for quite a while. I don't know why I didn't continue going to church. I just walked away from it."

"Dad, I don't know much about Jesus, but from what I've been learning these last two days I can bet that you may have walked away from Him, but He's still here for you." Randy stopped in his tracks. "Wow, Trudy would pass out to hear me talk like that! I really mean it though, Dad. Tony said that Jesus will never leave me or forsake me."

Randy felt uncomfortable when tears filled his dad's eyes. *What on earth is going on here? My dad is about to cry. He's looking at me funny.* Just as Randy recognized the look, his Dad pulled him into an embrace. It was…pride.

The walk back to the motel was filled with conversation. *I love being with my dad like this. It's been such a long time since I've even wanted to spend time with him. He's usually too busy or demanding.*

"I wish you would've been able to meet her, Randy. She used to make the best meals and she was so in tune to our needs. When I was Katey's age, I became withdrawn. My dad was busy and it seemed he never had time for me. I needed him, although I'd never actually admit it, but she knew. One night she called my dad and demanded he come home early. He came home, and she didn't come back until after I was in bed. She must have thought I was asleep because I overheard her questioning my dad about how things went. 'I need you home one night a week so I can do some errands. I want you to develop the habit of spending quality time with that boy again.'" Al laughed. "At first it was awkward, but soon those nights became boys' night. We don't do it as often, but sometimes you and I still get together for boys' night."

"I remember when we used to have a boy's night," Randy said.

"Yeah, but we don't really have any time together anymore, do we?"

"No. Trudy and sports pretty much take up my time," Randy admitted.

"I've let work take up mine. Maybe we could start, once a month, a few hours," Al suggested. "Reading the Bible has brought me back to who I was years ago. I'm not sure how that will play out, but I want to continue to read the Bible. Maybe even get the family to go to church and get to know Jesus again."

"Really? I think that would be great. I'm pretty serious about growing in my faith and learning more about God." *What a difference from a few days ago. God really does work in people's lives the way Trudy and Tony said.*

"I was hoping you were feeling the same way." He put his arm around Randy. "I want to show your mom and Katey what the Bible says too."

Randy liked the closeness that this newfound belief in God brought between him and his dad.

"This time with you has been nice," his dad said wistfully.

"I was thinking the same thing."

His dad patted him on the back and started running, "I'll race you back. Winner gets to use the shower first."

Randy ran after his dad. "That's no fair! You had a headstart." Then he sprinted past him, laughing.

* * *

"Okay, sweetie, let's get you into your bed." Bill carefully laid Trudy down on her bed while Sheryl pulled back the covers. The sound of the doorbell echoed down the hallway.

"That must be Kay. I'll go let her in." Sheryl hurried from the room.

Bill tucked the blankets around Trudy. His heart melted when he looked at her face. It was one big bruise with swollen eyes from crying. *She won't look at me.* He reached under her chin, lifting her face up to him, and laid a gentle kiss on her forehead.

"I love you, baby, and I'm here for you. I'm sorry I freaked out at the hospital. This whole thing scares me, to tell you the truth," he whispered, gently blowing her hair with his breath. He could feel fresh tears against his skin. "Shhh...you're going to be okay. Your daddy is here for you, pumpkin, he's here."

* * *

Sheryl and Kay watched the interaction from the hallway. Turning to each other, they signaled to go to the other room and let Trudy and Bill be alone.

"Thirsty?" Sheryl asked, reaching into the fridge for a bottle of water.

"No honey, I'm fine." Kay entwined her arm through Sheryl's and directed them to the couch. "How are you?"

"I don't know, really. Shell-shocked." Sheryl busied herself with moving the couch pillows out of her way. Sheryl finally glanced at Kay before sipping from her bottle. Her eyes looked weary. "She told you?"

Kay nodded.

"I assumed so. I knew Friday night something was brewing. It didn't bother me because she was going to your house and, well, you two had become so close since Elwood passed. I trust you. You've always been like a mom since my parents stopped talking to me." Sheryl took a deep breath, holding back emotions threatening to spill out. "I didn't have a clue. Why would I, though? I mean, we've taught her the ways of the Lord. I trusted she believed the same way we did. Never in my life would I think Trudy would make the same mistake as me." Sheryl pounded the pillow she was holding on her lap. "I made sure to teach her to make the right choices, especially about this. Why did she end up like me?" She sank bank onto the couch. "I just don't get it."

"I understand. I'll never forget how I felt when the two of you told us about the abortion. I struggled with so many questions and was sure I had done something wrong. But Sheryl, this isn't your fault. That's something I had to learn." Kay gently laid her hand on Sheryl's knee.

"I'm so sorry, Kay, it seems history is repeating itself."

"No, history is not repeating itself. Trudy has a good foundation. When she came up against the choice, she kept her baby. Abortion had just become legal when you were young. I don't think anyone was equipped for what was about to play out in the following years. Trudy had good teachers, but only God can cause her to believe and give her a desire to do things His way."

"Yesterday, when I saw the heartbeat on the screen…"

"What? You saw the heartbeat?" Kay interrupted.

"That's how I found out."

"What! That's horrible."

"I about died. Poor Trudy, the look on her face broke my heart." Sheryl stared off in thought. "Maybe I should've been honest with her about my choices when I was her age. What came out of them, the abortion, the end of my relationship with my parents. But how do you tell your child about aborting their sibling? Or, how do I tell her I almost aborted her?" Sheryl scanned for a box of tissue. Kay reached inside her purse and handed one to her.

"I'm so disappointed. I wanted the absolute best for her, and she compromised all of that. Why couldn't I have figured out she was having a physical relationship with that boy? He wants her to have an abortion, for crying out loud! They were at a clinic. She came this close to experiencing the worst thing a woman could go through."

Kay reached over to hold her.

"It terrifies me. I was so blind to what was going on in her life. I merely assumed she was making the right choices. Now she's about to be a mommy while still in high school." Sheryl placed her hand over her face, exhaling loudly.

"Well, kids are pretty clever at hiding things. I think what's important is, she knows you understand. Part of the reason kids hide what they're doing is they fear their parents' reaction."

"That's obvious," Sheryl said shortly.

"You love her so much, and you do understand. You understand her fear of losing you and the shame. Let her know. I believe she needs to hear that right now. Open a door of communication to stop every reason she has to hide things in the first place. She has you on a pedestal. Maybe it's time to let her see where God brought you from, my dear child."

"I don't know if I can do that. I'm afraid. She may not forgive me for aborting her sister and for almost aborting her. She may blame me for the miscarriages. I don't know if I'm strong enough to go through that."

"Oh, sweetie, I don't know what Trudy's initial reaction will be. It may hurt you, but you're her mom and she loves you so much. Just keep on loving her," Kay encouraged.

"I was hoping to keep my life a secret. I didn't plan on ever telling her." Sheryl shut her eyes. "Oh, all of this, plus the poor thing was hurt in a car wreck."

"Bill said the other driver ran a red light and turned left in front of Brenda. Does anyone know how he's doing?"

Sheryl shook her head. "I honestly haven't thought anything about him. After we got the phone call, it felt like we were moving in slow motion. I wanted to see my baby. I was so afraid I'd lost her." Sheryl began sobbing.

Kay took her in her arms, rocking back and forth as she cried. "Go ahead and cry sweetie, go ahead and cry," Kay whispered.

* * *

Every fiber in Brenda's body hurt. *I wonder how the baby is doing. I hope it didn't get hurt in the accident.* She heard the bedroom door open. Her mom was checking in on her.

"Brenda, you awake?" her mom asked.

"Yeah." Brenda tried to pull herself up on to her elbows. "Ow, okay, I can't do that."

Lorinda came to her aid. "Careful sweetie." Lorinda helped her lay back down and tugged the quilt up around Brenda. "Snug as a bug in a rug. That's what I used to say when you were young. It made you giggle. How are you?" She sat down carefully on the side of the bed.

"Sore."

"Well, I talked to Dr Wayne. You remember him—I worked for him a few years ago—and he's going to meet us at his sports therapy clinic first thing tomorrow morning." Lorinda brushed her hand across Brenda's face. "I'm so glad you two came out of the accident without any broken bones or worse."

"Mom, do you know what happened to the people in the other car? Are they okay?"

Lorinda shook her head. "I don't think so, honey. Your dad found out the driver was an older man. He must have had a heart attack or something and turned in front of you. He's been admitted to intensive care."

Tears filled Brenda's eyes.

"Honey, please don't let this worry you. Dad went over to the hospital to see if there was anything he could do and to talk to his family."

"Do you think he's going to live?" Brenda whispered.

"No one but God knows that answer. Maybe I should have waited to tell you this. You're probably going to have a hard time sleeping now."

"Well, that's not the only reason I'm going to have a hard time sleeping." Brenda mumbled, hiding her eyes with the covers.

"What's the matter, sweetie?" Lorinda folded down the blanket and searched Brenda's eyes.

"Mom, I hope Trudy doesn't get mad at me for telling you without asking her but…" She exhaled a long, shaky breath. "Trudy's going to have a baby, and I'm scared the baby got hurt in the car accident."

"What!" she exclaimed. "No way! Do her parents know?"

"Not yet," Brenda peeped out quietly.

"I can't imagine what they're going to go through. Oh, no."

"She was scared to tell them. Grandma Kay knows, though."

"Oh my goodness, I need to call Sheryl." Lorinda started to get up.

"Mom!" Brenda panicked. "You can't call her! What if Trudy hasn't told them yet?"

"You're right. I-I just feel like I have to do something. I can't imagine how she'll feel. Do you know how far along she is?"

"No. I'm scared, Mom. I'm afraid the baby got hurt."

"Oh, honey." Lorinda gathered Brenda close.

"Mom, oww! Don't hug me right now, okay?" They both started to giggle.

"I can't even hug you, poor thing. Better watch it. If you get smart with me, I'll just threaten to give you a hug."

"And I'll shape up believe me." Brenda smiled.

"Seriously, we need to pray for them and the baby. They've got a tough road ahead." Lorinda clasped Brenda's hands, and together they lifted their friends in prayer.

* * *

"I'll be back tomorrow after my meeting to help out," Kay called to Sheryl right before Kay ducked her head into her car.

Sheryl waved from the porch as Kay backed out of the driveway, closing the front door behind her after the car disappeared around the corner. With a sigh, she walked back down the hallway. Collages of pictures were plastered on the wall. She frowned, stopping at Trudy's most recent one, searching the face that smiled back at her. *How did I miss the clues? Why couldn't I tell you needed me?* She continued to Trudy's room, where Bill was kneeling beside Trudy's bed. Sheryl knelt beside him, putting her arm around him. Trudy looked so sweet and innocent as she slept. Bill cleared his throat.

"This is the first time in her entire life I'm not able to fix her problem," Bill said in a gruff whisper. Sheryl rubbed his shoulder comfortingly, scooting closer to him. "I was so angry."

"Or scared?" Sheryl suggested.

"Yeah, scared." Bill nodded.

Sheryl motioned for the two of them to go to the other room. They each gave Trudy a kiss and slipped out quietly. Sheryl stole one more glance at her before shutting the door; she looked as peaceful as a baby.

"How are you doing?" Bill asked.

"Oh, Bill, I'm so overwhelmed. Our baby is pregnant. What on earth are we going to do?" Sheryl exclaimed.

"What can we do?" Bill shrugged. "It's so frustrating. Now I know what my parents felt like. We'll have to do like them—walk beside her, and make sure the baby is okay."

"Kay thinks I need to be honest with Trudy. Tell her our story."

Bill looked surprised. "Huh? Serious? Do you think you can do that? You've always wanted to keep it secret."

"I don't know. It terrifies me. I can't even begin to think of telling her. Kay said she would help."

"It's up to you, honey. I'll support you whatever you decide." Bill held her close. Sheryl leaned her forehead against his chin.

"Who'd have thought this is how our day would end?" Sheryl asked.

"Not me." Bill held her tighter. "Not me."

7

The warmth of the heating rub massaged into her neck by the therapist caused Brenda to give a happy sigh. Her face was smashed into a donut connected to the massage table. *No need to wear any makeup next time. It's probably smeared all over my face.*

"Okay, Brenda, time to roll over and lay on some ice, then we'll heat." The therapist helped her sit up.

"Are you sure you're finished with the massage? I think I could tolerate about an hour more," Brenda said, getting a smile from the therapist. This Physical Therapist was new at the clinic, but so far all of the patients raved about her.

"Hey, Tony! How's it going today?" someone called from the front desk. Brenda glanced over. *No way! It's Tony! I bet I look terrible. Oh, he certainly doesn't.* The bangs of his dark hair fell lightly on his forehead and the dark gray from his letterman's jacket accentuated his good looks. Brenda started to smooth her curls. The therapist gave her a curious look and then peered toward the door. A knowing smile crossed her pretty face.

"Don't worry. Messy curls are considered cute."

"Great," Brenda mumbled before Tony recognized her.

"Brenda?" Tony walked over with a concerned expression. "What are you doing here? You okay?"

"Car accident." Brenda always had trouble speaking around him.

"What? I saw you at church yesterday. Did it happen afterward?"

Brenda nodded.

"Was Trudy with you?"

"Yes, she seems fine, though. She'll be here later today."

"How about…?"

Brenda shrugged with a sad look.

"This is terrible. I hope everything's okay."

"Okay, pretty lady. Time for the ice," the therapist interrupted as she brought the ice pack over and laid it on the table. "Lay down right here, and I'll put some hot pads on top of you to keep you from freezing." Tony helped the therapist give Brenda a lift and situate her.

"Hey, don't you have some exercises to do, young man, instead of bothering this gorgeous young lady?" The therapist laughed.

Brenda felt herself blush. Surprisingly, Tony's cheeks turned red, too.

"I'll talk to you later, Brenda. Hope you get better quick," he said before swiftly turning to leave and bumping into another therapist. Head bowed, he mumbled apologies and strode to the other side of the clinic. Brenda felt bad for him when she heard the laughs between the two PTs. *I've never seen Tony be clumsy before. He's normally so cool and confident. I wonder what's wrong with him?*

* * *

Brenda's dad, Steve, held the door open for Brenda while she slid into the front seat. "You okay?" he asked before shutting the door.

"Yeah, I feel much better after the therapy." Brenda busied herself with buckling her seatbelt while her dad got in the car. "Do you think we could stop by my school? I have a few things to pick up."

"Are you sure?"

Brenda nodded.

"Well, I could, but I have a meeting in half an hour. I'd need to come back and pick you up. You'd have to hang out at school for a while."

"That's okay." Brenda shrugged.

"Do you have a test to study for or a project?"

"Actually, Dad, I feel I need to talk to someone today; I can't let it go." She proceeded to explain to him about the phone call she'd received from Jodee Saturday morning.

"Hmm, and you're afraid she's going to spread the word about Trudy," her dad said with understanding.

"Exactly," Brenda agreed. "I know how this girl operates. I can't believe some of the things she does and says to me—they're horrible. She does *not* like me, and I get the idea it's because I'm a Christian."

"What makes you say that?" Steve asked.

"She's always bringing it up in one way or another. And she calls me Miss Goodie-Two-Shoes all the time." Bitterness tinged Brenda's voice.

"Obviously she's not happy about something. Usually when a person is nasty there's something bothering them."

"Yeah, in her case, it's *me*." Brenda pointed dramatically at herself.

Steve chuckled.

"It can be quite embarrassing, especially when there's a group of people around," Brenda grumbled.

"What do you do when she's rude to you?"

"I try my best to ignore her."

"Why don't you begin trying your best to be nice to her and pray for her? See what happens."

"Dad, I guess I could say I do pray for her, but in all honesty, my prayers are more for myself and how she affects me."

"Well, maybe you could change the way you pray. Pray for her needs, her hurts. Just make it about her."

"I suppose," Brenda said as they pulled up to her school. "I'll start praying for her later, but right now I need to pray for me. I've never started a conversation with her, and I'm one nervous girl!"

"Here, let me pray for you before you go in." He grasped her hand. "Lord, I pray you will go before Brenda and that You would encourage, strengthen, and comfort her. Whatever is bothering Jodee, I pray it would be revealed, and bring her to a loving relationship with you. I pray for Your goodness to be in their conversation, in Jesus' name, amen."

"Thanks, Dad." She drew his hand up and planted a kiss on it before getting out of the car. "I'll see you in a bit." She blew another kiss over her shoulder at him as she walked into the door of the school.

* * *

Randy looked out the car window thinking about the conversation he had with his dad the night before. *It's been a long time since I've had any kind of relationship with my dad. It feels good.* He shook his head, smiling over all the things that had happened since last Friday.

Then a feeling of sadness came over him. *I don't see how it's going to last, though. No matter what, I can't hide from what's happening in my life. Dad will be furious when he finds out about the baby.* He thought about what Tony had said about the dangers of abortion. *But not everyone goes through that. I'm sure there are girls who do just fine. If only she would have done it, we could go on with our lives and no one would have to know.* He stared at the back of his dad's head. *Mainly him…now everything's going to be ruined.*

Randy gritted his teeth in anger. *Why did Trudy have to put me in this position?*

"Hey, Randy, do you mind helping me carry this stuff out to the car?" his dad had asked.

Normally, his dad demanded him to do things. *It sure felt good to be asked instead of ordered around.*

Randy looked down at the Bible perched on his lap. *What's the use? It's not going to last. The Bible isn't going to help me with this problem. No amount of Bible reading is going to change anything. The baby isn't going to go away.*

Taking a deep breath, he stared out the window, not noticing the beautiful clear sky and the mountain ranges passing by. *No one had to know!* Randy felt even more frustrated because there was nothing he could do about it. *I feel trapped.* He knocked the Bible off his lap.

"I would know." The thought went through his mind.

What? Who would know?

"I would know." The thought was firmer.

Well, of course I would know. Randy squirmed in his seat.

The blue sky caught his attention. It was a pretty blue and so big. *The Bible said God created it in one day.* Pushing the thought away, he peered back inside the car. *Who cares? What does that matter now? It doesn't help anything.*

Strangely though, he felt drawn once more to the view outside the window. The sky seemed so incredibly large. *God created that big sky and mountain range. Obviously, God is bigger than both of them. I must seem awful small to God. What?* A surge of hope filled him. *My problem…it seems huge, but it has to seem small to God. The Bible said God created everything! The whole world! This sky!*

Randy was getting excited. *This God I'm reading about is bigger than anything I can see.* He reached over to pick up the Bible. *Now I understand why it's worth it. This Bible is teaching me about this God, who didn't think, in the entire universe, I was too small to be bothered with.* Randy took a deep breath. *I get it! People may not have known about the abortion, but there isn't anything I could hide from God's eyes. God would have known.*

As he started paging through the Bible, his smile spread. He could feel his sister looking at him. He gave a glance her way. She was turned toward him with a strange expression. He gave her a smile. *Why is she staring at me? Oh no, she's must be up to something.*

"You're weird," she stated firmly.

"What?" Randy asked.

She sat up straight. "I've been watching you, and you're really weird."

"Katey, that's enough. Don't talk to your brother like that."

Katey sat back in the seat and looked out the window.

Randy shook his head and started to read the Bible again. Once again he could feel her glancing at him with the kind of look that said he was from

83

Mars or something. "What's the matter?" he asked.

"That's what I'm wondering. What's the matter with you?" she asked.

"What do you mean? I'm just reading."

"You're not being mean back to me, and you actually helped Dad this morning. Last night you didn't make fun of me when I couldn't go along with you and Dad on your special walk." She sat up. "As a matter of fact, you haven't made fun of me since yesterday morning."

Randy thought about it. *She's right.* "Shouldn't you be glad? I mean, you've been getting a break."

"Yeah, but when I was watching you, it was like you were having an argument with that book. You looked at it the same way you look at me when you're mad. Then you got all happy and now you're reading it again. You're being very weird." She crinkled her eyebrows.

I hadn't thought of anyone watching me argue with God. Argue with God? Whoa! I guess that's what I've been doing. He smiled.

"See. There you go again! What are you doing?" She leaned away from him.

"Okay, leave your brother alone," Randy's mom called back.

"But, Mom, this is really weird! He's acting psycho. It's like he's talking to this book," Katey explained.

His dad smiled back at Katey. "Well, it is like talking to someone. The Bible teaches you about God. Go ahead, Randy, tell her about it."

"Tell her about it? I don't know what to tell her!" Randy lifted an eyebrow.

"Well, give her a story to read about Jesus," his dad answered.

Randy's mom was looking at his dad like he was the one who needed a shrink. "Are you really serious about this Bible thing?"

"I'm starting to be." He then went on to explain about what they had talked about the night before when they had gone for a walk.

Randy peeked at his sister. *How do I do this? I can't believe I'm so nervous. I mean, what do I care what she thinks?* Katey really was a cute little kid—hair in the messy braids she insisted on doing herself, which drove his mom crazy, blue eyes with curly long lashes, and such a stinker. He gave her a smile. She jerked back with a grimace. *I need to find just the right one. Lord, please show me the right story for Katey….the beginning. I'll have her start at the beginning.*

"Here." He placed the Bible on her lap. "Start right here. It's a story about God creating *everything*. Later I can even show you where rainbows come from and why."

Katey looked a bit hesitant. "I just hope I don't start talking to books when I'm done reading this," she mumbled as she started reading.

Randy laid his head back, closed his eyes, and listened to his dad talk to his mom about God. *And Katey's reading the Bible. Wow. Too bad we can't get reception on our phone out here. I'd love to talk to Trudy. She won't believe what's going on in my family.* Randy gave a silent chuckle. *Yes, she would; Trudy knows God better than I do. I can only imagine amazing things happen all the time.*

* * *

She was surrounded by white. It hurt. She pushed against it to try to relieve the pressure. Her arms throbbed; her head hurt. "Randy, help me," Trudy screamed.

Randy's laughter seemed to float around her.

"Randy, help, I need you." Trudy pushed again, but it was too painful. Her arms fell to her sides. She opened her eyes; she was wrestling with her blanket, and her body ached from the effort. "What a nightmare."

With a long sigh she remembered the events of the day before. "I think I probably had the worst weekend of my life. First Randy dumps me, then I get in a car accident. And to top it off, my mom finds out I'm pregnant at the hospital," she moaned to herself. Carefully she swung her legs to the side of the bed. "Ow! That hurts."

Gripping the top of the nightstand beside her bed, she pulled herself up to a standing position. "Okay, I can see this isn't going to be easy," she grumbled. With a lift of her head she came face to face with Randy's picture that hung on a completely covered bulletin board. Her fingers tenderly touched his lips. *Nothing is harder than losing you. I miss you so much.* Tears dropped unchecked to the carpet as she stared into his eyes. She scanned the contents of the board that used to give her such delight and hope. Tickets to a game and a movie, and notes he'd written: *Tru, missed seeing you after school today. I wish I could spend every minute with you. Love, Randy.*

And now it's been three days since I last saw you. Her hands fell to her side. *How can you just leave me like that?*

"Tru?" Her mom knocked on the door. "You awake?" She peeked in the room.

Trudy plopped back on her bed, hanging her head, not caring about the pain that screamed throughout her body. She could feel her mom enter the room. Her shoes stopped right as they came into Trudy's view.

"Tru, you okay? Need help?"

Trudy responded with a shake of her head, allowing her hair to hang over her face. "Tru, honey? What's going on?" Trudy flinched when Sheryl sat on the bed and started to stroke her hair. Sheryl's sharp intake of breath pierced Trudy's heart. "Oh, sweetie, don't hide. I—you don't realize this, but I—know what you're feeling right now."

"I doubt it," Trudy whispered.

Sheryl's hands gripped Trudy's shoulders firmly. Trudy fought the impulse to melt right into her mom's arms and cry on her shoulder.

"Trudy, please look at me," Sheryl pleaded.

Trudy looked into her mom's eyes, surprised at the tears that were welling over.

"Oh, Mom, I'm sorry. I'm sorry I disappointed you. I can understand if you…" Trudy stopped, unable to imagine her mom, like Randy, not wanting her around.

"What, honey?" Sheryl gripped both sides of her face. "Do you think I want to leave you? Send you away? Never…" Trudy found herself caught in a tight embrace. "I will always be here for you even when you make mistakes. You're facing some hard consequences. I wouldn't walk out on you now."

Trudy relaxed into her mom's embrace and let her emotions flow, soaking in the tender words her mom whispered in her ear. The shame and emptiness that came from Randy deserting her were lessened as she nestled into her mom's arms of love.

* * *

Brenda felt a little nervous walking down the hall. She said "hi" to her friends as she passed them. When Brenda reached her locker, she glanced over to see if Jodee was around. After breathing a sigh of relief, she scolded herself for being such a wimp. Grabbing her books, she shut her locker and started down the hall. Jodee was with a group of her friends walking toward her. *Lord, give me Your courage and let my words be yours, not my own.*

Taking a deep breath, she plastered on a smile as she approached Jodee. "Hey, Jodee."

Jodee looked at her with surprise. "Uh, hi, Brenda."

"How are you?" Brenda continued.

Jodee's friends rolled their eyes. Jodee joined them and answered sarcastically, "I'm just fine, Brenda." Jodee looked Brenda up and down. "What's with the bruises?

Brenda just shook her head. "Umm, do you think I could speak with you for a moment?" She smiled at Jodee's friends. "Privately."

Jodee wrinkled her brow and stepped toward Brenda. "Whatever. But make it quick. I don't want to be late for class."

"Oh, this will only take a minute." Brenda blew out some air, wringing her hands together. "I want to talk to you about last Saturday. I thought you'd want to know what happened after you called me."

Jodee smirked. "Yeah, sure, that's something I'd like to hear."

"Well, I went to see Trudy at her grandmother's. And yes, Randy and Trudy were at the abortion clinic on Friday, but she didn't have an abortion."

Jodee snorted. "Yeah, right, Brenda. She sure fooled you."

"No, she didn't go through with it. As a matter of fact, she's at home right now. Uh, we had a car accident yesterday," Brenda said firmly.

Jodee's lips were drawn tight, and her brown eyes squinted. "You're okay with this? Like it's perfectly okay for Trudy to be pregnant? I thought you Goody-two-shoes preached to people to wait until marriage before you had sex, let alone have children."

Oh Lord, give me wisdom, please. "Yes, that's true. The Bible teaches God's will is to wait until you're married."

"Well, hello? Trudy isn't married, so what about that, huh?"

Brenda felt the heat of her temper spark. *Lord, help me to settle down.*

Jodee looked down the hall, then back at Brenda. "I'm waiting." She smiled like she'd just won a contest and was waiting for a prize.

"Jodee, I still believe this. So does Trudy."

Jodee snorted loudly again.

"Everyone makes mistakes. I'm not going to justify what Trudy did. It was wrong. But when she failed, she made a good choice and ran to God. She'll still have consequences, but Jesus forgave her," Brenda explained boldly.

Jodee leaned in close to Brenda's face. "The whole thing is, she got caught. Now she's going to play a Miss Goody-two-shoe role again." She sneered.

Brenda stepped back. "I'm sorry you see it that way. She's going to have a relationship with Jesus, not play a role. We all make mistakes, and Jesus knows that. That's why He died for our sins. Only *He* is perfect. No one else is perfect, Jodee. Not Trudy, and certainly not me. It's Jesus in me who makes me able to not do what I shouldn't do." Jodee just stared at her, so Brenda dared to ask, "Why does it bother you that Trudy and I love the Lord?"

"You know why it bothers me?" Jodee snarled. "It bothers me because you walk around like you're so high and mighty. Like you're better than everyone else." Jodee put her nose up in the air. "Jesus loves me," she mimicked Brenda's voice, "I'm better than you." Jodee leaned in closer. "What, may I ask, makes you think you're more special than me?"

"Nothing." Brenda shook her head adamantly at Jodee. "I'm sorry it seems that way. Please forgive me. I wish you knew how much Jesus loves *you*. I want you to have a relationship with Jesus, too."

Jodee looked down at her feet and said something quietly.

"What?" Brenda asked.

"Nothing, I've got to go." Jodee kept her head turned from Brenda and walked quickly down the hallway. She glanced back once and then quickened her pace almost to a run.

Brenda stood there, watching her. *What just happened, Lord?*

* * *

Jodee's hands shook so that it was hard to light the cigarette. Finally! She drew a deep drag off of it and leaned against the brick outside wall of the school. She knelt down in case anyone saw her hiding in the nook where the garbage cans used to be stored. Her friend Karen had discovered this little hideaway at the beginning of the year. It was the perfect place for skipping a class.

Karen's probably going to be all over me for not making it to cooking class. She always hates it when I skip without her. I don't care. I need some time to myself.

The conversation with Brenda played through her head. Jodee smirked. *What did she mean, she wished I knew how much Jesus loves me? Not me. She would never say that if she knew.* Jodee exhaled in disgust. *I guess it's easy to run around and tell people how much Jesus loves you when you have a simple little life like hers. I don't see any love from Jesus in my life.*

Jodee took another puff from her cigarette. *If she had to deal with what I dealt with, she'd be singing a different tune.* Jodee glared at her cigarette. *I wonder how that girl would be if she had a dad like mine. A dad who taught me how to smoke, drink, and duck when he had too much alcohol. I wonder what tune she'd be singing? Probably not "Jesus loves me."*

Jodee threw her smoke down. She quickly lit another, hiding behind the veil of smoke from emotions she'd learned to hide deep within herself. Jodee's eyes stung with tears. She fought to keep them back, recalling the one time her dad had come and picked her up from school....

It was during the happiest time in Jodee's life. Her mother still lived with them. One night her mom was crying softly as she talked with someone on the phone. Jodee's dad was out as usual. Jodee crept quietly to her mother's room and stood outside the door, hoping to hear what was wrong with her mom.

"I'm pregnant." her mom said softly to the phone.

Pregnant! Jodee's heart jumped with excitement. *My mom's pregnant!* She was so excited she didn't listen to the rest of the conversation. She hurried back to her bedroom and crawled under the covers. She was so happy! Dreams did come true! She'd always wanted a brother or sister. She didn't care which one. If she had a brother, she could go play ball with him. If she had a sister, she could play dolls.

During the next couple of months, she planned for the baby. She cleaned her room and made space in her closet and drawers for the baby's things. She gave extra help to her mother. Her mom spent her time on the couch crying. Jodee made sure to be extra helpful.

Then one day her dad picked her up from school. Jodee kept looking over at him, wondering what was going on; he'd never done that before. He made her walk even when it was pouring down rain.

She thought her life was changing for the better. Her mom was pregnant, and now Dad was picking her up from school. But they didn't turn down the street to their house.

"Where are we going, Dad? You went past our street."

"I realize I went past the street. Do you think I'm an idiot? I know where I'm going," he growled at her.

Jodee knew it was better to sit in silence while he drove. He surprised her by breaking the silence.

"Your mom isn't doing too well. She's at the hospital."

Jodee was alarmed. "Mom's at the hospital? What's wrong with her?"

"Just some private stuff. I thought you'd want to see her before you went home," he replied.

Jodee had been anxious. It must be bad if he was doing something so nice. She worried that something was wrong with the baby. She peeked at her dad to ask him but saw his scowl and decided not to. She definitely knew better than to bother him when he looked like that.

When they reached the hospital, Jodee walked with her dad to her mother's room. She'd rather have known which room her mom was in so she could run as fast as she could. Finally, they reached the room. She pushed past her dad and rushed to her mother's bedside.

"Mom! Are you all right?"

Her mom brushed Jodee's hair back from her face. "I'm fine, honey. Don't worry. I just had a little problem. I'll be home in no time."

Relief filled Jodee. She leaned over, laying her head on her mommy's stomach. "I was afraid something happened to you and the baby."

Her mother jumped. "What?! What did you just say, Jodee?"

Jodee looked up at her mom, puzzled. "I was afraid something had happened to you and the baby," she repeated.

"You knew about the baby?" Her mom looked afraid as she caught her dad's eyes.

"What?" her dad growled. "Jodee." He grabbed her arm and turned her around to face him. "How did you find out?"

Jodee was too scared to admit she'd been eavesdropping while her mom talked on the phone.

"Jodee." Her dad shook her. "Tell me how you knew about the baby!" His voice was rising to a dangerous level.

"I...I...," she stuttered, "I heard...I heard Mom on the phone." She looked down, afraid he would hit her.

He pushed her aside. She slid on the hospital floor but was able to catch herself before she fell. When she gained her balance, her dad was spitting words into her mother's face.

She wanted to cover her ears to shut out his voice, but she stood frozen in horror. The baby was gone. Jodee felt herself die inside. Her mom was calling and reaching out to her, but Jodee couldn't move. She couldn't look at them any longer and stared at the floor.

Dad dragged her over to her mother, who tried to explain why they did what they did. "It wasn't the right time for a baby, honey."

Jodee lay there with her head on her mom's shoulder, staring at the wall. She'd never been so sad. Her baby brother or sister was gone.

Soon after, her mom was gone too. She just disappeared one day without even saying good-bye....

Yep. Jodee threw her cigarette down. She wiped the tears from her eyes. *Brenda would be singing a different tune.*

8

Sheryl turned on the cold water tap in the bathroom sink. Trudy sat on the toilet seat nearby with her head hanging. Her mom soaked the wash rag and gave it a good hard twist, wringing it out. She knelt in front of Trudy. "Look at me, baby." With gentleness she placed the cold rag on Trudy's swollen eyes. Trudy took it from her, placing her face hard into it.

"Honey," Sheryl began tentively. Trudy peeked over the rag. Clearing her throat and with a deep sigh, she continued, "I was pregnant."

Trudy held on to the rag and squinted at her mom. "Uh, duh, I kind of figured that out myself. I'm here, aren't I?"

"Yes, but that's not what I mean. I…" Sheryl's voice shook. She wiped the sweat from her palms on to her jeans. "I mean, when I was your age." Silence. "I ended up having an abortion."

Trudy dropped the rag to her lap, mouth open, eyes wide. "You've had an abortion?" Trudy asked, shocked.

"When I was a year older than you are now, I was dating your dad…"

"Dad? Dad knows about this?" Trudy asked.

"Yes, of course he knows," Sheryl answered, confused.

"Well, what did Dad say when he found out you had an abortion?"

"What? Trudy…"

"Well, he must have been pretty upset. I mean Dad is so against abortions. He's always going to fundraisers and counseling people. But then…" Trudy stopped. "So do you…I don't get it."

"That's now, honey. I was a different person then and so was your dad, but please let me finish telling you my story." Sheryl looked at the clock. It was already 10:30. Kay would soon be over. She reached for Trudy's hand. "You haven't had breakfast. Let's go downstairs. I'll finish telling you while you get something in your stomach."

Trudy didn't take her hand but did follow her without complaint. The kitchen welcomed them with the morning sun brightening up the room. The red geraniums hanging from the outside window ledge were getting stocky, adding to the Italian look Sheryl strived to create. Sheryl was quick to grab a bowl and a box of cereal, placing them in front of Trudy. After fixing espresso drinks for the two of them, Sheryl sat down across from her.

"I have to be honest. I hoped I wouldn't ever have to tell you about this part of my life. I went through so much emotional pain afterward that I never wanted to talk about it again," Sheryl admitted. When Trudy started to speak, she raised her hand to silence her. "I need to tell you. It's important for you to know. Maybe I should've told you sooner, but…"

"But…what did Dad say when he found out?"

"He's the dad."

"What! I don't get it. All my life I've heard about how important it is to do this and do that, but you and Dad…Mom, do you know what I've put myself through this last year just because I didn't think you'd understand? Why did you lie to me?" Trudy yelled.

"Trudy…I didn't lie. I believe in everything we've taught you. It's what I've learned from my mistakes. Now I know this is hard, but if you could please calm down and let me tell you the entire story," Sheryl pleaded.

"Fine." Trudy threw her hands up dramatically, rolling her eyes.

"I met your dad the summer before my senior year. I fell head over heels in love with him. And I loved his family. They were quite a bit different than mine. Although they went to church and had high expectations for your dad, they seemed to teach him and let him learn, rather than demand he did what they said. I was from a very strict home. I was told from morning to night what was expected of me, and that was that. It was a miracle I even got to date your dad, but when my parents met him, they really liked him."

"Your parents? You've never really mentioned your parents before."

"No, I try to avoid talking about them. I'll get to that later in the story. Anyway, one day I discovered I was pregnant. I was terrified. I knew beyond a shadow of a doubt my parents would kick me out of the house and never speak to me again. Your dad was afraid of hurting his parents because of their beliefs and because he didn't follow their values. A girl at school told me about someone who had an abortion. It had just become legal. She told me it takes a minute and no one knows or ever finds out you were pregnant. So I met with the girl. She helped me set up the appointment in a city where no one would know us."

Sheryl leaned back in her chair. "Little did we know at the time that what would only take a minute would last for a lifetime. Bill and I skipped school that day." Sheryl's thumb fiddled with the design on her red cup. "It was the most horrible thing I ever went through. Your dad was in the room with me. He almost barfed a few times. I was in excruciating pain afterward and bled very heavy. It scared us bad, so we told his parents."

"What about your parents?"

Sheryl shook her head. "No. No way. I didn't tell them. I ended up breaking off with your dad, dropping out of school, and waddling around in depression for about two years. I went from one bad relationship to another. I got my own place, and it just happened to be down the road from Grandma Kay. She'd faithfully check up on me. I started drinking heavily. I have no idea how I kept my job."

Sheryl closed her eyes. "Honey, I don't want to get into the details, but one day I couldn't take it anymore; I made plans to end my life. Your Grandma happened to come by that day, which is another long story in itself, but without knowing it, she hindered my plans. Instead of committing suicide, I ended up giving my heart to Jesus and…" Sheryl gave a smile, tears threatening to fall. "My life was completely different from the moment I gave my life to Him. And I mean the very moment.

"I got back together with your dad; I can't believe he waited so long for me. He had his own adventure during that time we were apart and had already given his life to Jesus. The two of us had a really special time loving God and each other. Still, we struggled physically; we were so attracted to each other. Your dad wanted to get married, but for some reason I believed a lie—that I wasn't good enough to marry him. One night my parents were out of town and we…well, we ended up spending the night together. I got pregnant again."

"What? Did you have two abortions? But, Mom, look what happened the first time."

"Yes, well, we were Christians who had messed up pretty bad. We didn't want anyone to find out we'd blown it. So we went back to the same abortion clinic, only this time they wouldn't let your dad in the room. I was alone and scared to death. Until this quiet voice started speaking to me. Not out loud, but words were going through my head. *'You go home. You don't belong here. Trust me.'* Over and over again the words went through my mind. I realized it was God, so I got dressed. While I was getting dressed, there was a knock on the door, I opened it, and there stood your dad. He had heard the same thing."

"What? Mom, something like that happened to me. I was waiting in a room, and by the time the doctor came I knew I couldn't have an abortion," Trudy admitted. Her face turned crimson. "I bet that's not something you wanted to hear."

"Honey, this is why I'm telling you my story. I want you to be able to talk to me."

"Really? To tell you the truth, this isn't very comfortable for me."

"Me either, Tru. This is the first time we've been honest with each other about things like this. I'm actually letting you know me, the part of me that isn't 'Mom,' but a girl, a woman, like you. It's important that I finish this story, though. On the way home your dad convinced me to marry him. We told Elwood and Kay. She knew right away I was pregnant. She told me she loved me and my baby. And she always has." Sheryl sniffed, biting her lip.

"Did you lose the baby?" Trudy asked with a baffled expression.

"No, honey, I didn't lose the baby." Sheryl creased her brow.

"Did you put the baby up for adoption? Where's the baby?"

"What? Honey, you…you're the baby."

"I'm that baby? Me?" Trudy sat back in her chair.

Sheryl moved over to the chair beside Trudy. She put her arm around her shoulder and drew her close. "I'm so sorry I didn't tell you sooner. I hope you can forgive me. I honestly didn't know how, or want to stir up things from the past, but I want you to know I'll be here for you. I won't leave you."

"Mom, I wish I would've known about this sooner. I needed to talk to you," Trudy whispered. "I can't believe I was almost aborted."

"God saved us from making the biggest mistake ever. Every time I look at you, I can't believe He allows me to be your mom. You're such a special girl."

"What about the other baby? Do you ever think about it? Do you miss it?"

"Yes, yes, and yes. Every year around the time that may have been her birthday. Every time you enter a different stage in life, I imagine what it would be like for her. I miss her."

"Her? Why do you keep saying 'her'?"

"I went through a Bible study to bring some healing into my life. I believe God let me know it was a little girl."

"Oh. What about your parents? Where are they? How come I've never met them?"

"They never talked to me again."

"Never? What about when I was born?" Trudy asked, astonished. Sheryl only shook her head. "Well, how did you deal with that? Didn't they want to get to know me?"

"I don't know, honey. I've never heard a word from them since the day I told them I was pregnant."

"Have you tried to contact them? Have you sent them my pictures?" Trudy pushed away, struggling to stand. Sheryl tried to help her up. "Oh, this is horrible, everything you're telling me. It's so much," Trudy said loudly. "I need some space. I'm going to my room." Trudy made her way up the stairs, away from everything her mom was saying.

Sheryl watched, feeling it best to not push her desire to make things right between them, but to wait until Trudy was ready to talk some more.

* * *

I can hardly believe it! I was almost aborted. Trudy dared to reach down and touch her belly. "Hey, little one in there, will you feel the way I do now the day I tell you I almost aborted you? I'm torn between feelings, like the rug was pulled out from under me. God, You saved my life."

Tenderness flowed through her while she caressed her stomach. She watched in the mirror while she moved her hand in a slow circle around her abdomen. "There's a little person inside of here. Wow, my mom was in the same position I'm in now. Well, except my dad wanted to marry her. I wish Randy would marry me." She gazed at herself in the mirror. "She was carrying me and was scared." *But look at her now. She loves me so much. Will I love my baby like that?* "She made it okay, even though her parents don't talk to her. That has to be terrible for her." *My parents and Grandma Kay are here for me. Grandma Kay was there for my mom. It had to be hard but...*

Trudy knelt. "Lord, I never knew how much You had saved me. Thank You, Jesus. I cannot express all my gratitude."

* * *

After lunch Grandma Kay came over and gave Trudy a ride to the Physical Therapy office while Sheryl went and ran some errands. Trudy felt a bit better after the appointment. It wasn't until they were on their way home from the therapist that Trudy brought up what her mom had told her.

"My mom told me about the abortion and how she almost aborted me," Trudy said quietly.

"Yeah?"

"Yeah, I had such conflicting emotions. I wanted to be mad at her because I felt like she'd pulled the rug out from under me and then, on the other hand, I was amazed and praised God for saving my life," Trudy admitted.

"I can only imagine. That was a very difficult time for all of us."

"I can't understand why her parents would stop talking to her. I mean, maybe for a little while, but forever?"

"It happens, kiddo. It's not right, but sometimes people don't handle things very well." Kay gave a sad smile.

"Mom said she tried to commit suicide, and you stopped her?"

Kay nodded. They sat in silence for a minute.

"Grandma?"

"I'm sorry, Trudy. I still can't get over how close we came to losing your mother that day. The whole thing ended in a miracle." Kay smiled. "I can still remember how beautiful it was outside. I could hardly wait to join Elwood in the garden, but I couldn't get rid of a nagging feeling I needed to stop over at your mom's house. She lived down the road from us. I'd make a point to stop by her place quite frequently.

"On that particular day, I brought some cookies and fresh lemonade in a jar. When I pulled into the driveway, the front room curtain opened as though someone were peeking out, but when I knocked, she didn't open the door. I had a nervous feeling in the pit of my stomach. I reached to open the door myself. It was unlocked. I called out to her, but there was no answer."

"She was sitting in front of the TV in a robe. Her hair was a mess, eyes red and puffy. My heart broke when I saw the pain in her eyes." Kay stopped. It was obvious she was fighting emotions.

Trudy found herself wiping at a tear that fell from her own eye.

Grandma settled herself and continued on with the story. "Anyway, she wasn't too happy that I showed up. Still, I went ahead and served her some of the cookies and lemonade I brought over. I knew she needed a friend, whether she wanted one or not. The place was an absolute mess, papers strewn all about, clothes on chairs, dirty plates lying on the coffee table."

"My mom had a mess? No way," Trudy interrupted.

"Oh, yes. It was bad. At one point she apologized for the mess but didn't make an effort to clear off a chair for me, even though she offered for me to sit down. So I picked a chair with the least stuff piled on it, to easily move it aside without causing any embarrassment. Then we sat in silence. She ate cookies and drank her lemonade. When she was finished, she put the glass on the coffee table along with the rest of the dirty dishes and went right back to staring at the television."

"I didn't know what to do. I prayed and prayed for wisdom. All of a sudden it was so hard to sit still. I needed to start cleaning up the mess. I mean, it was a struggle. I had the strongest urge to clean. I argued with myself. Surely He wouldn't ask me to clean her house. She might think I was being rude. But I ended up doing it, complaining the entire time inside my head that I didn't appreciate having to do this job." Trudy let out a soft giggle.

"I cautiously picked up a few newspapers and folded them neatly. Then I asked your mom if I could take her glass into the kitchen. There wasn't an answer, so I picked it up, along with a few others to bring to the kitchen.

While I was in there I cleaned, cautious at first, just in case it made her mad. After awhile a new sense of boldness filled me, and I cleaned the entire house. While I was in the bathroom putting stuff in the cabinet a bottle caught my eye. I didn't know why, but I felt I was to read the label. It was a new prescription of sleeping pills, not more than two days old. I opened the bottle, and every capsule was empty. The powder had been poured out of them."

"Did she already take them, Grandma?"

"No, fortunately not. When I asked her if she had taken the pills, she admitted it was in a glass on the kitchen counter." Kay gave a chuckle. "When I cleaned the kitchen, I'd wondered why she had cleanser or something in a glass. I prayed God would open a door for me to talk to her heart, and He did. She had so much guilt from the abortion and breaking up with your dad. She couldn't take it anymore. She had gone to a doctor who told her she couldn't have children in the future."

"Well, we know that's not true." Trudy smiled through tears.

"Your momma told me she didn't expect love to come from me—after all, she'd aborted my grandchild, hurt my son, and I was a Christian. She was amazed I kept coming around. Anyway, I held her while she cried and told her how much Jesus loved her. At first she told me it's a nice story and it was nice I'd want her to be like me, but it wasn't for her." Kay sighed.

"I thought my mom said that's the day she got saved?" Trudy interjected.

"She did, but not until after a whole lot of crying, talking, and praying. I told her, the way I see it, you can continue down this road of pain and sorrow and not receive forgiveness. You can continue to get so low you almost take your own life. Or you can turn to Jesus Christ and confess to Him and allow Him to wash you clean. And if you ask, He'll come right in and live in that worn-out, beat-up heart of yours. I've been coming here for quite a while, and I can tell beyond your pain that God created a wonderful person. But right now you're lost. Why don't you let Jesus take your hand and lead you down the road He made just for you?"

"Trudy, before I said another word, your mom was praying to Jesus with no direction from me. When she finished, she looked into my eyes and I'm not lying, the hopeless pain was gone. I saw a light of hope that only comes from our God."

"Woohoo!"

"She's never been the same since. Oh, how that woman loves Jesus. She knows where she came from and where He is leading her to." Kay waved her hand in the air. "And that, my dear grandchild, is the way our Jesus works."

9

After he picked her up from school, Brenda's dad agreed to let her have his car to go over to Trudy's. The two of them had a great time together. It was as though nothing had ever happened to separate them. Brenda and Trudy hardly had time to share everything that had happened during the day. Just like old times, they held hands and prayed about all they talked about before Brenda left to go home.

When she started home, the light sprinkling on the windshield soon turned into a heavy rain. It made her nervous since it was hard to see, even with the wipers on high. She slowed down to be extra careful. As she turned on the main street to her house, she saw a girl walking alone. *Oh, the poor girl is soaking wet.* She took a second look at the girl. *Hey, that's Jodee!*

Brenda pulled the car to a stop in front of Jodee. Through the rearview mirror she saw Jodee had stopped walking and was looking cautiously at the car. Brenda rolled down her window. "Jodee, it's me Brenda, from school. Get in, and I'll give you a ride."

Jodee's shoulders fell, but she trudged over to the car. Brenda turned the heat up on high when she saw her teeth chattering. "There's an extra jacket in the back if you want to take off your wet one and put a dry one on. Isn't it amazing this time of year? It can be warm one minute, then rainy and cold the next. I can hardly wait for spring to start," Brenda rattled.

"Oh! Neither can I!" Jodee sarcastically answered in a high voice, rolling her eyes. She struggled to get the wet coat off.

Brenda held back her own snarky response while checking her mirror before pulling out into traffic. She hummed under her breath to the music on the radio as they drove. She wasn't exactly sure where Jodee lived, but she knew the general area, so she drove in that direction.

"Do you normally listen to this type of music, or is today a special day?" Jodee asked.

"I listen to this all the time," Brenda answered.

Jodee pulled a cigarette from her pocket. "I don't believe you. You *are* from another world." She searched her purse again. When she came up empty, she peered at the lighter in the car. "Do you mind if I use your car lighter?"

"Jodee, this is my parents' car, and there is no smoking allowed in it."

Jodee blew out a disgusted breath. "I should've known."

They were near the area where Jodee lived. "So where do I go from here to get to your house?" Brenda asked.

"Uh, let's see." Jodee peeked over the dash. "Why don't you drop me off at the store up there, and I can walk the rest of the way?"

"Jodee, I can drive you all the way; it's no problem," Brenda offered.

"Really," she said firmly, "you can just drop me off."

"Do you need to get something at the store? I can wait. It's really awful out there."

"Brenda, get the message. I just want to be dropped off!" Jodee said shortly.

Brenda felt hurt and angry. *Why is it always like this with Jodee?* When she calmed down, she noticed Jodee fidgeting. *Why, she's nervous. Now I feel sorry for her.* Brenda stopped the car in the store parking lot. Jodee opened the door and got out. She leaned back in and started to take off Brenda's jacket.

"Don't worry about the jacket. Just give it to me tomorrow."

Jodee actually smiled at her. "Thanks." She waved as she shut the door and started walking across the parking lot.

Jodee smiled at me. The only smiles Brenda usually got from Jodee were unfriendly, mocking ones.

Suddenly a car sped into the parking lot and screeched to a stop close beside Jodee. The driver stuck his head out the open window and shouted at her. Brenda could hear his shouts even though her windows were closed. When Jodee walked away, the driver door opened and the man charged after her. Grabbing Jodee's arm, he yanked her close to him. His face red with anger, he began yelling in her face, then drew a fist, as if to hit her. Jodee turned away and shrunk down. She pointed toward Brenda's car.

"Oh no! Why is she pointing over here?" Brenda said, panicked.

The man glare in the direction of Brenda's car. Still gripping Jodee, he dragged her along with him. The man pounded on her window and put his face up to it. "Hey! Open the window."

Brenda shook her head. "No!" She screamed.

He hit the window again so hard Brenda was afraid it would break. She barely opened the window a crack.

"Is this your coat she has on? Did she steal it from you?" he yelled. He turned toward Jodee. "If you stole this coat, I'll beat you till there's nothing left of you!"

"No! She didn't steal it." Brenda was tense. It was hard to breathe. The man's foul breath—alcohol and cigarettes—seeped in through the crack.

"How'd she get the coat? Huh? Charity? We don't take charity."

"No!" Brenda answered. "She didn't steal the coat. I let her borrow it for the night. Her coat was wet from the rain."

"What were you doing out in the rain, trying to get sick? I can't believe you! Don't you have a brain? Is your head empty?" he screamed at Jodee.

Brenda was horrified, unable to imagine her own dad talking to her that way. With a rough shove Jodee fell to the ground, and the man stalked off to his car. Brenda jumped out of her car and ran to Jodee, watching to make sure the man didn't turn back. With relief she saw the man speed off in his car. Jodee wiped at her face.

"Are you okay? Here let me help you up."

Jodee pushed her away. Brenda didn't let that stop her. With determination she reached down and put her arms around Jodee to help her stand. Brenda led her over to her car. Jodee was shaking, and Brenda had no idea what to do. She had a feeling that if she said the wrong thing Jodee would only put up a wall. Brenda got a towel from the car. Jodee kept her head down, staring at her feet. Her wet, dripping hair hung down, covering her face. Brenda waited, not wanting to push.

Together they stood silent in the rain. Jodee threw her head back, water spraying as her hair flew back from her face. Brenda stepped back at the hard, cold gaze.

"Well, my little Miss Do-gooder, you've had your show for the day. You can go on your sweet way. I hope the entertainment was good. Why, when you go home to your little do-gooder daddy, you won't even have to watch TV! No. You can tell your little family all about the show. And it only cost you a ride down the road. Why, I believe that's not even a tank of gas." She drawled out the words with bitterness.

Brenda simply offered the towel to Jodee. As firmly as she could muster, shaking as she was inside, she said, "Here. Use this to wipe your face. When you're done, I want you to get in the car. I *will* drive you to your house. You're not walking in this rain."

Brenda turned and got in the car as the passenger door opened and Jodee got in. Brenda kept silent while Jodee gave directions. At Jodee's house, her dad's car was in the driveway. "Jodee, do you think it's a good idea to go in?"

Jodee stared at her house. "He's dead asleep by now," she answered in a low voice and moved to get out of the car.

"Are you going to be okay?" Brenda didn't want to leave her alone.

Jodee nodded. "I'm fine." She shrugged. "This is life for me."

"You can come and stay at my house."

Jodee's head jerked back. "What?" Then she added, "That's okay. I need to be here when he wakes up."

Brenda looked at the house. "Do you still have my number?"

Jodee nodded.

"Please call if you change your mind and decide you need a place to stay."

Jodee shook her head. "You are something else, Do-gooder." Then, for the second time that day she smiled at Brenda before making her way up the sidewalk to her house. Brenda pulled away after Jodee waved before shutting the front door. *I can't believe it! It's no wonder Jodee is so mean and nasty. I know, God, You let me see this for a reason.*

When she reached the driveway of her own house, her dad came hurrying out the front door before she even parked the car.

"Where have you been? I'm late now for my meeting." Her dad stopped in his tracks. "Brenda, what's wrong? Are you hurt?"

"No, I'm fine. I just…" Brenda clung to her dad. "Thank you for being so awesome, Dad."

"Honey what's the matter!!" Lorinda called from the porch. Brenda clung to her mom when she reached her. "Why, you're shaking. What happened? Were you in another accident?" Lorinda pulled Brenda away from her and looked at her face. Brenda shook her head. "Okay, honey, come inside and settle down for a minute."

Lorinda situated Brenda on the couch with a fluffy blanket and wrapped her arms around her. Brenda told her parents what happened with Jodee. She could see the worry on their face.

"Brenda, that's horrible. I'm not sure I want you put in that position again. You could've been hurt. Who knows how far he would've gone? Maybe we should call the police," her mom said in her worried tone.

"But she needs a friend. I can't shun her. It's her dad who did it, not her. It's not her fault. I think that's why she's so mean all the time; she must really hurt inside."

"I believe you're right, but you've never experienced anything like this before."

"Mom, God put her in my life for a reason. He thinks I can handle it."

"I realize that. But I don't want you around that kind of danger," her mom said firmly.

Steve finally said what was on his mind. "I think we need to think of a way you could be her friend and still be careful."

Lorinda turned toward him. "How? Her dad could show up anytime, like tonight!"

"It scares me just as much as it scares you. But we both know Brenda's right. God brought Jodee into her life for a reason."

"True, but this girl has been in Brenda's life for years. Brenda can witness to her in other ways, like being kind even when she's horrible to her. She can pray for her. Why does it suddenly have to be different? The first day she has a conversation with her a wild man comes and puts his face in her window and threatens her." Her mother's voice was higher than usual. "I can't let her go out there and be eaten alive like that. You saw her when she came home!" Lorinda's arm tightened around Brenda.

"Mom, it's been different this week. I promise I'll be careful," Brenda pleaded. "Jodee really needs a friend."

"I think we need to let Brenda determine if God is asking her to witness to this girl." Steve remained calm.

Lorinda was silent for a minute. "I know you're right, in a way. But I don't agree with allowing her total freedom. It's a dangerous situation, and this is new to her."

"I agree. We'll need to be guided by God and not our own fears." He gave her a tender smile.

"Mom, I promise to be careful."

"Okay, I know you're right." Lorinda gave her a hug, then grasped Steve's hand. "Can we pray?"

* * *

The house looked dark and silent as Bill unlocked the front door of his house. *That's strange*. The morning paper and a coffee cup were set on the coffee table. A blanket was thrown carelessly on the couch and clothes hung over the stair railing. "That's not a good sign," Bill muttered.

He made his way through the kitchen. Dirty dishes sat in the sink and on the counter. No dinner in process. "Note to self: Take Sheryl out to dinner tonight, or order takeout," he mumbled.

Peeking out the back door, he saw his wife, sitting in her favorite rocker out on the back porch, wrapped up in a blanket with her Bible perched on her lap. She seemed lost in thought.

"Hey, Sheryl," he said in a quiet voice so she wouldn't get startled.

"Oh, Bill." She turned toward him. "You're home. I didn't realize it was so late. I haven't even started dinner."

"That's okay. We can get some pizza or Chinese. Is Trudy home?"

"No. Brenda came over for a while after Trudy's physical therapy appointment. Kay was still here when she left. She asked us if we wanted to go get a bite to eat and then see a movie. I declined obviously, which Kay knew I would. I needed some time alone."

"Hmm, want to talk about it?"

"I told Trudy."

Bill sat on the chair across from her. "Wow. That's big." Bill scratched his head. "How did she respond?"

"Better than I thought. She needed time alone after she found out we almost aborted her." Bill only nodded in response. "Your mom told her about…" She didn't need to explain any further.

Bill knew. He gazed into her eyes.

"We haven't had time to talk privately since, which I think is a good thing. She needs time and I don't want to say the wrong thing."

"I think you're right. Hey, why don't you and I go out to eat and just have some fun?"

"That sounds great." Sheryl's eyes lit up. "I need to pick up a bit first. I haven't done anything all day."

"Oh, yes, you have. You've done a lot today, just different than your normal routine. I'll pick up while you go change." He held out his hand to help her up out of her chair.

"What—you don't think I should wear this to go out?" Sheryl gave him a gentle poke, then wrapped her arms around him. "Thank you."

Bill stared into her beautiful blue eyes. "You're welcome, my sweet princess." He gently kissed her forehead before holding her close. "You've done a brave thing today, honey, and I'm very proud of you, very proud."

* * *

Kay watched Trudy fiddle with her French fry, moving it back and forth, smearing the ketchup on her plate. They were at their favorite hamburger joint. Bright colors splashed on the booths and floor. Paintings done by local artists decorated the walls, and the jukebox volume stayed on "loud." On special nights a band from the area would be pounding out their tunes from the small stage in the back corner.

"Hey, Tru, you in there, honey? I seem to have lost you."

"Oh." Trudy sat up. "Sorry, Grandma, I was just thinking."

"I noticed. Anything you want to share?"

"Well…it's kind of strange that my mom and dad almost aborted me. It's making me wonder. Why did God save me and not the other millions of babies? Why didn't He save my sister?"

"Oh, that's a big question. I'm not sure I have 'the' answer for you, Trudy. It was such a hard time for all of us. I've often asked that myself. I can only think it may be as simple as your mom and dad listened to Him that day."

Trudy cocked her head.

"I'm serious, honey. You know your mom and I have counseled many women and told them the facts. Still, they choose to go through with having an abortion. I don't understand why some hear and some don't. It goes way back to the beginning. We all have a choice to obey or not obey."

"But why couldn't she hear God with the first baby?" Tears welled up in Trudy's eyes. "Why didn't He speak louder?"

"Honey, I don't know if your mom had the capacity to hear Him. They were running from what they were afraid of and not listening. Maybe they simply ignored His voice."

"That's what I did. Grandma, can I tell you something? I mean, this is something really personal."

"Of course, honey. If you're comfortable sharing it with me, sure."

"The day I…" Trudy stopped. Tears trickled down her cheeks. "That day after I was with Randy, I heard God's voice speak to me. I was alone in the bathroom. For just a moment, the reality of the step I had taken hit me. It hit me hard. But there was no going back. I felt like I had stepped into a world I didn't know. I wondered if Randy knew the value of the gift I'd given him. All my life I was taught it was meant for my husband. Instead of stopping and turning to God, I ran back into Randy's arms, ignoring His voice." Trudy could see her grandmother's sympathetic smile and the compassion in her eyes.

"I convinced myself we would be together forever. I believed everyone else in my life was wrong to say I couldn't be with him sexually. Now I wish I'd never done it." Trudy ducked her head

Kay laid her hand on Trudy's. "Sweetie, I think your mom and dad probably did the same thing. They ignored His voice. And young love can be very confusing. I remember. I was young and passionately in love with your grandpa. Only God's Word kept any balance in my life at that time."

"I don't understand how Randy can just shut off all the feelings he had for me. He may not want the baby, but how come he doesn't want me?"

"I can't speak for him, but it's probably not you, rather the whole situation, honey. It may be too much for him to deal with right now."

"It's not fair. I have to deal with it."

"I know, and you're very brave to decide to keep your baby. You could've made a different choice. I'm so proud that you listened to God."

"It doesn't make me feel any better. It's overwhelming. I wish I would've known about my mom."

"Hmm, I wonder if that's true?" Grandma Kay said thoughtfully.

"What do you mean? If I'd known about her, I would've had someone to talk to about what I was feeling," Trudy protested.

"Why would it be different?"

"Because she faced the same thing I'm facing now."

"Yes, but you came to me and talked to me, knowing how I believe. I think you still would have hid your actions with Randy."

"No, I would've been able to share with my mom."

"With what you know today about your mom, how do you think she'd have responded about you having sex? Think hard for a minute."

Trudy twiddled her French fry in the ketchup again. Someone put some money in the jukebox, and an oldie-but-goodie tune floated through the air. "I would've done anything to be with Randy. I love him so much. I turned from God. I suppose I still would've hid it."

"I went back and forth on whether you should have known your parents' story throughout the years. One day I saw what an incredible effort they were making to teach you about God's truths. That's when I decided in my heart when the time was right they'd share, but not until the time was right. Now that time has come when your mom let you know a part of her life that causes her great pain. She understands what you're dealing with, Trudy. It's better to go with things as they are today. Not with what-ifs. What-ifs confuse things."

"Yeah, I suppose you're right. I'm still amazed that God protected my life; that I'm here."

"I remember the first day they told me. I loved you instantly, and your mama was so protective of you. When her parents stopped talking to her, it hurt her deeply, but she still considered you one of her greatest blessings."

"She gave up so much for me, Grandma."

"I think you'll be the same way." Kay stole a look at the clock. "Do you want to stay, and talk some more, or catch that movie? We have just enough time to get there."

"Umm, let's go to the movie. And Grandma, thanks for always being there." Kay gave a wink as she scooted out of the booth.

* * *

Sheryl and Bill walked hand-in-hand down the sidewalk at the waterfront after eating a dinner of Sheryl's favorite comfort foods—nachos and chocolate.

There was quite a bit of activity going on around them. People on rollerblades and bicyclists zoomed past, and couples pushed strollers. The river was full of sailboats, making the occasional speedboat seem out of place.

Finally, they reached the path leading to their favorite spot. It hid them from the early evening fun people were having all around them. Bill helped Sheryl over the fence that blocked the stairs from others' view and then held her hand as they picked their way down the rocky steps, left over from an old building. The water was high enough tonight to cover part of the stairs, so they didn't get to go down as far as they usually liked to. Still they were hidden away in their own secret place, where they let themselves dream or share their deepest thoughts with one another.

Sheryl cuddled close to Bill, leaning her head on his chest, his arm wrapped tight around her. In all their years together, no matter how hard it got between the two of them, he was faithful to hold her close.

"Do you think Trudy thinks less of me now?" Sheryl asked.

"Hmm, I don't know. I hope not. I hope she doesn't think less of either of us," Bill answered softly.

"Us?"

"I was there, too. I kept our secret just like you did."

"But you didn't have the abortion or almost kill yourself." Sheryl peered up at his face. "You were there supporting me the entire time."

"I was also there supporting you during the abortion. I was a part of it, too. I didn't protect you or the baby. I also knew more about abortion than you did. When it became legalized, I'd overhear my mom talk to her friends."

"That's funny. I've never thought about you in that way. I only saw you as my support, and that I left you. Hurt you."

"Well, I drove you to the clinic after we both knew better and almost had you abort Trudy. That was plain stupidity after all we went through with the first abortion. How irresponsible."

"Bill, I honestly didn't know you had these feelings."

"I don't talk about them. Until now, we never talked about the abortion." Bill sucked in his breath. "I can't begin to imagine what Trudy is feeling."

Sheryl squeezed his arm with loving tenderness. "I can't either. I am glad we're finally talking about it ourselves. I'm sorry it took so long."

"Well, I think we're going to have to keep communication open between us and Trudy in order for our family to finish strong."

"And prayer. Lots and lots of prayer," Sheryl murmured.

* * *

At Aunt Cissy's, Randy would sleep in his older cousin Charlie's room, who was away at college. He finally had a chance to call Trudy, but no one answered the phone at her house, and she wasn't answering her cell phone either. *I miss her so much.* He put down his dad's phone and settled back against the pillows on the bed, trying not to think about her, but ended up scrolling through the pictures he had of Trudy on his own cell. When he came across a group picture from youth group, Tony was in it. Randy decided to give him a call.

"Hmm, I haven't talked to him since he prayed with me. I hope I didn't lose his number." After a short look in his wallet, he found it. He started to punch the number in his phone, then remembered he'd used his amount of minutes, so he grabbed his dad's phone and punched the numbers in.

He listened with impatience. Three rings, four...

"Hello," Tony answered.

Randy hadn't realized he was holding his breath as he let it go. "Tony, it's Randy; Randy Hunter."

"Hey, what's up? Are you still out of town?"

"Yeah, we just got to my aunt's. Probably be back in a couple of days."

"So..."

"Tony," Randy interrupted, "I just tried calling Trudy and couldn't get hold of her."

"Oh, so you don't know."

"Know what?"

"Brenda and Trudy had a car accident. I guess they're okay. I saw Brenda at the physical therapist's office and she was okay. Banged up and bruised."

"Oh, now I really want to reach Trudy. I hope she's okay. You know I left town without talking to her. During the drive here God's been talking to me. It's unreal. I hear Him. I can't tell you if it's in my mind or if it's out loud, but I'm hearing His voice."

"That is so awesome Randy! What's He been saying?"

"Abortion isn't the answer. God clearly let me know that. We could've gone through with the abortion and nobody would've known, but nothing is hidden from Him. He would've known."

"Wow!"

"Tony, I need Trudy to know. Honestly, I don't know what to do from this point. Whether we're to get married, give the baby up for adoption, I have no idea. I just know I've been a complete jerk, and I'm sorry. I dropped her off at her grandma's…"

"Hey, Randy, I'm here for you. You keep trying to get hold of her, and I'll try on this end."

"Thanks, Tony. Thanks a lot," Randy said, relieved.

"I'm excited for you, and I'll be praying."

"Oh wait, my dad…he started reading the Bible too, and we've had some great talks. He gave his life to the Lord when he was young, but walked away after his grandma died. We're doing this together."

"What? Oh wow…" Tony laughed. "All I can do is say praise Jesus. That's so exciting! Does your dad know yet about the baby? What about your mom?"

"No. I haven't had the guts to tell them. And I haven't connected with my mom about God yet. She hasn't shown any interest, but we'll see."

"Huh. Well, I'll be praying for you, for courage. Thanks for letting me know what God is doing and trusting me with what's going on with Trudy."

"Tony, I'll be honest with you. I don't have a lot of guys I'd call friends, but I believe I want you for one."

"Right back at you. I'll call after I've talked to her."

"Thanks, Tony. Bye."

Randy smiled. "He's a good guy, Lord, thank You. And help me know what I'm to say to my parents." He drifted off to sleep at peace.

* * *

Randy was the first one awake in the morning. He wandered around the living room and kitchen not sure what to do. He couldn't remember ever being the first person up. It was so quiet. Every step he took seemed so loud. He went and took a shower, then headed into the kitchen to get something to eat. He smiled. *There's Dad already at the table reading the paper.*

"Morning, Dad," he said.

"Well! Good morning!" His dad peered over the paper in surprise. "Is today a special holiday or something? I haven't seen you up this early since you were little and wanted to open your Christmas presents."

"Ha! Ha! Very funny. Maybe I'm starting to get old, and I'm going to start doing things like the old people in my life, like not appreciating a good sleep in the morning," Randy teased back.

"The morning is for those who appreciate a day. Say, muffins are over on the counter. Cissy made them last night before she went to bed. She's going to sleep in. She's another one who's not a morning person."

Randy found the muffins and started stuffing them in his mouth before he sat at the table. "Hey, these are good!" he mumbled with his mouth full.

"What was that?" His dad shook his head. "You better get something to drink before you choke."

Randy got some juice out of the refrigerator. Out of habit he started to drink straight from the bottle.

"Randy! You know better! Pour yourself a glass! What do you do when you don't have someone telling you what to do? You'd think you could think on your own by now," his dad scolded him.

Yeah, Yeah, I hear it all the time. So when does it stop? When do parents just let you be? Probably not until I'm a parent. And I am going to be a parent. He shook his head. *I can't get away from thinking about it. How will I be with my kid? I hope I don't nag at him all the time.* Randy stared at his dad reading the paper. *When did he stop being a kid? Did he simply wake up one day and just know what to do and how to do it?*

Randy's dad lowered his paper onto the table and looked up. "Something wrong, Randy?"

"Huh?" Randy snapped back into reality. "No, I was just thinking."

"Hmmm, you're sure?"

"Yeah."

His dad started reading the paper again.

"Dad?"

"Yes, Randy?" His dad looked at him.

"Dad, when did you stop being a kid? I mean, when did you stop messing up all the time?"

His dad smiled. "I don't think you ever stop being a kid, not really. Inside I feel young. But I started getting responsibilities that took more time. Well..."

"Yeah, but when does that happen? I mean, like when did you stop drinking out of the bottle when you drank milk or juice, or when did you stop stuffing your mouth?" Randy persisted.

His dad eyed him seriously. "Randy is something wrong? Is there more to this than you're asking?"

Randy scratched the back of his neck nervously. He hadn't planned to tell his dad right then, but, on the other hand, he hoped he could tell him now. Just get it over with. "Sort of, Dad, but it's hard to talk about."

His dad got up from the table, pushed in his chair, and headed for the door. "Come on, let's go for a walk. If you feel like talking about it, you can. Otherwise, we'll just enjoy the fresh morning air!" He opened the door and breathed in deeply. "Feel that fresh air fill your lungs!"

Randy rolled his eyes at his dad and put his glass in the sink. *Maybe this is why I'm afraid to be a parent. One day I might act like my dad does.* He chuckled to himself as he followed his dad out the door.

Whenever they passed someone, whether the person was in their yard or jogging past them, his dad would wave or call out a "good morning." Randy would only smile self-consciously at the person's response.

They walked to a little park close to his aunt's house. It had a little jogging path with a couple of picnic tables and a few things for kids to play on. Randy and his dad walked on the jogging path. When they heard joggers coming up behind them, they moved. He was surprised so many people were up this early jogging. *What for? It's not even seven yet. That's not something I do until later in the day.*

"Dad, I just don't get it."

"Get what?"

"Why are these people up so early? And jogging? Are they crazy?"

His dad laughed as he surveyed the joggers and the walkers, then reached over and messed up Randy's hair.

Randy pulled his head away. "Dad!"

His dad grinned. "I guess it does seem kind of silly to someone who thinks a day starts at noon."

"Ha! Ha!" Randy said sarcastically.

Then his dad got serious. "Some people enjoy mornings, as hard as that may be for you to believe. You're not a morning person. That might change, though. I wasn't a morning person when I was growing up, but now I love the morning. It's my time to relax or get things done."

"Did you like sleeping in when you had me?"

"Yeah, at first, but then I started getting up and watching you sleep in the morning. Your mother would take a shower and do all the stuff she needed to do. I started enjoying that time."

"You would watch me sleep?"

"Yep! Sometimes I still like to check in on you and your sister."

"Why?"

"I don't know how to explain it. There were plenty of nights your mother and I would stand at your door and watch you sleep." His dad looked a little embarrassed. "When you're a parent, you have this feeling inside like I can't explain. It just grows and grows, even when the kid is driving you crazy!" He winked at Randy. "When they're asleep, you can take in everything about them. Kids look so peaceful and sweet. That's when, no matter what kind of day you had or what troubles are lurking around the corner, you can really see that it's all worth it. You can see it in your child's peaceful expression."

Someday I'll be looking at a kid while he or she sleeps and think it's all worth it. A picture of Trudy and him standing at a doorway watching their baby at the end of the day floated through his mind. He smiled. *Hmmm, that doesn't look so bad. But what about all the work! I'd have to get up every morning, go to work, come home, work in the yard and on my car, pay bills. Bills? What if I can't find a job? What can I do anyway? I've never worked. Taking out the garbage is work!*

His dad sat at a picnic table patting the bench beside him. "Come on, sit down," he said firmly.

A nervous twinge twisted in his stomach. He tried taking a deep breath but couldn't. His heart started beating fast. *I think I'm going to lose my breakfast.* He sat down, folding his hands with head down and eyes closed. He felt his dad's hand on his back, and started taking deep breaths, fighting the urge to cry. Still, tears stung his eyes.

"Hey, whatever is bothering you, you have to get it out. Nothing can be that bad," his dad said, concern lacing his voice.

Randy couldn't talk. The words wouldn't come out of his mouth. *God help me to talk to my dad.*

"Even if you did something horrible, we can get through it. If you're afraid I'll get mad, I'll get over it. You know that. Don't worry about it." He patted Randy's back. "No matter what's bugging you, I'll be here for you."

"Dad," he started. *God, how do I tell my dad I got my girlfriend pregnant? He's probably going to think I'm an irresponsible idiot when he hears this. Okay, I have to get it over with.* "Dad, I've got a really big problem, and it's not the type you solve."

A funny look appeared in his dad's eyes, as if he were trying to swallow a baseball caught in his throat. "Ah, is this about you and uh, Trudy?"

Randy nodded, then averted his eyes. The words slipped quietly from his lips. "She's pregnant."

"Randy?"

"She's pregnant," he said a little firmer. *Oh God, I want to run away from here. It feels so real now that I said it to my dad. I'm going to be a dad, and I'm scared to death. Will my dad hate me? I can't look at him. I can't stand to see what might be in his eyes.*

10

"She's pregnant." The words seem to echo again and again throughout the park. Stunned, Al fought the urge to start yelling. He stared at Randy. The poor kid looked like he was expecting to be hit with a blow harder than ever.

Instead, Al reached to give Randy a reassuring pat on the back. Randy flinched. He tried to pat Randy's back gently again. When he felt Randy relax, he pulled him close and wrapped his arms around him tight. He knew he didn't need to yell or tell Randy he'd done something very wrong. He believed deep in a place in his heart that his son knew all that. What he needed most was to know his dad still loved him.

Neither said much on the way back to Aunt Cissy's place. Every once in a while Al would turn his head toward Randy. Randy would return his gaze for a nervous moment, then stare back down at his feet. It was going to be a rough road, but Al was more concerned with how Randy was feeling.

Al was known to react in anger before he did anything else. He didn't study the situation and try to work it through. But today, he found himself listening for the voice of wisdom that comes from God. Although he had only been reading the Bible and praying for a few days, it was obvious God was already changing him. His main concern right now was making sure everyone was okay and then, who knew what? He needed to be strong for the family and Randy was one scared guy. He seemed to be waiting for the moment that Al would start to yell and tell him how wrong he was and who knows what else would come out of his mouth.

Al nudged Randy on the arm. He could feel Randy stiffen. "Hey, Randy, are you waiting for the other shoe to drop? Are you wondering when this news is going to hit me, and I'll react and jump all over you?"

"I don't know." Randy shrugged.

"Come on, Randy, be honest. You are, aren't you?"

Randy stopped and nodded, but his eyes didn't look directly at Al. "Yeah, I guess I am," he admitted.

"I was just thinking to myself how I would normally react. I get angry, and you usually get the raw end of the deal."

Randy stared at the sidewalk.

"I'm really sorry I do that. You know I feel different inside. I don't know how to explain it, but I can almost hear God guiding me. It's like He's showing me the whole picture. How you may be feeling, and how this is going to affect your mom, even how Trudy may be feeling right now. My anger has no place in this. The only reason I'd yell is to make me feel better, but then you'd feel worse than you already do."

Randy half smiled and nodded.

"I'm sorry, Randy. I'm sorry you were afraid to come to me. Listen, if you're in trouble or you mess up in the future, I hope you'll know I'm here to help you, not to yell at you. I may get upset, but someday, I hope, no matter what, you can come to me without being afraid."

Randy's face turned red with embarrassment. "Dad, I didn't want to tell you because I always want you to be proud of me, but I blew it and I let you down."

Al tousled Randy's hair. "I've always been proud of you. I just don't let you know. I'm sorry. I admit I'm disappointed for you, because the choices you've made have hard consequences. It's going to be tough, but you can still have a great life. But it'll be different than the one we planned for you."

Randy stuffed his hands in his pockets and kicked at a rock with his foot, "Yeah, a lot different. I can't believe I blew it like this."

Al put his arm around his shoulder. "We're going to get through this together. I'm here for you and Trudy. And there happens to be someone else on our side now to guide us, and that's Jesus. I believe He'll show us the way."

Randy smiled. "Thanks, Dad. There's more to the story. When Trudy told me she was pregnant, I insisted she have an abortion." Randy watched his dad's expression before he proceeded. His dad looked like he was listening and ready to help instead of getting angry. "We were at the clinic, and she left without aborting the baby. Dad, when she told me she didn't go through with it, I dumped her." Tears sprang to his eyes. He put his hands on his head and turned away. "I left her. I can't imagine how she felt. Then I tried again to convince her to have an abortion, but she'd turned her life back to following God. I was so upset. I went out, and that's when I met Tony. You know the rest of the story, except when I talked to Tony last night he said she had gotten into a car accident Sunday, and I haven't been able to reach her."

"Is she okay? What about the baby?" his dad said, alarmed.

"Tony thinks they're okay, but I'm such a jerk. She needed me, and I left her. God showed me through Tony and the stuff you were talking about this morning that abortion isn't the right choice. This is my baby and I need to be there. I don't know if we're supposed to get married or what, but…"

"Hey, hey." Al put his arm around Randy's shoulder. "You made a mistake and fortunately she didn't go through with the abortion. Now what we need to do is let Trudy know you are here for her, and so am I. I'm going to help you two. First, though, I need to talk with your mom."

"Oh," Randy groaned.

"I honestly think I need to talk to your mom privately about this. I'll ask Cissy if you and your sister can hang with her while I take your mom out."

"You sure, Dad?"

"Oh, yes, son, I'm sure. Very sure." Al gave Randy's shoulders a squeeze before they walked up Cissy's driveway. Katey came running out the door demanding to know where they had been and, of course, why didn't she get to go with them.

* * *

Jodee stood by her locker talking with Karen before school that morning. Karen glanced over Jodee's shoulder. "Oh my, here comes your goody-goody buddy, Brenda. You know, she's pathetic," Karen said snidely.

Jodee looked down the hall and swallowed nervously. Brenda was coming their way. Jodee's heart started pounding. She didn't want Karen to know anything about what had happened. Even though Karen was her best friend, Jodee had never told her about the problems at home. She didn't want people to think she was some sort of weirdo.

Jodee watched Brenda walk toward them with a smile. *Oh no!* But Brenda merely said a friendly hi and walked on. Jodee breathed a sigh of relief.

"What's the matter with you? You acted like you're afraid of Brenda or something." Karen eyed her strangely.

"Yeah, right, like I'd be afraid of Brenda. Get a grip." Jodee turned toward her locker and acted like she was searching for something as she tried to get a grip on her emotions.

"No, really, when she was walking up to you, you had the strangest look on your face," Karen persisted.

Jodee turned to Karen with impatience. "Look—if you have to know, lately Brenda has made it her mission to show me how much Jesus loves me. It's driving me crazy!"

Karen started laughing.

"Laugh all you want, but just be thankful it's not you she has her eye on!" Jodee changed her voice to a high sing-song tune: "Jesus loves you, I love you!"

Karen leaned against the lockers, laughing. "Are you kidding?" she screeched. "That girl is such a freak! What next? Will she chase you down the hall yelling, 'I love you! Don't run away, I love you!'" Karen laughed harder.

"No, she follows me in her car. I love you! I love you!" But as Jodee watched Karen holding her sides laughing, images of the night before flashed to mind. Even though she was the one making the jokes, it wasn't funny anymore. She didn't like it that Karen was laughing at Brenda.

"That girl should be in the circus! It's a wonder Trudy ever wanted her for a friend." Karen choked out in between giggles.

Jodee stared at Karen. She had started to figure out why herself. Brenda obviously cared about people. She wanted Karen to stop laughing. It was irritating! Disgusted, Jodee said, "Karen, it wasn't that funny. Come on. We'll be late for class."

Karen straightened up, but was still laughing. "Like you've ever cared if we're late for class." She put her arm around Jodee. "Ohh, you've always been good for a laugh. Whew!" She held her side. "My stomach's tired from laughing."

Jodee stared straight ahead, angry over the remarks she'd made, and that Karen had a laugh at Brenda's expense. Karen was talking on and on, not noticing Jodee scarcely paid any attention to her for the rest of the morning. Jodee had to sort out what she was feeling. Something about Brenda had set Jodee off negatively from the day they met. Why was she getting under her skin now?

Images of the times she'd ridiculed her in front of other kids paraded back. For some reason Brenda was always nice to her, but it grated on Jodee's nerves like someone scratching a chalkboard. She couldn't figure out why a nice person would bug her so much. Jodee continued to think about this for the rest of the morning.

* * *

Trudy made her way to the back room, where she could hear the sound of the television, to say good morning to her mom and see if she could go to school. She wasn't as sore this morning as yesterday. She made a quick stop in the kitchen to pour a bowl of cereal and spotted her cell phone on the counter next to the phone book.

"There it is." She scrolled through the missed calls. Her heart started pounding. Randy had called. Hand shaking, she pressed *Redial*. It went directly to his voicemail. "Bummer, well at least he called me. I can't believe he called me."

With a little skip and a smile she continued on to find her mom. She found her standing at the ironing board, staring at the television.

"Good morning." Trudy gave her a hug.

"Good morning. You're in a good mood. Did you have a good time with Grandma Kay last night?" Sheryl returned the hug and gave her a kiss on her cheek. "I considered waiting up for you, but when your dad and I came home from dinner, I was exhausted. I went to bed and didn't even hear you come in."

"I did have a good time. We had a good talk. I'm also not as sore. Can I go to school?" She sat down to eat her cereal and watch the program.

"Well, if you want to go, I don't see why not."

"Good. You'll have to drive me," Trudy stated, getting captivated by the show. One of her favorite movie stars was being interviewed. She never missed a movie he was in.

"Trudy." Sheryl tried for her attention.

"What?" Trudy stayed fixated on the program.

"Trudy…"

"Sorry, Mom, but he's so cute. I want to hear about him."

"Whatever, hon." Sheryl rolled her eyes. "After school I'd like to show you something."

"Okay." She shrugged. "That would be great. Are you going to pick me up, or should I take the bus home?"

"I'll pick you up. But for now, I'll be about fifteen minutes if you want to leave for school."

Trudy took one more look at the show as they closed up the interview and shoved a spoonful of cereal in her mouth before nodding that she'd be ready. Butterflies started dancing in her stomach at the thought of seeing Randy in less than an hour.

* * *

Trudy could hardly wait for class to finish. She struggled to swallow the lump stuck in her throat and blinked hard to stop the tears from flowing. *Come on, clock, move! What…are the batteries dead?* She counted the squares on the floor under a desk, and how many girls wore something in their hair, whether a barrette or ponytail holders. She'd look back at the clock, and it seemed time stood still. *I want out of here.* She squirmed in her chair. Her hopes for school this morning were dashed when she hadn't found Randy or Brenda before class, and now she was humiliated listening to what a few girls sitting behind her were saying. Oh, how she wished she couldn't hear them.

Don't they know I can hear every word? They're talking so loud they might as well have a megaphone.

According to the story they were whispering back and forth, Randy had dumped her after finding out she was pregnant. "Do you think Randy knows whether it's his baby or not?" They giggled. "I bet she's pretending to be pregnant. She had an abortion, or else why would she be seen leaving a clinic? She's probably using it to hang on to Randy."

"Who wouldn't? I'd do everything I could to hang onto a guy like him," one of the girls answered back.

"If she is pregnant, she'll get big and fat. And afterward she'll probably be overweight with messy hair. That would make him run for sure." The girls howled. The teacher glared at them to quiet down.

Trudy didn't care much about their opinion of what she may look like later. They would see the truth soon enough. But she did care about Randy. *Was he really telling people he broke up with me because of the baby? How could he do that to me? I can't imagine him doing that!*

She flashed back on the night they stopped at the park and how he responded after finding out she didn't go through with the abortion. He did act in a way she'd never seen before. He shut her out. He hadn't called until this morning.

Tears welled in her eyes, and she blinked hard to keep them from falling. She did not want those girls to see her cry, so she stared down at her desk. She felt so alone. She didn't have anyone there to help support her.

Then she heard a voice. Not so anyone else could hear. She heard it in her heart, in her mind. *"I will never leave you nor forsake you."* He was here. Jesus was here to support, comfort, and strengthen her.

Oh, Lord. Thank you for being here with me. She felt led to pray for the girls who were talking about her. When she was done, her heart felt lighter.

The bell rang; class was over. She had made it. *Thank You for being there to support me.* With determination she went to find Randy.

* * *

Jodee was still deep in thought during lunch, oblivious to the noise of the cafeteria around her. Kids were laughing, food was flying, and Karen was busy telling everyone at the table the latest exciting thing going on at school. Brenda sat at a table with her friends across the cafeteria. Fascinated, Jodee watched them. It wasn't like Brenda and her friends were doing anything out of the ordinary. They were eating and laughing like any of the other kids at lunch. Yet, there was something different, and Jodie was trying to figure it out. She felt embarrassed for Brenda and her friends when they prayed before they ate. *Brenda doesn't get it! You don't do stuff like that in public. People will think you're a freak.*

Jodee stopped herself midthought. *What do I care about what people think of Brenda?* She focused on her own food, trying to pay attention to what Karen was saying, but found herself drawn back in Brenda's direction. *What is wrong with me today? What's the big deal about Brenda? We've eaten in the same lunch room since we were kids! They're only a bunch of do-gooders.* Yet she continued to watch and even caught herself smiling when they smiled.

"Hey, Jodee!" Karen's voice was loud. "What are you doing? You haven't heard a word I've said this entire lunch." She eyed her. "In fact, I don't think you've heard a word I've said all day! What's with you?"

Jodee shrugged, embarrassed. "Nothing."

"What do you keep staring at over there?" Karen turned around. "Is there a new, cute guy in school?" she teased.

Jodee made a face. "Very funny. I was just thinking, that's all. Anything wrong with that?"

Karen glanced over her shoulder. "Hey! Miss Do-gooder is over there!"

A tightness formed in Jodee's stomach.

"I wonder what Miss Do-gooder and her friends are talking about. The latest way to walk an old lady across the street?" Karen hooted at her joke. The other kids at the table joined her. Jodee didn't laugh. "What's the matter, Jodee? No sense of humor today?"

"I didn't think it was funny, Karen," Jodee replied quietly.

"Getting soft? Is Miss Do-gooder getting under your skin?" Karen needled.

"Karen, have you ever stopped to think why we say and do such mean things to her? She's never done anything to us!" Jodee exclaimed.

"Oh, please, she is such a Goody two-shoes. She gets on my nerves. All that Jesus talk drives me crazy!"

"Why?" Jodee asked. "Just because someone is a really nice person, and believes in God, does it mean we should be mean to her?"

Karen sighed. "Listen, all I did was make a joke, which obviously you didn't think was funny. Somewhere you lost your sense of humor, but don't get all over me about teasing Miss Do-gooder. You've made it your main event for years."

"I know," Jodee murmured as she stood. "And now I'm trying to figure out why. She didn't do anything to me." Jodee scanned the others faces at the table, then quietly picked up her bag of food and walked away. Her friends' mouths dropped open in shock. They stared at each other quizzically.

"Do you believe it?" Karen snorted, and they all joined in laughing at the situation together.

Jodee could hear them laughing behind her and knew it was at her expense, but at the moment she didn't care. She threw her lunch bag in the garbage, but when she turned around, she bumped right into Brenda and knocked her tray on the floor. *Great!* Just something else for her so-called friends to get a good laugh about. *Just great.*

"I guess I wasn't paying attention." Brenda smiled. "I'm sorry. Did I get anything on you?"

"No, I'm fine." Jodee picked up the mess and put it in the garbage. Brenda put the tray where it belonged on the tray stack. "It was probably my fault. I wasn't paying attention."

"Oh, well, neither of us was hurt or covered with food." Brenda laughed. "Well, I'll see you later." She started to walk away.

"Wait!" Jodee called. Brenda stopped and turned toward Jodee. "I...wanted to thank you."

"Thank me?"

"For last night. I really appreciated your help."

Brenda nodded sweetly.

"And for not saying anything this morning. I mean"—Jodee looked at her—"no one knows."

Brenda put her arm around Jodee's shoulder, and Jodee found she didn't mind. "It's no one's business unless you feel it's their business."

"You've got that right." Jodee pulled away as she snapped at Brenda. Immediately she regretted it. She knew Brenda wasn't against her. "I'm sorry."

"Hey, don't worry about it. I'm not going to tell you I understand what you're going through because, well, I honestly couldn't even begin to imagine," Brenda started saying. Jodee felt sad inside. "But I will tell you that I can imagine what you are *feeling*. And if you ever need someone to talk to, I'm here. I may not have all the answers, but I know Someone who does." Brenda gave her a big, comforting smile.

Jodee found herself smiling back. "Thanks, Brenda." She felt self-conscious then. "I better get to my class now. I'll talk to you later." *Wow, Brenda really cares,* she thought as she walked off. Her smile grew bigger the more she thought about that. And the thought put a good feeling in her heart.

***

Trudy put her lunch tray on the table where she usually sat with Randy. Before she sat down, she glanced around the cafeteria for Brenda. She caught a glimpse of her as Brenda walked out a door to the outside area and sighed. She'd have to try to catch up with her later. *But where's Randy?* It was all so strange. Except for last night, he hadn't called her since Saturday, and some friends told her in the lunch line he hadn't been to school yet this week. Obviously the girls in class were only spreading rumors, but who started the rumor?

"So, what's up with your friend Brenda?" Karen asked with a scowl.

"What do you mean?" Trudy asked.

"Why is she so interested in Jodee all of a sudden? I just saw her give Jodee a hug."

"I don't know." Trudy was as surprised as Karen. The last she'd heard from Brenda about Jodee was on Saturday. Jodee had called her to gossip about Trudy being at the abortion clinic.

"Don't give me that, Trudy. You know exactly what's going on. Your friend is trying to turn Jodee into a geek, just like you used to be, until you got smart," Karen commented. Karen had hit a sore spot with Trudy, and she knew it. It was all Trudy could do not to lash out at her. But Trudy chose to stay silent.

"You've gotten a taste of the good life—being a part of the popular crowd. You even learned to cover your mistakes. I think it's rather fun to watch your little scheme of pretending you're still pregnant. But I know better. What else would someone do at an abortion clinic? Are you going to pretend to lose your baby soon?" Karen's words dripped with sweet sarcasm as she batted her eyes.

Trudy laid her fork down quietly. *That's it. I've had it with her remarks.* But right as she opened her mouth to lash out, Trudy saw the picture she had painted of herself this last year. She'd turned away from her faith, friends, and family. She'd done things she wouldn't have done before, and she did go to have an abortion. How she wanted to wipe that smug look off of Karen's face, but the other part of her knew what she needed to do.

"I hate to admit it, but you're partly right. I did go to the clinic. I'm not proud of it, but I did it. However, I'm not going to sit here and argue. You'll see in a few months whether I had an abortion or not. And I did walk away from my faith." She stood, lifting her tray. "Now I'm going back. I hope I never turn my back on it again. It's not worth it. You know, Karen, you can get to know Him to," Trudy finished.

At that moment Jodee appeared behind Karen to retrieve her purse from under the table just as Karen threw back her head and laughed.

"What's so funny?" Jodee asked. She looked back and forth between Trudy and Karen. Trudy wasn't laughing.

Karen slapped her hand on the table as she continued to fake laugh. "Trudy just told me a good one. She told me she's decided to go back to her faith," Karen said. Jodee shot her a look that Trudy couldn't decipher. "I can, too. Did you know that?" Karen said sarcastically.

Trudy met Jodee's eyes. Trudy couldn't figure it out, but Jodee didn't have the same tough-girl look.

"Karen, I don't think this is something to laugh about." Jodee spoke in a quiet tone close to Karen's ear. Karen gave Jodee a glare that caused Trudy's stomach to do a flip.

"What? First you're over there hugging Brenda, and now you're getting a soft spot for Trudy, too. Well, don't forget who's responsible for spreading the word about Trudy. It's not me." Karen stood, picking up her tray. "You're really getting on my nerves today, Jodee," she threw back over her shoulder as she walked away.

Trudy studied Jodee. Tears were in her eyes as she watched Karen walk away. "What's up, Jodee?"

"What?" It was obvious she was trying to put her tough-girl face back on.

"Don't give me that. Why? Why are you spreading rumors?"

"I didn't think they were rumors. I saw you come out of the abortion clinic, and then I saw Randy at The Cave Saturday night without you. I only told a few friends. So shoot me."

"I'm still pregnant."

"Well, congratulations!" Jodee said with animated sarcasm. "Gotta go. See ya!"

Trudy let out a sigh. *What's the difference anyway?*

"Hey, Tru! I've been looking for you today." Tony was walking in her direction. "Are you getting ready to leave? Here—let me carry your tray. I got something to talk to you about."

I'm so not ready to have a talk with Tony.

"It's a nice day out. Would you like to go outside?" Tony continued.

"I guess." Trudy watched Jodee walk away while Tony put the tray on the stack. *I wonder what's going on with her? Oh, well, I have other things to worry about, like having a talk with Tony.*

11

The courtyard at school was outside of the cafeteria. Most everyone hung out there after lunch before returning to class. There were different levels, each with cement benches to sit on and a five-foot width of grass before you had to step down to the next level. It was set up like an outside auditorium but normally wasn't used in that way, except for a very few pep squad rallies. Tony led Trudy over to an empty bench.

"So are you okay, Trudy? Did you get hurt much in the car accident?" Tony asked.

"I'm okay. A little sore." Trudy exhaled, relieved the topic was the accident and not her pregnancy.

"I saw Brenda at the PT's office, and she mentioned your accident."

"Yeah, it was so freaky. I'm not even sure what happened. We were talking, and I was putting lotion on when *bam!* We were hit."

"Well, just so you're okay. Is there anything you need?" Tony asked.

Trudy shook her head. "No. I'm fine."

"Listen, I talked to Randy last night," Tony started. Trudy felt her breath catch in her throat. "Did he end up getting a hold of you? He told me he'd tried right before calling me and didn't have any luck."

"No, I forgot my phone at home." Trudy tried to sound nonchalant, but inside she was dying to know what Randy had said.

"He felt pretty bad about the way he left things on Friday, and he mentioned he was sorry."

"Sorry?" Trudy sat up straight. Hope filled every fiber of her being.

"Yeah, hey, I haven't had a chance to tell you about the time I spent with Randy Saturday night. Actually, I didn't have his permission to share it, but after talking to him, I don't think he'd mind if I did."

"Oh, tell me." Trudy couldn't wait to hear.

"Randy showed up at The Cave where I was playing pool. I invited him to join me, and we started talking. A couple of his friends came up and when their conversation turned ugly, he ended up leaving, and I followed him out." Trudy started to ask him about the situation, but Tony held up his hand. "I really don't want to get into all that ugly stuff. It's not worth the time to say it or hear it. Anyway, we started talking, and I told him some things about abortion and my family's experience and well…" Tony stopped and searched

Trudy's face. "I told Randy something very confidential, and because I told him, I feel I need to share it with you. Please don't let this go any further."

"Okay, I can't imagine what it is. Our families have known each other since forever. I doubt if I haven't heard it before," Trudy said.

"I don't even know if my parents have shared it with your parents or not. We agreed to keep this secret. Remember when my brother's girlfriend died after the car accident?" Trudy nodded her head. Tony then went on to share everything he'd told Randy about what really happened that day.

"But I thought she died in the car accident."

"Her family didn't want anyone to know how she died. We've honored that. I felt it was important for Randy to know how serious abortion can be."

"Tony, that's awful. It's no wonder your brother had such a hard time after her death." Trudy gave a shiver. "I still can't believe I even went to the clinic and how close I came to taking the life of my own child. Just the thought of abortion now gives me the creeps."

Tony's gaze was compassionate. "You ended up making the right choice. I'm proud of you."

"I wish I would've made the right choice from the beginning."

"Trudy, everyone faces temptation, and sometimes we fall. The important thing is, you turned back to God." Tony gave her one of his winning smiles. "I do have something to tell you that will make your day."

"Oh, what?"

"After I told Randy everything, we talked about having a relationship with Jesus. Randy prayed and gave his life over to Jesus."

"What?" She nearly screamed in delight. "You've got to be kidding me!"

Tony took hold of her hands and laughed, delighted over her response.

"Tony, this is beyond my wildest dreams. I had no idea this had happened." Trudy sat back. "Hey, wait a minute. Where is he anyway?"

"They went to see his aunt. Apparently he'd forgotten all about this trip his family had planned. And he used up his minutes for the month. Both his parents' phones were unable to get reception through the mountain passes."

"Oh," Trudy said quietly. She faintly remembered him mentioning the trip before they found out she was pregnant.

"He was sorry, and he agrees abortion isn't the answer."

So many thoughts went through Trudy's mind. *Does this mean he would be there for her and the baby? Were the two of them still together as boyfriend, girlfriend?*

"Trudy!" Trudy's thoughts were interrupted by Brenda calling out to her. "I didn't know you were at school." Trudy stood to greet Brenda.

"Brenda, you're not going to believe this. You just are not." Trudy's voice bubbled with excitement. Brenda's eyes flashed in response. "Randy gave his life to Jesus."

"What? That...oh my word, how incredible is that? Tony, did you know about this?" Brenda asked.

"Tony is the one that led him to Jesus," Trudy screeched.

"Wow. That's incredible." Brenda dragged out the words and gave an admiring smile to Tony.

Trudy giggled when Tony blushed. Their excitement was interrupted by the school bell. Tony stood and put his arms around both of their shoulders as the trio walked to class, the joy of the news spread across their faces.

* * *

It was dark by the time Randy and his sister returned with Aunt Cissy from their day out. They'd had quite a day—an amusement park, a movie, and then dinner. Randy carried sleepy Katey into the house, but as soon as she saw their mom she pushed out of his arms and started talking a mile a minute about their day. Randy noticed his mom's eyes were swollen from crying, and she only gave him a half smile in greeting as Katey pulled on her for attention. Randy looked at his dad. His dad nodded toward the bedroom. Randy felt relieved to be excused.

Closing the door behind him, he went and sat on the bed without turning the light on, recalling his mother's expression. He leaned over his knees and put his head in his hands, angry at himself. "God," he said, his quiet voice loud in the dark, "I'm so sorry for hurting my parents, for making my mom cry, for what I did to Trudy." Randy glanced up when the door to his room opened slowly.

"Randy?" his mom whispered.

"Yes," he answered.

"What are you doing?"

"I'm, uhh, praying."

She sat next to him on the bed. Randy felt uncomfortable when he heard her take a deep breath. She did that when she wanted to talk but was trying not to cry. He heard her take another one. He wished she would stop it.

"We're going to go home tomorrow," she said quietly.

"Tomorrow? We just got here!" Randy exclaimed.

"Randy," she said like he didn't know, "things have changed. We have things to take care of at home. Honey, why didn't you tell us before we left?"

"I don't know."

"You don't know?"

"Mom, I was scared to tell you. I didn't even plan on telling Dad today; it just happened."

"I don't know what you were thinking, Randy." She leaned close to him and, as low and as firmly as she could, asked him, "Just what were you thinking? We taught you better than that. Sex is not something to play around with. It's something shared between two people who are married." She stood and peered down at him in the dark. It was very effective. Randy's heart rate was up as she continued. "And do you know what else I don't understand?" She didn't wait for an answer. "In this day and age, if you were going to go against everything we ever taught you," her voice started to rise, "why on earth didn't you use birth CONTROL?"

"Mom," he said nervously.

She walked to the door, then back toward him, leaning down again. "Randy, I love you, but I have never been so angry with you! What you two did was very irresponsible. Do you realize that? Do you realize the responsibilities of raising a child? Right now I am so...." She headed toward the door. "I will talk to you later. Right now I may say something I will regret. Good night!" She left, shutting the door firmly.

Randy sat stunned, thankful he hadn't told her about trying to make Trudy get an abortion. Randy flopped back on the pillow on the bed. *I think she would have said everything on her mind and not regretted a word of it.* Randy lay stiff, biting his lip. Every once in awhile he would hear a noise outside of his room, and he was afraid it was his mom coming back. His stomach was in knots. He knew he had to walk very, very carefully the next few days. His mother had never gotten that mad at him. He stared at the wall across the room until he drifted off to sleep.

* * *

Earlier that evening, Trudy had received a call from Brenda, asking her to come to youth group with her that night. Trudy readily agreed. She wanted out of the house. After school, her mom ended up having an important errand to do for her dad, so she had cancelled her plans with Trudy. Trudy was relieved. She spent the rest of the afternoon busy in her room listening for her Mom to come home and realized she dreaded the thought of it. So it didn't take too much convincing from Brenda for Trudy to say yes, write a note, and leave it on the counter.

While on their way, they realized Brenda had forgotten her purse at home, so they had to go back and get it. Trudy waited in the car. *Hmm, what's wrong with me? Why don't I want to be around my mom?* Trudy wished she could figure out her feelings. Brenda dashed into the house to get her purse and dashed back out again. *I'll have to think about this later. I don't know if this is something I want to share with Brenda.*

"Do you believe it?" Brenda asked as she got back into the car. "Forget my purse!" She backed out of the driveway and started driving down her street.

Trudy noticed someone jogging down the street. When they drove past, the person looked down toward the ground. Trudy recognized her when the girl glanced up toward their car.

"What is Jodee doing by herself in the dark over here? Doesn't she live quite a few miles away?"

"What?" Brenda asked, stopping the car. She had panic in her voice.

"Yeah, it's Jodee. She's out alone at night. Maybe we should give her a ride," Trudy suggested.

"Okay." Brenda hadn't shared with Trudy about Jodee, since she had told Jodee she wouldn't tell anyone.

"Hey, Trudy," Brenda said as Trudy was rolling down her window to talk to Jodee. "Ask her if she wants to come with us tonight."

"Come with us?" Trudy asked, then shrugged. "All right. Hey, Jodee!" She called out. No response. She called out again.

Jodee walked slowly over to the car. "Uh, hi, you two. What are you guys doing?"

"We were about to ask you the same thing. Do you want a ride?" Trudy asked.

"Well...," Jodee hesitated.

"Come on, Jodee. It's not safe to be walking around at night alone. Let us give you a ride!" Brenda leaned over and pled persistently.

"Okay." She got in the back seat.

"So, any place you'd like us to take you?" Trudy asked, turning to face Jodee in the back seat.

"Well, I was just going to the coffee shop by my house."

"By *your* house? Hmmm, you're quite a ways from there," Trudy answered.

"So, Jodee, we're on our way to youth group. Want to join us? We'll drive you home afterwards."

The car was silent for a minute. "Okay, sure." Jodee surprised them with her answer.

"What have you been up to tonight?" Trudy asked again.

Jodee sighed, frustrated. "Since you probably know already about…"

Brenda interrupted her. "I haven't told her anything, Jodee. I told you I wouldn't. It's not my business to tell."

"What? You haven't told anyone?" Jodee asked.

"Just my parents. And only because I was upset when I came home and, well, it could hardly be avoided," Brenda confessed.

"I can understand that. But thanks for not telling anyone else."

"I don't suppose this is something anyone wants to share with me, now is it?" Trudy ventured.

Jodee stared for a long time at her. Just when it seemed she was about to speak, they pulled into the church parking lot.

Trudy turned, making herself busy collecting her things before getting out of the car.

Jodee hung back staring at the building.

"Come on, Jodee," Trudy and Brenda called out.

"You know, I think I've changed my mind. I think I'll go on home. This really isn't my type of place."

"How do you know?" Brenda asked.

"Yeah, ever been to a place like this before?" Trudy added.

"No, but I'm not that type of person."

"What do you mean by that? How do you know that for sure, Jodee? Now come on, give it a chance. If you don't like it, you don't ever have to come back." Brenda wrapped her arm through Jodee's. Trudy joined her.

"Well, for one thing, I don't act like you two or your friends. I'm not a sweetie do-gooder. I'm quite a bit tougher."

"If it was a matter of being a sweetie do-gooder, do you think I would be going in?" Trudy patted her stomach. "I mean, come on. It's a matter of how much God loves you. Not how good or bad you've been."

"That's right."

"Yeah, but I know I can be a jerk and get into lots of trouble. Besides, whoever said God loved me?"

Trudy and Brenda smiled at her. "God," Brenda and Trudy whispered in her ears with a giggle.

Jodee gave them both an odd look. She also gave in and let them lead her in the door.

* * *

Jodee sat between Trudy and Brenda. Quite a few kids from school were there, and none asked why she was there. They all welcomed her and acted like it was a normal occurrence. They sang a bunch of songs that had really good music. Although Jodee didn't sing along, she found herself tapping her feet to the beat and sometimes even nodding a bit. She watched the others clapping and raising their hands. It made her feel weird inside, in a good way.

When the music finished, a couple named Mike and Janice stood in front of the group. They didn't look that much older than the rest of the people there. Jodee found herself only half listening until the guy started talking about problems kids may experience at home. He asked if anyone had anything to share or needed prayer. A boy raised his hand.

"John." Mike pointed at him.

"Uh, I just wanted to tell you about answered prayer," he said.

"What? Did he get an A+ on his test instead of an A-?" Jodee whispered in Brenda's ear. "He'd flip out if I shared a story or two." Brenda only gave her a sad smile in response.

"Well, my dad has a real problem. He beats my mom. Last time he put her in the hospital," John began, but then stopped, seeming to be overwhelmed with emotion. He took a breath and continued. "She won't press charges; she's too scared. Well, while she was in the hospital, he started beating on my older sister. I guess because my mom wasn't there. My grandparents called the cops, and now we're staying with them until my parents work out their problems." Tears were rolling unchecked down John's face. "Thanks for the prayer, 'cause now my sister is safe."

The girl next to John put her arm around his shoulder. Jodee watched him in shock. The leaders suggested they break up into small groups and pray for one another. Jodee became even more shocked when Trudy admitted to the group of girls she had been at an abortion clinic.

"I tried to cover my sin. I almost destroyed an innocent person's life." Trudy's face was wet with her tears. "I've hurt my family deeply and found out some things about my family through this situation that really hurt."

"Trudy, I was in that same place last year. I didn't make the right decision like you," another girl said. "I covered my sin. I was so afraid, and I didn't trust God. I've never gotten over what I did. It's all a big lie. It doesn't make your life easier. I'll never forget. But I know finally that I'm forgiven by Jesus. It was hard to accept, but I finally believed in His forgiveness."

"Were you ever able to forgive yourself?" Jodee looked at her, horrified.

The girl smiled and nodded. "Yes, but only because of Jesus' love for me. If Jesus can forgive me, I realized I had to come to a point of forgiving myself.

I still regret what I did. Hopefully, someday when I'm *married,* I'll have another chance to have a baby."

Jodee stared at the floor. "My mom had an abortion. Would Jesus forgive her?" she found herself asking.

"If she believes in Him, yes, He would."

"But what about someone who, like that kid's dad, who beats his wife and kid? Would Jesus forgive him?"

"Yes. If he repented and believed in Jesus."

"But what about the people who get hurt 'cause they're beaten? Or they hurt because their brother or sister is aborted? What will Jesus do for them?" Jodee asked. Anger tinged her voice.

"Whoever turns to Jesus will be forgiven. Jesus will bring comfort and healing to those who have been victims of others' actions," Brenda said gently.

Tears filled Jodee's eyes. "All my life I've been told I'm a bad person. My Dad told me I was a mistake from the very beginning. I would love to pretend I'm good enough like all of you and have Jesus forgive me and bring me some comfort, but I don't belong here." She leapt to her feet, knocking her chair over, and ran to the exit doors.

"Jodee, wait!" Brenda yelled out.

She didn't look back but started running across the parking lot. She could hear footsteps keeping pace behind her.

Wait!" Brenda called out.

Jodee only ran faster.

"Wait!" Brenda gasped out. "Please Jodee...wait! Please!"

Something in Brenda's persistence slowed Jodee's steps until she stopped. Jodee panted raggedly. Brenda stopped close by, bent over, trying to catch her breath. Jodee plopped onto her back on the grass next to the sidewalk. Brenda slid down next to her. Both sat catching their breath.

Trudy came up to them.

"Are you two okay?" Trudy asked.

"Yeah." Jodee looked embarrassed. She started to get to her feet.

Brenda held onto her arm. "Please, Jodee. I don't want to chase you again. If you want to go, then let us drive you home."

Jodee sat back on the grass and began to sob. She couldn't control herself. All the pain she'd stuffed deep down inside since the day she knew her mom wasn't coming home to get her poured out. Both Brenda and Trudy put their arms around her.

"It's okay, Jodee, we're here for you," Trudy whispered. "Just cry it all out."

"I can't. I have to be tough, but I hurt so bad inside. Why did my mom leave me? Why doesn't she come back for me?" Jodee was beyond caring what anyone thought. It felt good to get it out in the open. "My dad said I was a mistake from the beginning. Jesus could never love a mistake like me."

"No disrespect to your dad, but I'm afraid he's wrong. Jesus doesn't make mistakes. He's the one who made you and placed you in your mom's womb. He loved you before anyone else even knew you existed," Brenda said.

Jodee lifted her head with a questioning look.

"It's true. He died for you on that cross just like He died for me and Trudy." Brenda gave her a smile.

"You two don't understand, though! Your lives are nothing like mine. I'm no good! I'm mean and hateful inside. My dad is a drunk and tries to beat me. My mom left me!" Jodee looked at them to see if anything she said was sinking in. Trudy and Brenda gazed at her with caring faces.

Jodee continued impatiently. "You two are so innocent! You wake up to a mom and a dad who love you. Your moms probably make breakfast for you every morning. It's a miracle if I can find something to eat in the cupboards most days!"

Jodee shook her head impatiently. She realized by their expressions they didn't understand exactly what she was trying to tell them. "Listen, you guys, to put it simply, I can sit and pretend I fit in with that group in there, but I don't." Jodee looked down at the ground. "I don't want to pretend, either. It only makes reality that much harder to deal with."

"Well, Jodee, both Trudy and I know you don't fit in with that group, and we don't want you to pretend like you do, either," Brenda stated.

"You do? I mean you don't?" Jodee sounded hurt.

"That's right," Trudy agreed.

"Oh," Jodee said quietly.

"Jodee, we can't pretend to fit in. The only way you'll belong in that so-called group is when you, yourself, come to know Jesus as your very own personal Lord and Savior," Brenda said gently. "That's the only way. Jesus knows our hearts. We can't pretend."

"This all doesn't make sense to me. It never mattered before now, but I want to fit in, and you're telling me I can't. I feel worse than before."

Trudy's arm went back around her shoulder. "Don't be sad, Jodee. Jesus wants you to be part of His family. He wants you to know Him."

Jodee gave her a look of hope.

"What do you mean?" She peered over at Brenda. "You mean…" She sat quiet for a moment. "You mean…are you saying Jesus loves me, too?"

"Uh, huh!" Trudy and Brenda nodded.

"How do you know? I mean, what if He doesn't?" Jodee asked.

"We believe the Bible is God's Word. It's how God tells us about Himself and how we're to live. And the Bible says Jesus loves you," Trudy answered.

"He does?" Jodee asked.

"Yes, the Bible says, 'For God so loved the world, He gave His only begotten Son, that whoever believe in Him should not perish, but have everlasting life."

Jodee thought for a minute, then asked, "What are you supposed to believe about Him?"

"Jodee, would you like us to tell you about Him?" Brenda asked.

Jodee nodded in answer.

Brenda started telling her the gospel. "Everyone sins. No one is good enough on their own to stand before God. God is perfect and holy. Sin separates us from God and leads to eternal death. God loves us so much He gave His Son so we could live eternally with Him."

"What do you mean, He gave us His Son? I don't understand," Jodee interrupted.

"Jesus died on the cross for every sin that was ever committed. And then three days later He rose from the dead and went to heaven. He's going to return someday for those who believe and live for Him."

"In the Old Testament, God's people had to follow a bunch of laws they couldn't keep. God is a holy, perfect God. Well, every year they would make sacrifices for their sins, usually a lamb or a goat. But no matter what they couldn't follow all of those laws. Jesus was the perfect sacrifice for all of our sins." Brenda stopped and took a breath for a moment.

Trudy continued for her. "Way back in the beginning when God created everything, He created a man and a woman, Adam and Eve."

"I've heard of them. They were in some garden, and Eve ate an apple and got them kicked out," Jodee interjected.

"Exactly. The reason they got kicked out of the garden is they disobeyed God and chose to listen to Satan instead, who came and tempted Eve. God told the two of them they could eat from any tree in the garden except the Tree of Life. Well, Satan came along, as a serpent, and basically called God a liar, telling Eve she could be like God. Eve believed the serpent and disobeyed God. But even then the Bible shows God's compassion. He didn't just leave them to fend for themselves. He made clothes for them," Trudy said.

"Why didn't He just wipe them out? I mean, He made them!"

"Because God loves them. There was a time, though, that God did wipe out the whole world except one family. Ever hear of Noah and the ark?" Brenda asked.

"I think so. When I was little, my mom read me some sort of story about the animals going into the ark two by two."

"That's right! God flooded the whole world and afterward promised to never do it again. As a sign of that promise, every time it rains, He puts a rainbow in the sky," Brenda said.

"A rainbow! That's where a rainbow comes from? Way back from when God flooded the world? He still puts it in the sky?" Jodee asked, astonished.

"God never breaks a promise." Trudy smiled.

"Whoa! That's kind of weird." They sat quiet for a minute. "I still don't know what to do," Jodee admitted.

"Well, Jodee, do you want to follow Jesus?"

Jodee slowly nodded.

"I can lead you in a prayer, and you can repeat it after me. Once you confess your sins to Jesus and ask His forgiveness, Jesus comes and lives in your heart. He becomes the Lord of your life. Through His Word and by the Holy Spirit, He leads you to follow Him."

"Do you mean I don't even have to figure out what to do afterwards? He does that for me?" Jodee asked.

"Yes." Brenda nodded. "The Bible says, 'He will never leave you, nor forsake you,' and the Holy Spirit guides you. Would you like to pray?"

"I'm kind of scared," Jodee admitted.

"God loves you, Jodee. You don't have to be afraid of love." Trudy patted her hand.

"Can we pray now? I want God to be in my life!"

Trudy and Brenda smiled at each other through their tears. All three held hands and led Jodee in a prayer to her Father who not only created her, but loved her.

12

Jodee picked up her cat, giving him a big squeeze, then turned to give a quick wave to Brenda and Trudy before she stepped inside her house. The cat squirmed himself free from her grip, running into the kitchen, stopping at his bowl. His eyes stared at her intently while he licked his lips.

With a learned quietness she followed him to the kitchen to put a scoop of dry food into his bowl. "You sure are a hungry fellow," she whispered. "Don't eat so fast; you'll make yourself sick." She patted his head, then went in search of her dad.

The sound of the television blared in the hallway. A tight knot began to form in the pit of her stomach with each step toward his room. Cautiously she peered in to find him passed out on his bed, clothes still on, even his shoes. Making a passing glance to make sure no cigarette was still burning, she sighed in relief and turned away. He wouldn't be yelling at her tonight.

She headed back down the hall to get ready for school in the morning, but something made her stop in her tracks. She turned back around, halting at his door, and watched him sleep. A funny feeling rose inside her. It wasn't the usual fear she normally felt with her dad around. No, it was something else.

She timidly crept close to the bed. Empty bottles lay on the floor below his messy nightstand. And what a mess it was. Papers and dirty dishes were stacked under and around an overflowing ashtray. A picture of him with her mom still hung on the wall above the dresser. It looked like they were happy. Jodee didn't like to look at pictures of her mom. It hurt too much.

She gazed for a long time at her dad's face. The feeling inside her intensified. Even while he slept, his face was a mirror of how she had felt inside before tonight. Empty. She smiled, realizing that so soon after giving her life to Jesus the empty feeling was gone.

For as long as she could remember, she'd feared this man who lay in front of her. Tears formed in her eyes as she realized her heart didn't have love for him that a daughter probably should have. The two had never had any relationship other than she was in his way or he was angry with her. There wasn't a time she sat on his lap or was given a hug, a kiss. There hadn't even been good night stories. He had only shown her disdain and violence. She never understood how her mom could leave her with him.

Normally, bitterness would start to boil within her when she thought of her circumstances, but not tonight. Instead she felt sadness, even a bit of compassion. She knew firsthand how it felt to feel so bad inside that you wanted to strike out at everyone. Hurt them so they could hurt just like you. This man had helped her in feeling this way. But who had hurt him?

Tonight she realized she had been given a gift beyond measure. This man was not a loving father, nor did he seem to care to be, but she had been introduced to her heavenly Father. He loved her beyond measure. And God was already changing her. He had filled her with his being. She could feel his comfort and love. And because of that she could feel compassion for this man who had caused her so much pain.

Jodee reached down and gently slid his shoes off his feet, being careful not to wake him, but willing to take the chance. She went to her room and took the extra blanket off her bed and brought it back into her dad's room to cover him.

She picked up the bottle of alcohol and emptied the ashtray in the garbage can. Then she turned off the TV and light. She had one more thing to do before she left. She said her first prayer for another person. A prayer full of the hope that God would free him from alcohol and that he would come to know the joy and love she had through receiving Jesus Christ as her Lord and Savior.

After putting the bottle away in the kitchen, she scooped up her cat and curled up in her bed with him. His purr vibrated on her chest. She tried to hold on to just a few more minutes of this day, but her eyes were heavy with sleep. She did something else she hadn't done before tonight. She went into a peaceful sleep.

* * *

Brenda and Trudy drove away from Jodee's house in silence, except for an occasional glance at one another, followed with a little giggle. Trudy broke the silence. "Do you believe what just happened, Brenda! I cannot believe it! I would never, ever have expected that, tonight of all nights, Jodee would become a believer!" Trudy exclaimed.

"And that Randy Hunter would become a believer last Saturday!" Brenda gave a low whistle. Trudy stared out the front window with a thoughtful look. "What's going on, Trudy?"

"Oh, I don't know really. So much has happened this week that my thoughts and emotions can't keep up. I'm so happy about Randy becoming a believer. I still don't know what's going to happen in our relationship, though. And I'm excited about what happened in Jodee's life tonight, but..." Trudy bit at her lip, seeming to be disturbed.

"But there's something else, right?"

Trudy nodded before looking down at her hands.

"Is it something you can share?" Brenda asked.

"I'm not sure if I want to," Trudy said softly. By that time they had reached Trudy's house. Brenda pulled up to the curb and turned the car off.

"Trudy, I hope you know I'm here for you no matter what. It must be pretty bad if Randy and Jodee's salvation doesn't erase the concern from your mind. I mean you've dealt with so much this week. You were under the impression you and Randy broke up, you had to tell your Grandma Kay and your parents about being pregnant, our relationship was restored, a car accident, physical therapy...the list seems to go on and on. What can be bigger than any of those things?"

"How about finding out I was almost aborted?" Trudy whispered.

"Huh?" Brenda turned herself to lean against the car door so she could see Trudy better. "Ummm, that..." Brenda was at a loss for words.

"My mom got pregnant before they were married. They went to a clinic to have an abortion. Both of them were guided by God to leave before going through with it and so...here I am." Trudy put her arms out wide, with a cock of her eyebrows.

"It's just like what happened to you."

"Yeah, it is, so I should be a bit more understanding, but it's kind of mind-boggling to think about *my parents, my own parents*," she pointed at herself, "even thinking of abortion. Especially aborting me."

"I don't know what I'd do or think. Honestly, I don't know much about my parents' past, except they were raised in unbelieving homes and came to know Jesus in college. That's about it. I never really thought to ask."

"Well, that's not the only thing."

"What? There's more?"

"Before my mom became a Christian, she and my dad did have an abortion. Afterward my mom broke up with my dad. She couldn't get over it, and she almost committed suicide after a doctor told her she wouldn't be able to have any more children."

"No!"

"Yes. My Grandma Kay was there for my mom and led her to Jesus. I'm trying to grasp all of this. Why did God save me and not my sister?" Trudy asked.

"Your sister?"

"My mom said she went through a healing group and believes God told her it was a girl. I would have had an older sister. You know how bad I've always wanted a brother or sister." Trudy exhaled long and slow. "My mom wanted me to do something with her after school today. Something came up, and we weren't able to. I was glad. I'm finding it hard to be around her. I haven't even been around my dad since she told me."

"That would be tough. Trudy, this is big news that was totally unexpected. It's like something that came out of the blue and smacked you on the head. I honestly don't know how I'd feel about it."

"I guess I should be happy I wasn't aborted, huh?" Trudy tried to lighten the situation.

"Seriously, that's a good thing, Trudy. You're my best friend. I can't imagine what my own life would've been like if you weren't in it." Brenda stopped for a second and gave Trudy a strange look. "Actually, I do know what it's like. I hated not having you as my friend. I felt emptiness in my life where you were supposed to be, but at least I could see you every day, even though we didn't talk or share things. If you would have been aborted, I wouldn't have all of those wonderful memories of what we did growing up together."

"You probably wouldn't know the difference though. I mean, if you never met me, then…" Trudy shrugged.

"Well, let's say your mom did go through with it, and I never met you. But everyone in my life is exactly the same as they are now. Can you think of one person, out of all the people we know, who I would connect with in the way we do? There isn't anyone else I connect with like you. Sure, I have a group of friends, but only one best friend."

"Hmm, what a weird thought. My mom and dad probably wouldn't be as close to your parents as they are now. Didn't they become friends because of our friendship?"

"Probably. And your mom talks to girls down at the clinic with my mom trying to help them choose not to have an abortion. And then you're her only child. She wouldn't have any children. That is a huge hole in itself."

"Grandma Kay wouldn't have her granddaughter. Isn't it funny I never asked my mom about any of the girls she counsels? Or why haven't I heard her when she speaks publicly? I've never taken the time to get to know what my mom is interested in or why."

"I haven't either. I wonder what my mom was like when she was young. The only other thing I know is she had to deal with a rare breast cancer just before my mom and dad had Jonathon. She shouldn't have been able to have any more children, let alone live, but she did both."

"Yeah, you've mentioned that before. I couldn't imagine going through that. I wonder what it was like for her."

"I'm kind of ashamed to say I never asked," Brenda admitted.

"I'm feeling a bit convicted to take time to get to know my mom. She's just always been my mom and I love her, but oh!" Trudy stopped abruptly. "I forgot to tell you. My mom's parents stopped talking to her when she got pregnant with me. They've never spoken a word to her since."

"Oh, your poor mom, how sad. She sure has had a lot to deal with."

"Oh, Brenda, I feel like a selfish jerk wanting to stay away from her."

"Trudy, anyone who finds out they were almost aborted would naturally feel a little freaked out about it and need to have some time to deal with it."

"Yeah, there's going to come a day my child will know how close I came to ending its life," Trudy whispered.

Brenda hugged her. "Yes, and your child will realize how wonderful it is that God stepped in to save his or her life, just like He did for you. That's a mind-blowing thing, that God stepped in so clearly and saved both of your lives. And how thankful I am He saved my best friend's life."

*　*　*

Sheryl and Bill were in the front room when Trudy went into the house. "Hi, honey! Did you have fun?" her mom asked.

"Yeah," Trudy answered without enthusiasm.

"What's wrong? Are you hurting?" her mom asked, sounding worried.

Trudy shook her head. She came in the room and sat on the ottoman in front of her parents. "Jodee received Jesus tonight. It was amazing. And I heard Randy received Jesus Saturday night."

"That's great!" her dad responded. "So what's the problem? Haven't you and Brenda been praying for this Jodee girl for a long time? And Randy? That's awesome."

Trudy nodded.

"So?" her mom prodded.

Trudy studied her parents for a minute. Both had expectant expressions.

"Brenda and I were talking out in the car about the information you gave me yesterday." Sheryl and Bill nodded in understanding. "It's been hard to grasp that I was almost aborted and that I had an older sister." Sadness crossed Sheryl's face. Trudy noticed her dad tighten his arm around her mom. "It's been a lot to deal with. But, after talking with Brenda, I realize I don't know you two very well. Except that you're wonderful parents, and you always pour a lot of love out to me. I'm very fortunate." Trudy put her hand up in a stopping motion when tears started rolling down her mom's cheeks. "Please, Mom, don't cry. Then I'll start crying."

Trudy took a minute to regroup while Sheryl reached for a tissue. Bill gave a half smile.

"I have to finish what I'm saying. I'm still trying to sort it all out in my head, so it may not come out very well."

"Go ahead, honey. We understand you have a lot to figure out right now. We all do," Bill interjected.

"Well, I need to know more about all of this. I also want to," she paused, unsure how her parents would react, "write a letter to my grandparents." Sheryl looked shocked. "And, Mom, did you have any brothers or sisters? Did they stop talking to you?"

"I had a younger sister. She wasn't allowed to talk to me. I doubt she was ever given our address after we moved away. I've sent her birthday gifts and cards on holidays. I miss her terribly."

"Why didn't I know all of this?" Anger rose in Trudy. "It's frustrating."

"We honestly didn't know the appropriate time, honey." Bill put his hand on her knee. "After we got married, got settled, we had you, and we just started living. For a few years we tried to reconcile with your mom's parents, but then we gave it to God. Except for the cards and pictures we still send, we learned to live with their silence. It was so hard to get to that point, and you were young, so we never brought it up."

"Maybe we should have told you sooner, but now is when the door opened wide for your mom to share our past with you, as much as it hurts." Bill stroked her cheek.

"Well, I wanted you to know I'm trying to deal with all of this information. Just like you're probably having to deal with me being pregnant."

"We all seem to have a lot to deal with right now, honey." Trudy saw the love shining in her dad's eyes. "But we're going to get through this together. No matter what, we love you. We are here for you."

"I know that, Dad, and I'm sorry I lied about my life this last year."

"I'm sorry we didn't figure out how to tell you about our life before."

Bill leaned back close to Sheryl. Both opened their arms wide, beckoning her to join them. Trudy felt a little silly, but with a giggle fell into their arms, like when she was a little girl. And just like when she was young, her heart felt better, as they squished her in their double hug.

* * *

Randy's eyes sprung open. He didn't know what time it was, but he felt an urgency to be ready to go before his mom was. Jumping out of bed, he grabbed fresh clothes out of his bag, showered and dressed, then brought his bag out into the living room. He turned on a lamp as he sat on the couch to wait. It sure seemed dark out. Getting up, he peered out the window. It was still night. He groaned. *What time is it?* He scanned for a clock and gave an exasperated sigh when he saw it was only three in the morning.

He went over to the couch and laid his head on the pillows. He couldn't believe he'd gotten ready to go at three in the morning. *Wow, I'm sure nervous. Oh well, I can lay here and be ready when everyone else wakes up.* He drifted easily back to sleep.

* * *

Katey had heard her brother getting ready. She watched from the hallway as he lay down on the couch. Her heart felt sad and scared. She'd overheard her mom and dad talking about Randy, Trudy, and a baby. Randy was in lots of trouble. She went back into her room, took a blanket off the bed, and brought it to the couch to cover her brother.

She knew she drove him crazy, but she was really proud of her brother. He was good at everything he did, and everyone liked him. She bragged about him to her friends all of the time. She knew for now she was only a pest, but she hoped someday they could be friends and do things together. Like maybe he'd drive her to get ice cream or take her to the movies.

Once back in her room, she folded her hands. "God, please help my big brother. I'd love to be able to do something really nice for him. Please help me not to be such a pest for a while. Thank You very much."

A smile came to her face as she thought of an idea. She crept back down the hall and found his Bible tucked in his bag. Randy didn't even stir. She opened to the place he had read to her from just yesterday. There was a really special verse they both liked. After finding a pen and paper, she carefully copied the words down. It was taking forever, and her hand started to hurt. She put the paper in his Bible like a bookmarker and shut it. Then she curled up on the chair next to the couch and went back to sleep.

* * *

Someone was shaking him. *Knock it off.* Whoever it was wouldn't stop bugging him. He woke to his pesky sister trying to wake him up.

"Randy, wake up! It's time to go!" Katey said.

He couldn't believe it. She was standing there dressed and ready to go. He didn't feel like he'd slept at all. He sat up, putting his face in his hands.

"What were you doing out on the couch, Randy?" his dad asked. "You better go wash up so we can get going."

"Yeah, I will," he said as he reached for his bag to get his toothbrush and a fresh shirt. Slowly he walked to the bathroom. *Where was all that nervous energy he had earlier this morning?*

* * *

Aunt Cissy was disappointed they were leaving so soon. Randy wasn't sure if they had told his aunt or not. She didn't say anything to him or look at him funny. He thanked her for the great time and got in the car.

When his mom got in, he realized she hadn't said a word to him this morning. A lump formed in his throat. His mom had always been on his side, no matter what, and he'd done some pretty bad things. They had a special bond between them. He fought the tears that threatened to fall. He didn't need his sister teasing him about crying, so he stared out the window. After a couple of minutes, he felt a gentle tapping on his shoulder.

He ignored the tapping, knowing his little sister's greatest ambition in life was to make him miserable, and he wasn't in the mood. He felt her tap him softly again and peered over at her warily. She was smiling at him.

What's she up to? She put his Bible in his lap and quietly pointed to it. She gave his arm a pat and leaned back over to her side of the car. After he started reading the first few words, tears fell from his eyes unchecked. *"Therefore I say to you, do not worry about your life..."* He was shocked and touched over the words his sister had found for him. They were perfect!

He reached for her hand and squeezed it. She turned toward him with a bright smile. "Thank you," he mouthed with no sound. She sat up a little taller and squeezed his hand back in return.

* * *

Jodee woke up, excited, before her alarm went off the next morning. It took her a moment to figure out why. Then she recalled the night before. God loved her!

She got up and ran over to look in the mirror above her dresser. She turned her head from side to side, studying her face from every angle. Then she smiled directly at herself. Standing back a little, she frowned, a little disappointed. She didn't look as special as she felt.

Would anyone else be able to tell she was different today? Brenda had a look about her. Sometimes it seemed like she glowed—so fresh and peaceful.

Then a thought struck: What if her friends could tell there was something different about her? Then what? What should she do? Tell them about Jesus? But how? Brenda could tell anyone about Jesus because she had known Him for such a long time, but Jodee had just met Him. What would she say? And would they turn against her and start teasing her the way she'd always teased Brenda? Thinking about Karen and what had happened the day before, Jodee got a little nervous.

She walked slowly down the hall to take a shower. She was so torn. On one hand, she was happy that she'd received Jesus as her Lord and Savior. But she was kind of scared to face the changes that might happen.

She surveyed her face again in the bathroom mirror, remembering the sad, angry, and lost girl of the day before. Now, even though her circumstances were the same, because she had received Jesus in her heart, she didn't feel that anymore. She couldn't explain it. She only knew that Jesus had changed her inside. She felt peace, happiness, and love like she'd never felt before. She never wanted to be that sad, angry, lost girl again, no matter what.

Awkwardly, she got on her knees next to the bathtub, folded her hands, and closed her eyes. "God" she prayed, "thank You for loving me and saving me. I'm new at this, and I've got to tell You, even though I am so happy to know You and feel so much love, I also feel afraid. I'm not sure what to do. Last night Brenda said that You would lead me and show me how to live…that I wouldn't have to figure it out. I haven't a clue what to do or say, especially if my friends tease me. I do know that I never want to be without You ever again. You've already filled that emptiness in my heart. Thank You. In Jesus' name, amen."

This time when she got up to look at the girl in the mirror, ahhh…. She did look different.

A smile was on her face.

13

When Jodee entered school later in the morning, she looked around for Karen. Jodee had to walk to school and would leave her house early, and Karen was normally already there waiting for her since her bus was the first to arrive at school. But not this morning. Jodee searched at all their normal hang-out spots, but there was no sign of her.

She went outside to wait for Karen. Leaning against the wall, she reached into her coat pocket for a cigarette. *Darn. It's empty. That's just great. What am I going to do all day without a cigarette?* Jodee checked her watch to see if she had time to walk over to the store. Nope. *Maybe I'll go to the store anyway. Karen isn't very generous with her cigarettes, and I don't want to go all day without one.* Today was supposed to be a good day—her first one as a Christian—and now she was going to be grouchy.

After standing there pouting for a moment, she decided to go in. The smell of other people smoking was making her feel worse. Inside she saw Brenda at her locker. She decided to go chat with her to pass the time quicker. "Hi, Brenda."

Brenda turned with her typical friendly smile. "Well, hi, Jodee! How's it going?"

"I'm all right. How about you?" Jodee asked.

Brenda's gaze was compassionate. "Are you sure you're okay? You seem like you might have something on your mind."

Jodee started to shake her head to deny it. Deciding against it, she nodded. "I do. It'll probably seem silly to you, but well, I'm a little nervous about today. You know, with my friends and all, and well…I forgot my cigarettes. When I don't have a cigarette, I get really grouchy."

"Oh," Brenda just said.

Jodee rolled her eyes.

"I didn't mean to make you feel bad," Brenda was quick to assure her. "I didn't know what to say, so I was praying."

"Oh. I prayed this morning about my friends. You know"—Jodee looked down at her shoes, shyly—"Jesus…" She looked up at Brenda, feeling a little embarrassed to share what Jesus had done for her already.

Brenda urged her on. "It's okay, Jodee, I love to hear about Jesus."

"He...well, I always felt sad and empty inside." Jodee peered at Brenda carefully to see how she was responding. Since Brenda smiled expectantly, Jodee continued, "I feel so loved by Him that the emptiness inside... it's gone."

"I'm so happy for you." Brenda patted Jodee's shoulder. "You know, although you prayed already this morning, sometimes it helps when you pray with someone. Would you mind if I prayed with you?"

Jodee shrugged.

"I realize this is all new, and it's okay if you feel awkward. We could also pray about your smoking."

"What?" Jodee asked. "For smoking? God will get me a cigarette?"

Brenda shook her head. "No, I doubt that, but God could help you get through the day without one."

Jodee was unsure of this news.

"So, do you want me to pray for you?" Brenda asked.

"Here? Now? Aren't you worried the others will think you're strange?"

"Um, no." Brenda shook her head. "Yeah, God hears us at school too. But if it bothers you to do it here, we can go someplace private. It doesn't matter."

Jodee stared at Brenda for a minute. "This is weird. Instead of giving me a bunch of rules, you're willing to pray for me, right here in front of everyone. That's amazing. You actually think my problem is worth praying for, no matter what others kids might think." Jodee grabbed Brenda's hand and closed her eyes. "Go for it."

Jodee ended the prayer saying, "Thank You, Jesus," and "Amen" with Brenda. "Thanks, Brenda. I have to admit I hardly heard what you prayed. It touched me so much that you care enough to bring me in prayer to God. Thank you." She checked the time on her watch. "Oops, I better let you go, or we'll both be late for class." Laughing, she turned to leave, only to be met with Karen's expressions of shock and horror. Her friend stared with her mouth open and then stalked off without saying a word.

Brenda's eyes met Jodee's, and they were full of compassion. She closed her locker, putting her arm across Jodee's shoulder, and they walked very slowly together to her class.

* * *

Trudy sat at the table, staring out the kitchen window. She'd finished eating her breakfast and was waiting for her mom to come downstairs to drive her to therapy before going on to school. Her thoughts were on Randy, as usual. Hoping against hope he would change enough, now that he knew Jesus, to at least walk with her through this pregnancy. Her imagination drifted away with her...Randy wanting to be with her forever, the baby being born and looking just like him, right down to his or her smile.

Trudy's stomach jumped in excitement at the thought of the way that Randy smiled at her. It was a smile just for her, no one else. Randy normally had a beautiful smile, and it could charm anyone he used it on. But for her, he got a special look in his eyes. He could make her feel like she was the only person in his world.

Frustrated, she folded her arms on top of the table and laid her head down on them. *What am I going to do? I miss him so much!* She wanted him to call her more than anything! She wanted to see his smile, hold his hand, laugh at his jokes. She just wanted to be with him.

"Oh well," she muttered to herself. She got up and cleared her dishes from the table and put them in the dishwasher. "Mom! Where are you?"

Trudy headed down the hallway from the living room to find her. The door to her parents' bedroom was partially open. She could see her mom's legs hanging over the bed.

"Mom?" She tapped on the door as she pushed it open the rest of the way. "Are you going to drive me to therapy?" Sheryl swiped at her face. "What are you looking at?" Trudy peeked at the book she had on her lap.

"It's an old photo album." Sheryl pressed her lips together in a smile. "It's from before I even met your dad."

"What? I've never seen any pictures of you from when you were young! Can I see them?" Trudy sat next to her, not waiting for an answer, and started turning the pages. "Who are you riding bikes with?"

Sheryl let out a long sigh.

"That's my little..." Sheryl put her hand to her mouth in an effort to control her emotions.

"Mom?" Trudy put her hand on her mom's arm.

"It's my little sister. We were very close. Isn't she pretty?" Sheryl stared at the picture. Love was written all over her face.

"Mom. I'm sorry you haven't been able to see her. Have you tried recently? Maybe your parents have forgiven you and will talk to you. Maybe if I write a letter or call them, they'll come to their senses and then you can see your sister again."

"I've tried so many times. I sent a card last Christmas." Sheryl continued to stare at the picture. "It was returned. All I can do is pray."

"Do they know about the abortion?" Trudy asked quietly.

"The abortion? No way. I was afraid they would stop talking to me if I told them. They're against abortion." Sheryl gave a funny sounding laugh, and Trudy hugged her.

"Can we spend the day together? After my therapy appointment, skip school?"

Sheryl put her arms around Trudy and held her close for a moment. "I think I'd like that. But more than that, I think I'd like to show you something that is very special to me. What do you say?"

"Okay. There isn't any chance you're going to tell me what it is, is there?"

Sheryl stood. "No, and don't try to get me to tell you either." Grinning, she tried to mess Trudy's hair, but Trudy dodged her hand and then pouted. "Nope, that look isn't going to work for me. You ready? Race you!"

"Race? I can't race, Mom!" Trudy called out to her mom as she ran out of the room. "You are a big cheater taking advantage of a helpless child." Trudy could hear Sheryl's laugh float back down the hall as Trudy limped behind her.

* * *

Jodee put her lunch sack down on the table, looking around the cafeteria to see if she could spot Karen. Usually, Karen waited for Jodee outside of her classroom and they walked to lunch together; today she wasn't there. Jodee had gone over to Karen's class, but Karen had already left the room.

Jodee shook her head, unable to believe the way Karen was acting. They had their first three classes together, and Karen hadn't said a word to her. Not one. She sat and listened to the teacher and when it was time to do their assignment she bent her head down and did it, not paying the least bit of attention to Jodee.

If Jodee asked her a question, Karen either shook her head or shrugged. She didn't even stop walking when Jodee dropped her books in the hallway between classes. By the time Jodee had picked them up, Karen was walking around the corner. Jodee's feelings hurt too much to even try to catch up with her.

The more Jodee thought about Karen, the more anger started to build inside her. They were supposed to be friends. Best friends. Karen hadn't even given Jodee a chance to explain. Not that there was much to explain. It was pretty obvious what was going on. Karen had plainly seen that Jodee was praying in the hallway at school.

But Jodee wanted a chance to explain why. She wanted Karen to be happy, to share this with her, and to know Jesus, too.

Jodee stopped chewing on her sandwich. *What am I thinking?* It normally would get on her nerves whenever one of those goody-goodies would preach at her. She'd even led her group of friends in teasing the preachers. Now today she wanted one of her friends to know Jesus?

She scanned to the table where Brenda and her friends were sitting. *I'm one of them now!*

Just then, Karen dropped her lunch tray on the table loud enough to make Jodee jump. She sat across from Jodee, who gave a nervous "hi," but another one of their friends came at that time, and Karen turned her head away to talk with her.

Jodee stared at Karen, unable to take it any longer. "Excuse me!" She leaned toward Karen. "Excuse me, Karen?"

Karen swiveled and gave her a stern look.

"I don't know if you noticed or not, but I'm here today. I've been here all day," Jodee said.

"So." Karen shrugged and turned her attention back to the others who were now joining them.

Jodee couldn't believe it. "Karen," she said firmly.

"What?" Karen asked.

"How long are you going to give me the silent treatment?"

"I don't have anything to say to you," Karen surveyed the cafeteria, and her eyes stopped when she found the table Brenda was sitting at. "I'll bet they have plenty to say to you. Better yet, maybe they could pray with you about me. You know, that I might suddenly have something I'd want to say to you." Karen's words dripped with sarcasm.

The other kids at the table gave nervous giggles, unsure of what was going on between the two of them, let alone whose side to take.

Usually Jodee would take the bait and come back with a much better snotty remark than the one delivered to her. She was great at cutting people down. There wasn't a kid at school who could talk her down, except Karen, She was just as good as Jodee was. But this time it was more important to Jodee for Karen to listen to her. *Really* listen to her.

"Karen, if you would let me explain what has happened…I mean, Karen, it's really great! Last night I found out that you and I have been wrong about them. All wrong."

Karen glared at her. "What exactly are you saying, Jodee?"

Excited, yet nervous, Jodee took this as a good sign to continue. "Last night I went with Trudy and Brenda to their youth group. It's a long story on how I ended up going with them, but anyway, that doesn't really matter.

What matters is that last night I received Jesus into my heart! I prayed and..." Jodee stopped talking as she watched the other kids eye each other.

Karen started laughing. Loud. It sounded strange, forced. "That's a good one, Jodee!" Karen pounded her hand on the table. "Wasn't that a good one, you guys!" She continued to laugh. The other kids started to chuckle but appeared unsure of what was so funny. "You sounded just like them, Jodee. You've got them down good."

Jodee couldn't figure out what was going on. Karen acted like she was taking deep breaths to stop laughing, "Oh, Jodee. You shouldn't make me laugh so hard right after I eat."

"But I wasn't..." Jodee tried to say, confused.

"I know you probably weren't finished. But if I laugh anymore, I'll probably get sick. Please, no more." Karen held up her hand. "Jodee's always got to be the funny one. She really topped what I said, didn't she?"

The others nodded. One by one they finished their lunches and got up to leave. The entire time Karen kept up the act. Jodee felt embarrassed. Finally, it was just Jodee and Karen at the table.

"Karen, what was that all about? I wasn't kidding around. I was trying to talk to you."

Karen's voice was low and firm. "Listen. You're my best friend. I wasn't about to let you humiliate yourself like that in front of everyone. It's obvious you're going through something right now."

"But...," Jodee tried to interrupt.

Karen held up her hand, "I was wrong to ignore you. I'll admit it. But, hey, whatever you're going through, remember that you've got a reputation to protect. You can't go around talking about Jesus. I mean, Jodee!" She stuck her face right up to Jodee's and cocked her head toward Brenda's table. "Those guys are freaks, remember! They're all a bunch of pains in the you-know-what. You're not going to turn into one of those. Not if I can help it."

Jodee shook her head, feeling sad. "Karen, we were wrong. Please, if you would just..."

Karen stood. "I don't want to hear any more about it! If you're my friend, you'll forget all about this nonsense and never bring it up again." With that she stormed off.

Jodee watched her walk away, then followed suit, throwing her lunch bag with more force than necessary into the garbage can.

"Hey, Jodee!" Brenda called to her.

Jodee stopped.

Brenda smiled gently. "Hard day, huh?" she said with sympathy.

Tears threatened, so Jodee simply shrugged, dermined not to cry.

"I'm sorry," Brenda continued.

Jodee knew of only one way to keep the tears from falling, and she used it. She put on her tough-girl act. Giving a huff, her glance grazed over Brenda like she wasn't worth anything. "And I suppose you were kind enough to pray for me too. Like that did a lot of good." With those words she hurried away.

* * *

Brenda watched Jodee depart with a shake of her head. Deep in her heart she knew Jodee was hurting and didn't know any other way but to lash out. She prayed that the Lord would show her how to help Jodee through this and that He would be with her.

* * *

Wind blowing through the open car window whipped Trudy's hair across her face. "Do you have a hair tie?" Trudy asked her mom.

"Check the glove box," Sheryl answered.

"Ah! Here we go." Trudy held the band up victoriously, pulling back her hair to make a ponytail. "Hey, this is the turn to Gran's."

"Yep," Sheryl said simply.

"Hmm, are we going to hang with her? Or is she coming with us?"

"Well, we're going to her place. Just wait, okay?"

"Yeah, I guess," Trudy mumbled.

Soon they turned on to the familiar gravel road that led to the farm. Trudy sang softly to the song on the radio until Sheryl parked the car at the beginning of Grandma Kay's long driveway.

"Why are you parking down here?"

"Come with me." Sheryl was quick to get out of the car and wait for Trudy. They walked over to the old swing. It swayed in the gentle breeze.

"You probably don't remember when Grandpa put this swing up, do you?" Sheryl asked, sitting down on the swing.

"I only know it's been here forever, and he put it up for me."

"After you were born, I took a class to heal from having an abortion. The lessons went pretty deep and opened a lot of wounds that were in my heart before the healing process. I spent quite a bit of time sitting right here under this old oak tree praying, thinking, and journaling."

Trudy crouched and sat cross-legged on the grass. Settling back against the tree, she stayed quiet while her mom spoke. She could sense she was being allowed into a very private place.

"Each time when I'd be sitting out here for a while, I would notice good old Elwood stroll over to his bench there." Sheryl pointed with a smile. "Part of the requirements for the study was to ask someone to be a prayer support and then each week touch base with that person. Grandpa Elwood was my prayer person. I don't know why I didn't ask Kay. I just knew he was supposed to be the one who supported me."

"It was very comforting when he appeared. Eventually, when I was ready, I'd give him a wave and he'd come join me. Depending on how I felt, I'd either talk his ear off or we'd sit in silence, listening to the brook. It didn't matter. Merely having him take the time to sit with me was enough for me. Before I left he'd say a prayer."

"Well, one week the assignment was to do something in memory of our child." Sheryl stopped talking. She stared off at the water going by.

Trudy could tell she was fighting with her emotions.

"I really struggled with it. I mean, did I want to have something tangible to remind me of what I'd done to my baby?" Sheryl sniffed.

Trudy blinked fast and hard to fight the emotions that were beginning to overwhelm her.

"The request made me angry. I wanted the whole thing to be behind me. I didn't want to deal with it every day of my life. I almost took my life because of such a stupid decision."

"Mom...you don't have to..."

"I do have to, Trudy. I do," Sheryl sat for a moment lost in her thoughts. "I explained the situation to Elwood. I sure miss his wisdom." She laughed.

"I do too, Mom." Trudy joined her giggles.

"He asked me if I truthfully could forget what I did. I had to be honest and say no. He reminded me of a trip he'd taken back East, and how he was so impressed with the grave of the Unknown Soldier. Such honor was given to someone who had died in a war, yet nobody knew who he was." Sheryl glanced at Trudy. "He suggested that instead of the memorial being a reminder of my choice, how about giving honor to her memory?"

"So did you do something?" Trudy asked.

"Yes. This spot is where I learned to receive forgiveness for my decision. This is where Grandpa Elwood truly showed me through his actions how loving and compassionate our heavenly Father is." Sheryl stood and turned the swing over. "He suggested we make a swing for you. Not only would it be a reminder to us of God's redemption when we watched you enjoy it, but it would allow Elisa to bring joy into your life."

Stunned, Trudy walked to the swing and read the words out loud: *"In memory of Elisa. Though not given the chance to experience the joy of life, she is given the chance to give joy in life to her surviving sister, Trudy."* Trudy stepped back.

Sheryl looked her direct in the eye. "I had to deal with something else in that class. What I almost did to you. Whenever you were on this swing, my heart bowed before the throne of God in praise and thanksgiving, that He was so faithful to protect you. I was so grateful you were alive." Sheryl pulled Trudy to her, and Trudy melted into her arms. "Honey, I love you with my whole being. Please forgive me."

"Mom, I forgive you. I do!" Trudy clung to her mom. "How could I not? Do you forgive me, for getting pregnant and for almost having an abortion myself?"

Sheryl stepped back and cupped Trudy's face in her hands. "I forgive you, and I will love your baby. I'm here for you and will not walk away from you. I'm sorry that you thought I would, but I won't. I don't know why or how my parents could disown me for such a long time, but that's their decision." She drew Trudy close to her again. "I could never let you go, never. You're my precious baby."

"I love you, Mom." Trudy's voice was muffled in her shirt. "I love you."

14

The woman unlocked the back door with silent ease. After years of doing this, she knew nobody could see her, yet she glanced over her shoulder anyway. Opening the door, her steps were quiet within the house. It didn't appear that anyone was home, but she'd come later than usual. She proceeded with caution. Placing the grocery bags in the kitchen, she moved stealthily down the hallway, trying to avoid the first bedroom.

Then she found she couldn't resist. The cat was lying on the bed. "Oh, I'm so glad she has you to love her," she cooed, picking it up and nuzzling her face into its fur. "Take good care of her, please."

Turning to the closet she opened the doors, reaching for a shirt. Her heart sank at how worn the clothes were getting. Nevertheless, she held the fabric up to her nose, inhaling deeply. "My baby, I miss you so. It's not fair I can't be with you."

A noise from the front room startled her back to reality. The front door opened and closed with a sound of keys dropping on the floor.

"Ow. Can't anything go right today? Ouch, that hurt my head," Jodee shouted from the living room.

"Oh, my goodness," the lady whispered. She put down the cat and searched for a place to hide. In all the years she'd never been caught here. She hurried to the back room, edging behind the door. A glance filled her with disgust. The place was a mess. Cigarette butts overflowed in the ashtray, an empty bottle of alcohol rested on the dresser, and papers were strewn on the floor.

She shook her head in wonder. How had he convinced the courts he was the fit parent? And what a dirty lawyer he must have had. A night so very long ago burned clearly in her mind like it was yesterday. He pushed her out the door and threatened her life if she were ever to come back. No matter how much she'd begged, he wouldn't let her have her baby. Instead, his laugh was so evil that her skin still crawled at the memory. Despite being soaked and shaking from the cold of the heavy rain pouring down, she'd stood for hours outside of Jodee's window, wishing for a way to get her daughter and hoping beyond hope it was only one of his cruel jokes. Surely when he sobered up, he'd let her in.

But when he found her in the morning, curled in a ball inside his car, he'd dragged her out by her arm. Through tight, cursing lips, he'd demanded she get off his property or he'd finish her off himself. Somehow the courts believed him when he said she'd abandoned them. He had full custody of the child he never wanted, and all visitation rights were denied to her. *I love her with my whole being and miss her dreadfully. Just to touch her precious face, look into her eyes, hold her one more time.* But somehow, someway, he'd even been able to get a restraining order on her.

Yet he never complained when she brought him money and groceries. She knew how it was to live with this man. Someday she'd find a way to be with her daughter again. Her only worry was whether Jodee would want to be with her.

Now she could hear Jodee moving through the kitchen to her room. Her heart lurched when she recognized Jodee was crying. "What's wrong, baby?" she whispered to herself. She longed to comfort her. If only she could put her fear of him aside and go to her daughter. Ask her to run away with her. For a second she started to step out from behind the door, but then the memory of his cruelty stopped her in his tracks. She stayed behind the door, listening to her daughter's cries.

Soon there was silence. Jodee's mom went over to the dresser and left her usual envelope, then tiptoed back down the hallway. At Jodee's door she stopped and dared to step in. She reached down and touched a tear that still lingered on her now sleeping girl's face. A strong boldness filled her being. Leaning over she tenderly kissed Jodee's brow, breathing in her scent.

"I love you, baby," she whispered.

Then she stole back out of the house, away from the most precious thing she'd had in her life. "Someday, sweetie, someday Mommy will be back to stay."

* * *

"Hey, how was your day?" Lorinda met Brenda as she came in the door. "I have some good news for you."

"For me? What?" Brenda asked.

"Well, your brother Jonathon called today. Instead of staying at college and working through the summer up there, he's decided to come home and see what he can do here during the break."

"Really? That's great." Brenda smiled.

Her mom lifted an eyebrow. "Hmm. I thought you'd be a bit more excited than that to see your brother."

"I am excited. I just have a lot on my mind. I can't wait to see him."

"Care to share?"

"I guess." Brenda shrugged. "Trudy wasn't in school today. I got a text that she was spending the day with her mom. And then I watched poor Jodee have a hard time with her friends. I didn't know what to do to help her."

"Oh, that's too bad."

"I had kind of a weird idea, but I'm broke, so it's not going to work out very well." Brenda gave her a sideways look.

"Do I need to hide my purse?" Lorinda teased.

"Depends. You might like being a part of my idea."

"Shoot."

"Well, I want to buy Jodee a Bible and cover. Also, I want to invite her over for dinner."

"Tonight?"

"Yeah. Can you give me some money?"

"I'll do better than that. I'll go with you." Lorinda stood and gestured in the direction of the door.

"You will?" Brenda followed, beaming.

"I think you've come up with a wonderful idea," Lorinda said in a funny accent.

Brenda laughed. "Give it up, Mom, give it up."

* * *

In a sleepy fog, Jodee tried to turn her alarm off but couldn't find the right button. She sat up, exasperated. Grabbing her alarm clock, she realized it was the phone, not her alarm. She jumped off her bed and ran to get it before the person hung up, just in case it was her dad. He checked in on her sometimes. If she wasn't there when he called, she heard about it later.

"Hello!" she breathlessly called into the phone.

"Jodee?" a girl's voice asked.

Jodee leaned against the kitchen wall and slid down it until she was sitting on the floor. All that trouble for nothing.

"Jodee? Are you there?" she heard again.

"Yeah, who's this?" Jodee asked unenthusiastically.

"It's Brenda. Were you busy?"

"I was sleeping," Jodee said plainly.

"Oh, I'm sorry!"

153

"Yeah, well, what do you want?"

"I'm with my mom, and we wanted to stop by for a second."

"You're with your mom?" Jodee shook her head to clear the sleep. "What do you want to stop by here for?"

"A surprise."

"I guess. See you when you get here." Jodee disconnected. "I wonder what it's like to spend the afternoon with your mom? That would be nice." She noticed some bags on the floor. "Where did these come from? Dad doesn't grocery shop." She peered inside the bags and, sure enough, there was more food than she'd seen in a long time. "Wow! What's up with Dad? He makes me do the shopping."

She started putting the things away, surprised to find some of her favorite things to eat. From the side of her eye she saw her cat moving down the hall to her dad's room. "Oh, no, you don't, little fella." He sprinted away from her. Jodee went after him, grabbing him right as he was about to jump on her dad's clothes. Her dad might be messy, but he didn't tolerate cat hair on his stuff. She noticed a fresh white envelope on the dresser. Not knowing what possessed her, she picked it up to see what was in it. She was shocked. The envelope was full of money with a note in it. Jodee's heart pounded, and she nervously looked behind her. When she pulled the note out a little to see who it was from, she was filled with wonder:

> Please be sure to use the extra money to buy some clothes for Jodee. She needs some new things....

Curious, now Jodee took out the entire note. Any fear of being caught by her dad wasn't even a thought now. Who would give her dad money for her to have new clothes? Jodee's heart seemed to stop beating as she read the signature: *Annette*. Her mom? This was a note from her mom? How long had this envelope been here? Why had her dad kept the money so long? As she read the note, she realized it had to be recently.

> Please be sure to use the extra money to buy some clothes for Jodee. She needs some new things. She may want to get a job for the summer and she needs to look nice. Please take good care of her and tell her I love her. Annette.

Annette. Her mom. Her mom loved her. Jodee could hardly breathe. She read the note again and again and again, wanting to absorb the words her mom had written about her. Her mom loved her! Jodee closed her eyes, holding the note close to her chest as though it would bring her mom closer to her. Over and over she heard the words in her head: *Tell her I love her....*

"What are you doing in here?"

Jodee spun, feeling like a trapped animal. "I...I." There was no way around him as he lunged toward her. Somehow she jumped out of his way. He missed her and hit the dresser.

"You little...what is that you're looking at?" He ripped the envelope out of her hand as she hid the note behind her back, trying to stuff it into her back pocket. "Money. You were trying to steal money from me, huh? Why, you no-good, little brat." His hand lifted as though to hit her. She scrambled over the bed and out the door. She knew he'd been drinking since he was slow to follow her and a bit clumsy. "Get back here."

The sound of the doorbell echoed in the hall.

"Dad! Someone's at the door." She ran for the front door, hoping to stop his actions.

"You open that door, and I'll kick your behind right out of it." The doorbell continued to ring. She made it to the door and heard him stumble behind her, cursing. It was Brenda and her mom. She'd forgotten all about them. She almost pushed them over as she jumped onto the porch.

"You dirty rotten...," she could hear as she closed the door behind her.

"Jodee?" Lorinda asked.

"Quick! I have to go. He's..." She eyed Brenda with desperation. "Please."

"Mom, let's go." Brenda pulled at her mom. Jodee followed close behind them, hopping in the offered open car door.

Lorinda backed out of the driveway just as Jodee's dad opened the door. Jodee could only imagine the things he was saying as they drove away.

* * *

Randy was glad to finally reach the motel they were staying at for the night. The car ride had been very uncomfortable. Hardly a word was spoken all day. Much to Katey's delight, his dad ordered pizza to be delivered to the room, and he let Randy have his phone. "Just don't use all of *my* minutes, okay? Try to make it short." Then his mom and dad put on their jackets and went for a walk.

Katey stared at Randy. "Boy, this sure is a drag."

Randy's first impulse was to tell her to keep her mouth shut—that he wanted to call Trudy—but instead he decided to talk with her. "You can say

155

that again. You know Mom has never really gotten mad at me before. It's an awful feeling," Randy confessed.

Katey threw herself on her stomach on the bed, resting her head in her hands. "I don't think she's really mad at you. I think she's scared, and I think she hurts."

Startled, Randy said, "How would you know something like that? I mean, you're just a little kid. How did you figure that out?"

"I'm not a little kid!" Katey said defensively.

"Okay, you're not a little kid. But you are young."

Katey rolled her eyes. "You'll never ever get it. It's not how old you are. It's who you are and how you act. I'm old for my age," she said as maturely as possible.

Randy stifled a laugh. He didn't want to fight with her. She'd been on his side all day, and he'd discovered he liked it. "You're right. You are a little more mature than other kids your age."

Katey smiled triumphantly. "You really think so?"

"Yeah, I guess. Anyway, you better be older acting, since you're going to be an aunt." His stomach jumped queerly as he said that.

"Are you going to marry Trudy?!" Katey asked excitedly.

"Hmmm." Randy was surprised at the question. "I don't know what's going to happen. But I know I'm going to start with saying I'm sorry." He shrugged. "If she'll talk to me."

Katey lay back on the bed, a big smile on her face.

"I have to be responsible about this and do the right thing. After all, I'm going to have a little kid!" Randy thought out loud.

"It's God," Katey answered quietly.

"What?" Randy asked, still deep in his thoughts.

"It's God. Ever since you've been reading the Bible and praying, you've changed. I think God is talking to your heart. I think He's telling you what you're supposed to do."

How did she get so smart? Randy wondered. He knew she was right. He nodded, staring at her, seeing for the first time that yeah, she was still young, but she wasn't a baby anymore.

"You're one smart"—he started to say "kid" but changed it to "girl."

Katey beamed.

Just then the door to the motel room opened. Their mom and dad entered. Their mom did not look happy. Taking her coat off, she grabbed her makeup bag and said she was going to take a shower.

* * *

Cassie closed the bathroom door tight, then slumped against it and closed her eyes. Her head hurt from all the tension she felt inside. Her whole world was falling apart. It was changing too fast. She wanted her old world back again.

Not only had her son gotten a girl pregnant, but her husband had turned into some sort of religious freak. The whole time on their walk he had talked on and on about how God had helped him to look at this situation in a different way than he normally would have. Not that he condoned what Randy had done. He was just as upset as she was. But he knew Randy knew how wrong it was, and it was more important for them to be strong for both kids and the baby. He told her how God had revealed Randy's fear to him and how he had to help his son.

She shook her head as she thought of how he sure picked a convenient time to be the so-called "good" parent. Right when she needed him to be strong, he was wimping out. Turning the shower on, she sank down by the side of the tub. She felt tired. She wasn't up for all that was happening. What was she going to do?

She'd gone to church as a kid. So what? She went to all the Sunday school stuff, and whatever else you were supposed to do at the church she went to, after all her parents made her. Her parents made her do other things to look good too.

Resentment rose in Cassie at the memory of how important it was for her parents to look good to their fellow church friends. It had cost Cassie a lot. After Cassie got married and had kids, she got too busy to go to church, especially since her husband didn't want to go with her. Her parents couldn't argue with that, although they pushed their opinion on her whenever she talked to them.

She didn't understand what the big deal was. Why would her husband get such a kick out of reading the Bible? It was written ages ago. He talked like it was a newly written bestseller. But he claimed it had changed him.

She rolled her eyes as she gathered her hair up in a ponytail holder so it wouldn't get wet in the shower. Her son was going to be a dad. Her husband and son had turned into religious people. She knew it was merely for convenience sake. It had to be. This way Randy wouldn't get into as much trouble with her and her husband, since he looked like a goody-goody who regretted what he'd done, and her husband didn't have to take a stand. He could be the good guy. She hated thinking this way about the two of them since she loved them so much, but she knew she was right.

Well, she wasn't going to trouble herself with it any longer. This religious stuff would pass and, if she had anything to say about it, it would pass quickly. With renewed determination, she got in the shower and snapped the shower curtain shut. No way was she going to allow religious stuff to control her house. No way.

* * *

Silence rang in the car on the drive to Brenda's house. Lorinda was deep in troubled thought when she got out of the car. She had driven on auto-pilot all the way home and hadn't even considered asking Jodee if she'd mind going to their house. When they entered the house, each of them seemed to just drop into the overstuffed chairs in the living-room.

"Thank you, Mrs. Sanders. I'm sorry I put you in a position to have to rescue me." Jodee's eyes were filled with pain.

"Oh, honey, you're welcome. I didn't quite get what was going on at first, but I'm more than happy that I rescued you. Do you mind sharing what was happening?" Lorinda asked with a gentle tone.

Jodee hung her head in shame.

"You don't have to, Jodee, if you don't want to. You don't know me very well so I can understand. Even so, I'm here if you need anything." Lorinda started to get up out of her chair to leave the girls to themselves.

"No!" Jodee reached out a hand. "Don't go. I've never had anyone who'd help me before. It's been my secret." Jodee nodded toward Brenda. "She's the only one who knows I've had any kind of trouble. Not even my best friend knows."

Lorinda sat slowly, keeping eye contact with Jodee. "What about your mom?"

Jodee slumped against the chair. "She's gone. Left when I was a little girl."

"Oh, sweetie, I'm sorry." Lorinda's voice rang with compassion.

Tears stung at Jodee's eyes. She reached in her back pocket and pulled out the note from her mom. "I found this on my dad's dresser this afternoon. I know I'm not supposed to mess with his stuff. I don't know what came over me. But when I saw an envelope, I looked inside and it was filled with money and this note from my mom." She handed it over to Lorinda.

Brenda stood to read it over her mom's shoulder. "Oh my word! I wonder when she left it?"

"I'm not sure. I think it was recently, because there was a bunch of money and, well, money goes fast at my house. My dad thought I was trying to steal from him, and that's why he was so angry. He gets angry easily when he's been drinking. Usually I leave until he goes to sleep. I know better than to do something to upset him like that."

Lorinda tightened her lips, listening to the two girls' conversation.

"So why did your mom leave? She says to tell you she loves you, and obviously she wants to care for you," Brenda asked, bewildered.

Wonder came over Jodee's face. "Hey, there was a bunch of bags of groceries in the kitchen this afternoon. I thought it was strange for my dad to buy them. Usually he gives me money to get groceries. Maybe my mom brings me food, too."

"Wow! I wonder why she'd do it secretly?"

Jodee's expression clearly revealed she knew why. "My dad can get pretty mean. Maybe he's mean to her."

"When did your mom leave?" Brenda asked.

Jodee sat for a moment and thought about it. "It was shortly after the baby. She was in the hospital. They had an abortion," Jodee whispered, teary-eyed. "One morning I went to the kitchen to eat breakfast, and she wasn't home. My dad was sleeping. It was kind of weird. I thought she was on an errand. At the end of the day I put myself to bed. I went to sleep believing she'd be back in the morning."

Brenda slumped next to her mom. Lorinda knew it had to be freeing for Jodee to tell someone her story.

"Every day I waited for her to come back. At the end of the day, when she didn't come home, I would tell myself, *She'll be home or come and get me tomorrow.* So I'd go to bed with hopes of seeing her the next day. Then one day, quite awhile after she'd left, I woke up, went into the kitchen to eat breakfast, and there wasn't any food. And that's when I knew. I knew she'd never be back. I sat at the kitchen table with an empty plate. If she was coming back, she would've been sure to be back so I didn't go hungry."

Streams of tears now flowed down Brenda and Lorinda's faces, too. Lorinda stood and approached Jodee cautiously. "I'm so sorry that you went through all that alone." She sat next to her, enfolding her in her arms.

Jodee's body was stiff at first but eventually relaxed as Lorinda held her close, making gentle rocking motions. *So it's been a long time since she's been held by anyone,* Lorinda guessed. "You're not alone anymore, honey. You're not alone."

Jodee snuggled into Lorinda's comforting embrace and let go of the tears she'd held since she was that little girl waiting for her mommy to return.

* * *

"Honey, your dad will be here in about half an hour." Sheryl clicked her cell phone shut. "Let's go see if Kay needs any help in the kitchen. It's pretty funny to set up dinner plans with her from the phone while standing in her own yard." Sheryl laughed.

"Yeah, I guess." Sheryl and Trudy walked arm-in-arm through the garden to the back kitchen door. "Mom, could I try?"

"Try what?"

"Could I try to contact your parents?"

Sheryl stopped in her tracks. "Honey, you mentioned this the other night, and, well, I'm not going to stop you, but I don't want you to get your hopes up. And I don't want you to get hurt. I've tried, Dad's tried, even Grandma Kay has tried, and they don't respond."

"Grandma Kay even tried? Well, I haven't, and I want to." Trudy was adamant. "They have to regret all the time they've spent away from you,"

"They don't show it, honey. But if it's that important to you, go ahead." Sheryl opened the door. "But don't get your hopes up too high."

"I already have, Mom."

Sheryl sighed, reaching over to mess Trudy's hair.

Trudy ducked and then made primping motions over it. "Don't touch the hair."

Sheryl just shook her head.

Soon after, Bill arrived, and the four of them had dinner together. It felt like old times, before Trudy had her secrets. She loved it and realized she didn't want to miss out on moments like this ever again. *My grandparents need to be a part of this, too. They're missing a lot not being with my mom.* Trudy watched her mom interacting with her dad and Grandma Kay. *She's so special. They'd be proud of her. Especially if they could see what a wonderful mom she turned out to be.* Trudy gave her mom a smile filled with love. Sheryl stopped and gave her an inquiring look, then blew a kiss across the table at her.

* * *

Lorinda and Jodee sat quietly in the chair together. Jodee was so quiet that Lorinda began to wonder if she'd drifted off to sleep. Brenda had left the room when Jodee broke down. She now came back in carrying iced drinks and a plate of chocolate-chip cookies.

"'Nothing better than sugar and chocolate when you're down' is what my mom always says," Brenda said as she entered the room.

"Yeah, I do say that. Probably not the best lesson I taught you, but…" She grabbed a cookie and took a bite. "A necessary one. Do you want one, Jodee? Here's some ice water." She handed Jodee a glass, along with the offered cookie.

"Sure." Jodee wiped at her red, swollen eyes. "I don't think I've cried that hard in my entire life. Sorry about that."

"You needed to cry, sweetie. Don't go apologizing. You probably have some more tears stored up inside you that need to come out," Lorinda said gently, taking another bite of cookie. "I can't imagine how hard it's been for you to carry that burden by yourself for so long."

"The thing I don't understand is how she could leave me alone with my dad. I mean, strange as it may seem, I love my dad, but I've also always been scared of him. The fact is, he has a problem, and my mom knew he had a problem, yet she left me all alone with him. I don't get it," Jodee admitted.

"Me either. But obviously there was some reason she had to leave and that it had to be without you," Brenda said.

"I've always wanted to believe that, but then I think: *So why doesn't she call?* Or, w*hy doesn't she try to see me?* Like she could show up at school or call while my dad is at work," Jodee said. "Now there's this note. She left money and says she loves me."

Brenda gave a sympathetic nod. Lorinda caressed Jodee's back.

"It would be the greatest thing if I could be with her again. And my dad wouldn't drink anymore or do all the other stuff he does. Do you think that could happen?" Jodee asked.

"It could happen," Brenda answered.

"Do you think my parents could be forgiven, like me?" Jodee asked wistfully.

"Of course, honey. Jesus died for everyone. They have to choose to believe in Him, though. It has to be their decision," Lorinda said gently. "We can pray for them and hopefully we'll get to watch Jesus work in their lives, like we've watched Him work in yours."

"Mine?"

Brenda nodded emphatically. "Yes, I prayed for you and look what I got to see Him do? You now believe in Him and you're sitting in *my* living room talking with me and my mom. I mean, come on, is that not amazing?" Brenda said with a flair of drama.

"I guess you're right about that. I never would have imagined sitting in little Miss Do-gooder's house, let alone talking about personal stuff *and* caring about my parents being forgiven for everything. Okay, I guess I better start praying." Jodee dodged the pillow that Brenda threw her way.

"Before we forget, we have something for you." Brenda got up and retrieved a colorful bag with bows attached to it.

"That's for me? What is it?" Jodee reached for the bag and started opening it.

"It's the reason we were coming by your house this afternoon. We had a little surprise for you." Lorinda moved over to the ottoman to give Jodee more room in the chair. Jodee pulled out a small spiral notebook with a picture of a young girl sitting by a rock praying on it and a matching pen. Next she pulled out a Bible.

"You bought this for me? How can I ever thank you?" Jodee asked.

"The notebook is to write prayers, thoughts, or Bible verses down on." Brenda got up and sat next to her. "Here, read the insert."

"*To Jodee, may you walk in how deep, wide, long, and high God's love is for you. Brenda and Lorinda.*" Jodee held the book close to her chest. "Thank you."

"Jodee, there's one more thing. Would you be comfortable staying over tonight? I'd feel better knowing you're safe," Lorinda asked.

"Wow. I...yes. That would be so fabulous." Jodee's smile was bright.

"Good. Then I'm going to start dinner, and you girls can set the table." Lorinda got up to go to the kitchen. "Maybe I'll call Steve to bring a movie home and we'll have popcorn with it later. Sound good, girls?"

"Yeah," Brenda answered.

"Sounds fantastic!" Jodee's face was filled with excitement. Then quietly she whispered, "I think Jesus is doing this for me. Thank You, Jesus, thank You."

15

The night air was crisp. Randy stood outside the motel room door with his hands shoved deep into his jacket pocket. The phone continued to ring over and over in his dad's Bluetooth. Excitement mixed with an urge to hang up the phone and run coursed through his body. "Answer, Trudy, answer," he mumbled.

"Hello?" Trudy answered.

"Tru!" Now that he had her on the phone, he didn't know where to start. "Are you doing okay? Tony told me you were in an accident."

"Randy!" Trudy held back a scream of delight. "I'm fine. Sore, but I'll be okay. Brenda and I are getting Physical Therapy, and we both feel better afterward."

"Do you know what happened to the guy in the other car?"

"Last I heard he was still in the hospital. He's older, and hasn't woken up since the accident."

"Oh, that's a bummer."

"Randy, where are you?" Trudy changed the subject.

"I'm on my way back home from my Aunt Cissy's place. I forgot all about going with my family to her place after everything that went down…the pregnancy…"

"Oh. When you didn't call, I figured you were done with you and me," Trudy said softly.

"Oh, Trudy, I was…listen, I just have a few minutes and a lot to say, but first, let me say, I'm sorry."

"What?"

"Trudy, I'm sorry I made you go to that abortion clinic and that I took off on you. I was stupid, and I'm sorry. Can you forgive me?"

Silence.

"Tru? You there?"

"Yeah, but why didn't you call?" Her voice was quiet.

"My minutes ran out on my phone as usual. The first couple days, I was going over so many things in my head, I didn't try to call you. I did call once and didn't reach you. I didn't know what kind of message to leave."

"Did you tell your mom and dad?"

"Yes, and I can't believe it—my dad and I have been reading the Bible together and, oh yeah, I spent Saturday night with Tony and he led me in a prayer, asking God to forgive me of my sins and then told me to start reading the Bible. Every day, Trudy, things are different for me. And my dad and little sister joined me in learning about God."

"Your dad? Wow, that's incredible! What about your mom?" Trudy's voice was returning to normal.

"My mom's mad."

"Oh."

"Hey, she's mad at me, or rather disappointed in me, not you. I mean, can you blame her?"

"No."

"Trudy, I have to get going, I promised my dad I wouldn't use up all of his minutes, but I have a question for you."

"What's that?"

"I don't know how you're feeling about us, but when I get back into town, can we talk? Try to figure us out…I mean, if there is an 'us' anymore, that is."

"I'd like that," Trudy murmured.

Randy let out a sigh of relief. "Good. I'll call you tomorrow, okay?"

"Okay!"

He could hear joy in her voice. His heart felt lighter as he pushed the button to hang up. "I still love you, Tru!" he said to the night air.

* * *

Trudy's hands were shaking with excitement as she punched one to dial Brenda. "Come on, Brenda, answer, answer!" she squealed as quietly as possible, not wanting to wake up her parents and grandma.

"Hello."

"Brenda, he called! Randy called! He wants to get together and talk about us, I mean, him and me." Trudy's words tumbled over themselves.

"Really? That is so, oh, I'm so happy for you! When are you getting together?"

"I don't know. He's still out of town and won't be back until tomorrow. I can't believe it! He must still love me."

"Of course he does. I'm so happy for you, but I have to go. Jodee is here for the night."

"Jodee? She's spending the night?" Trudy interrupted.

"Yeah, it's a long story. I'll have to tell you tomorrow."

"Okay, okay. I'll talk to you tomorrow. I might be late for school—I'm not sure. We're at my grandma's for the night. Oh, Brenda, I'm so happy."

"I'm happy for you, too, Trudy, I really am."

Trudy tossed her phone down and dived onto the bed, doing a few carefree jumps of joy before landing in the fluff of pillows. A "thank You" escaped from her smiling lips.

* * *

The sun was beginning to rise, and the birds were starting to sing. It looked like the start of a beautiful day. But the beauty went unnoticed by Karen as she climbed the trellis on the side of her house to sneak back into her bedroom.

She cursed when her foot slipped from the slickness of the morning dew. Careful not to make too much noise, she opened her bedroom window. *I wish the stupid birds would quit chirping. They'll wake my mom up.* Although Karen did wonder why she bothered worrying about this, since her mom never woke up when Karen cried out during the night, after her stepdad or stepbrothers came home.

Karen recently had found a safe place to hide during the night hours when they were on the prowl. So far nothing had been said to her mom about Karen not being in her room at night.

She snuck through the window and grabbed some clothes to change into for school. She'd learned to get her shower done before the so-called men of the house woke.

Karen didn't get it. Her mom had changed so much from the patrol guard in the house she used to be. There was a time that even if her mom wasn't home at the time it happened, she would know who left the milk out on the counter, or what time Karen went to sleep and got up in the morning. She would spaz out about stupid things, like a towel on the floor, or Karen's unmade bed. But she couldn't figure out what had been going on under her own roof for years.

Karen resented her mom for allowing these disgusting men into their home; for not protecting her from them. She felt abandoned and couldn't wait for the day she never had to see her mom's face again.

She had tried desperately to tell her mom when everything first started, but her mom had betrayed her. *Why would she think I'd make up a horrible story about them because I was jealous? What was there to be jealous about?*

They were gross pigs. And then to tell me I was ungrateful for all Mr. Stepdad did for me, and to realize how good I had it now…oh, the nerve of that woman. Karen's heart had hardened against her mom that day.

After getting ready for school, she went in search of her mom's purse to take money for cigarettes and lunch. Next, she made a speedy exit out the door. *I made it safely out the door again.* It was the one thing that put a smile on Karen's face.

* * *

"Hey kiddo, if you hurry, I'll give you a ride. I have to meet Steve for coffee this morning," Bill called to Trudy through her bedroom door.

"I'm ready." The door swung open. Trudy's face beamed.

"Well, good morning! I like the happy look on your face!" Bill smiled. Trudy hummed and made little skip movements down the hall to the stairway. "Okay, what is going on, young lady?"

"Randy called me last night and apologized. Dad, he wants to talk—about us, me and him."

"Oh."

"OH? That's all you can say? Dad, this is huge for me! Maybe Randy and I can stay together." She touched her stomach. "Wouldn't that be great?" Bill nodded but didn't look convinced. "I thought you'd be glad about this bit of news." Trudy pivoted to face him when she reached the bottom of the stairs.

"Don't get me wrong. I'm glad for you. I just know there's quite a bit to work out. I've been there, remember?" He caressed her cheek. "Maybe I'm only feeling protective, and I want to be sure you know what you want out of your relationship with Randy."

Trudy leaned in for a hug, then rested her head on his chest. "Dad, I love you. After Randy and I talk, I promise I will talk it over with you. No more secrets, okay? I'll even listen to your advice; well, I'll *try* to listen."

"Promise me, even if you don't think I'll agree with you, you'll still talk to me. Let us be there for you. Please don't hide from us ever again. Got it, Tru?" He kissed her on the forehead.

She stepped back, stood at attention, and saluted him. "Yes, sir."

"Ha, ha, very funny. Now come on—I'm going to be late." Bill put his arm around her shoulder as they called good-bye to Kay and Sheryl.

Trudy wrapped both her arms around his waist as they walked out the door.

* * *

Jodee sat at her desk, lost in thought. It had been so much fun at Brenda's house the night before, and Lorinda was one of the nicest ladies she'd ever met. Brenda's dad, too, was incredible. When he got home, the whole house seemed to be so animated. He actually gave Brenda a big hug and talked to her about her day. Not only that, but he included Jodee.

Lorinda encouraged Jodee to tell Steve what she'd shared earlier with her and Brenda. Steve listened with intensity. Once her stomach knotted up when anger flashed across his face, until she realized it wasn't directed at her. He must have noticed her reaction because he apologized. *Apologized? Wow. I've ducked my dad's fist, been ignored by him all my life, and never has my dad apologized. What is up with this guy Steve?* He asked if it was okay if he helped her to find out more information about her mom. Jodee's heart jumped at the thought. She couldn't even let herself begin to think about the possibility of being reunited with her mom.

And earlier this morning had been like a fairy tale. After getting ready for school, Brenda and Jodee went down to the kitchen. Lorinda was already there and had set the table. Glasses of juice sat in front of each place setting, and cereal and toasted muffins were in the middle of the table. It was so hard to grasp. The last time breakfast had been on the table at her home was sometime before her mom had become pregnant. And since her mom had left, Jodee had to get her own breakfast.

I've never been this happy! Oh thank You, God!

"Hey! Spacehead!"

Jodee looked up to see who was responsible for bringing her back to the real world, and Karen scowled back at her. Jodee sighed. *I'd probably be acting the same way before I met Jesus and got to stay at the Sanders' house. Karen probably feels deserted.* Jodee worked up a smile for her friend.

"What are you thinking about? Got a crush on someone?" Karen teased.

"Yeah, right." Jodee nonchalantly leaned back in her chair.

"So, where were you last night? I tried calling you, a *lot!*"

"Well, um, you're not going to believe this, but yesterday I was having a pretty bad time and Brenda…" Jodee started explaining but was interrupted by the loud remarks coming from their friends entering the classroom. With no regard to who got bumped or how they may be intruding on conversations, they bombarded their way down between the desks to the back of the room where Karen and Jodee were sitting. Of course the guys started goofing around with Karen. She was popular with all the boys.

Jodee didn't care, because the interruption allowed her thoughts to drift back to her time with Brenda's family....

Lorinda had joined the girls for breakfast. They talked about reasons her mom may have left. It may have been because of all of the ugliness between her and Jodee's dad. Maybe her mom did have a hard time living with herself and the decision she had made about having an abortion. Still the unanswered question hung out there: Why would she leave Jodee with a man who obviously didn't care for her? *Does Mom ever worry about me, or does she wonder how I'm doing? Isn't she afraid my dad will hurt me like he hurt her?*

Lorinda had suggested she pray for her parents. Yes, even her dad. Jesus could touch anyone's life. He had died for the whole world, not only people who we think are good.

Wow, that's something to think about. Maybe God will heal my whole family. Lost in her thoughts, she didn't pay attention to anything going on.

* * *

Karen was watching Jodee like a hawk. *I don't get what's going on, but if Brenda thinks she can take Jodee from me, she has another think coming.* Karen clenched her fists. She wasn't about to lose her best friend to anyone, especially do-gooder Brenda.

* * *

Steve stood outside of his office building waiting for Bill to pick him up. Earlier that morning over coffee Steve had shared about Jodee, and how both he and Lorinda desired to help her, even offer her a place to live. Bill had agreed to go with him to visit Jodee's dad at lunchtime.

Steve waved as Bill's car turned the corner and pulled up. Steve got into the car quickly and latched his seat belt. "How's it going so far today?"

"It's going great, considering all the stuff on my mind. It made it hard to want to stay in the office. How about you?" Bill asked.

"Well, a few of my cases got put off so I was able to look up some information on Jodee's situation. Seems in the divorce settlement Mr. Grant Myers got full custody of Jodee, and there's a restraining order against her mom. Her name is Annette Spelldor."

"Wow, do you have her last address?"

"Yep. How would you like to make a visit to her after we visit with Mr. Myers?"

"I'm right there with you, bud. Hey, is this the house?"

"Yep." Steve sighed. "Let's go see what we can do for little Miss Jodee Myers."

"Hey, Steve, wait a minute. I know you have high hopes you can take Jodee home with you and help her out, but let's not do this on our own."

"You're right. Will you pray about this?" Steve asked.

Bill nodded. Just as they began praying, a knocking sounded on the car window on Steve's side of the car.

"Hmmm, Mr. Myers comes to us," Steve mumbled while rolling the window down.

"What do you guys want? You here to sell something? I don't want anything, so take your business elsewhere," Jodee's dad snarled.

"No sir, actually we're here to talk to you about your daughter," Steve started to explain.

"My daughter? What has she done? She causing trouble?"

"No sir."

Bill got out of the car and walked around the back to the driver's side and stood by the passenger door. He held out his hand for a handshake. "Sir, my name is Bill, Bill Thomas. My daughter, Trudy, goes to school with Jodee." Bill put down his hand after receiving no response from Jodee's dad.

"So, what do you want?" he barked.

Steve squeezed his way out of the car. Grant barely moved to make room for him. "My name is Steve Sanders. Last night my wife and daughter picked up Jodee, and she stayed at our home."

"Last night? Jodee wasn't here last night? That no good..."

"No, it seems she felt like she was in danger over a note she'd found in your bedroom, so we allowed her to stay over with our daughter. She's at school today," Steve explained.

"A note? It wasn't about a note. I remember now. That no-good brat was trying to steal money from me. I should call the police. And what was she doing out all night? She knows better than to stay out all night!" he yelled.

Steve and Bill looked nervously around, wondering how many neighbors were watching them.

"I'm sure it was all a misunderstanding. Anyway, I have reason to believe that she may have been in danger due to your actions that my wife observed when she picked Jodee up here."

"What are you going to do about it? You can't prove anything. She's no better than her hussy mom," Grant said smugly.

"Well, sir, my wife and I would like to offer Jodee our place to live during the rest of the school year." He had not intended to be so blunt.

"What are you saying?" Jodee's dad asked. "You don't know her. It's none of your business."

"Actually, sir, not to be disrespectful, but I have made it my business. It seems there are numerous times Jodee left your home in order to find safety when you were intoxicated. We'd like to offer her a safe place while she finishes school, or we will document every time she has to leave her home seeking shelter and turn it in to foster care," Steve said firmly.

Bill stood behind Grant, eyes big. Steve tried not to laugh at his expression. He hadn't meant to be so forward or sound like he was blackmailing the guy.

"What do you mean, stay with your family? Who will cook and clean the house? And what about her stupid cat?" he asked.

Bill took in a deep breath to try to calm down.

"Well, sir, who you find to clean your house and cook for you will have to be something you work out. But our house is open for your daughter to come and stay for a while. We'll be more than happy to set up a schedule so we are always accountable to you, and you can come to visit her," Steve finished.

"How much are you going to pay me?" he asked.

"Pay you?" Steve asked.

"Yes, pay me for letting my daughter stay with you?" he asked.

"Nothing, sir, nothing at all," Steve answered.

"That's right sir, nothing," Bill agreed.

"I don't see why I should let her go stay with you then. Oh, well, I don't care. It'll save me from having a headache every day. I never wanted her to begin with. Kid just gets in the way."

"Here is my address and phone number. You can call anytime, especially if you want to come to visit her," Steve offered.

"Visit? Whatever. Tell her if she wants any of her things she better get them before I get home. Tell her to leave your phone number on the refrigerator. She's like her mother, just like her. Tell her if she doesn't come get her stuff today, while I'm gone, she can't have any of it," he growled. "And keep her away from her mother. She keeps coming back, trying to take Jodee. I fixed her. She can't get within a hundred feet of Jodee, or she'll go to jail. If she shows up at your house, call the police. I have legal custody and a restraining order. The no-good woman needs to stay away from Jodee. If I find out she's even near Jodee, I'll call the cops on all of you." He turned, stormed into his house, and slammed the door.

Bill and Steve eyed each other in shock.

"Wow," Steve said as they drove away. "I'd never believe it if I hadn't seen it myself. He doesn't care about Jodee. She is just a pawn to him. I don't understand why he won't let her poor mother have custody. That child has not been loved. It breaks my heart."

"She's obviously loved by her mother, but yeah, it's unbelievably sad," Bill added.

"At least she'll have a safe place for a while. Now if we can just connect with her mom. Are you up to visiting her mom?"

"Steve, I'm up to doing anything to help that girl right now. She needs some joy, and I know she wants her mama. I hope we don't scare her mom, though…two strange men coming to the door."

"Hmm, never thought of that. Let's try to call her first. And maybe I can get that restraining order dropped. Who knows? We'll see after we talk to Annette." Steve dialed information for Annette's number.

* * *

Annette had agreed to meet the two of them at a coffee shop down the block from where she lived. Her back was toward the door, but both knew who she was the moment they entered the restaurant. She seemed to be completely oblivious to her surroundings, lost in her own thoughts, facing a window, sniffing and continually bringing a tissue to her face.

"Excuse me, Annette?" She took an obvious deep breath and barely raised her eyes while they sat down across from her.

"I'm sorry. Your phone call took me by surprise."

"I can imagine," Steve said in a soft tone. "Can we buy you a coffee?" She gave a nod, and Bill got up to get the order.

"Jodee is a school friend of my daughter's," Steve said. "It came to our attention recently that she had a dilemma in her life. To make a long story short, she'll be staying at our house during the rest of the school year."

"She's at your house?" A smile beamed through the unchecked tears pouring down her face. "Can I, can I see her?" Sobs shook her shoulders. Steve grasped the shaking hand that was trying to brush the tears away.

"If I could let you see her, I would, but I made an agreement to honor the restraining order."

Annette grabbed her purse with obvious anger and started to rise from her seat.

"Wait." Steve almost lurched himself across the table. Bill sidestepped so he didn't spill the coffee on her back. "I want to help you. I'm a lawyer." Her body relaxed, and a cautious expression was planted on her face. "From what my wife tells me, it would bring Jodee no greater joy than to let you see her. She wants her mom and doesn't understand why you left." Tears sprang to Steve's eyes.

"I didn't leave. I was kicked out. Do you know how many times I tried to get her away from him?" Annette's voice rose in anger. Some of the customers turned in her direction. She lowered her voice. "He never wanted Jodee. He used to beat me. Sometimes after he was drunk, he would get a kick out of threatening me with awful things he'd do to Jodee just to get a rise out of me. Honestly, I can't tell you how many times I tried to leave. I felt like a caged animal. Then when I was finally free, he wouldn't let me have my baby. He told me she would take my place." Her eyes stared off to a place she lived years ago. "Every night I pray for God to give me my baby back. I try to leave money and food for her. He drinks up the money, but at least she has some food."

Steve's pager sounded. His shoulder sagged. "Listen, I've got to get back to the office. Let's meet again. First thing I have to do is check out the conditions of the restraining order."

"Do you think you'll be able to help me?" A desperate hope rang in her voice.

Steve nodded. He noticed Bill wiping at his eyes.

"Can you give me a moment to write her a note, please?"

Again, Steve could only nod. They waited as she pulled out paper and pen from her bag and wrote to her daughter.

"Thank you—both of you. I'm so grateful. Whatever your fees are, it doesn't matter; I have a good job and will get another one if I have to."

"Let's just take this one step at a time and worry about everything else later." He smiled. The light of hope in her eyes was payment enough.

* * *

Karen sat on the sidewalk, leaning her back against the wall of the school. She was partially hidden by a bush that was on the side of the stairwell. She needed some time alone. Her life was changing at school, and she didn't like it. She'd come to depend on the stability of school. She knew she was safe each day when she entered the doors in the morning. No one could hurt her. She went to class, laughed with her friends, and ate a hot meal at lunch. Jodee was always right beside her.

School was a place where she could pretend she was normal, she was from a rich, classy family, and that others were beneath her. She could hurt others, but they had no power to hurt her—except Jodee.

Jodee was always by her side, someone she could depend on, ever since she was a little girl. Jodee didn't know the truth about Karen, so when they were together, Karen was able to still pretend that her life was something it wasn't. When Karen missed school, she'd let Jodee believe she had gone on some trip with her parents, to the beach, skiing or whatever. She always made something up. She never let Jodee know the truth about her stepdad and brothers.

Nobody knew.

Nobody knew she was the type of girl that men only liked for one reason and one reason only. Her stepdad said she could probably bring him quite a bit of money. He just had to figure out a way that her mom wouldn't find out about it, though.

At first she would scream and cry, hoping somehow, some way, it would stop them. Instead they laughed and accused her of leading them on. They said her "no" meant *yes!* They liked a woman who played hard to get.

They stopped her screams one day with their threats. They told her what they wanted her to say and that if she didn't comply, they threatened to hurt her more. The day she stopped screaming was the day her heart shut down, and her mind shut off. She no longer existed when they were around. In her mind she was somewhere else, someplace where no one could ever touch her.

Now that she was older and had more freedom, it was easier for her to stay away from them. At night it was easy to sneak out her bedroom window. One night she made a discovery, a hangout where other kids like her would hide out for the night. Or she'd have Jodee come home with her. Fortunately, they left Jodee alone.

No matter what she went through at home, she could always come to school and pretend with Jodee. But now her friend seemed to be slipping away. Now she had new friends—geeks.

There wasn't anyone else that Karen could depend on to hang out and not get too close. Jodee faithfully hung out with Karen, but she only got so close or let Karen get so close to her. It was safe.

She threw her cigarette down in the dirt. As she stepped on it she thought of Brenda. Anger rose within her. Miss Do-gooder was messing with Karen's life. She needed to find a way to keep Brenda away from Jodee.

* * *

"Tony!" Trudy called out, trying to move through the throng of kids walking through the hall to class. "Tony." She jumped up to see over the heads of the three guys she found herself stuck behind. Putting her hand between them with a gentle push, she squeezed through the human barricade. "Excuse me, I'm sorry." She flashed them a smile.

"Tony," she called again, relieved when this time he turned in her direction. She gave him a wave. He nodded and moved closer to the lockers to get out of the throng of classmates to wait for her.

"What's up with this hallway? It's like a herd of cattle," Trudy complained when she finally landed in front of Tony.

Tony chuckled. "A toilet overflowed and ran into the hall up by the auditorium. Besides being gross, the janitor blocked the hall off until he could get it cleaned up," he informed her.

"Eww. You always know everything. How do you do that? Anyway, I wanted to talk to you. Randy called me last night."

"That's great, Trudy."

"I think so. Tony, I'm so grateful you've become his friend. He doesn't have any real friends, you know. You've been wonderful for him."

Tony shrugged with a sheepish grin. "At first I was only being obedient and also protective of *you*." He pointed his finger toward her nose, and his grin broadened. "But now I'm getting to know him, and he's a great guy. I can see why you fell for him."

Trudy hugged him. "Thank you, Tony. You're a wonderful friend."

"Oh, what do we have here?"

Trudy swiveled in the direction of the voice. *Karen.*

"Two little love birds. Tsk, tsk, tsk…little mommy looking for a daddy, hmmm?"

Trudy could feel the heat on her face. Tony stiffened. Just as both of them were about to respond, Jodee approached.

"Hey, Trudy! Tony! It's packed in this hallway. Whew! So, what's up with you guys?" She put her arm around Karen's shoulder, oblivious to what was going on.

"Not much, just talking with the two lovey-doveys. Little momma looking for a little dada," Karen cooed, then threw her head back, laughing.

Jodee dropped her arm to her side and shot a concerned look to Trudy. She leaned toward Karen and said in a low voice, "Do you think that's appropriate?"

"Excuse me!" Karen tossed her head and snarled at Jodee, "Appropriate? Whatever, Jodee!" Karen put her hand up. "Talk to the hand."

The four stood in an awkward silence. Karen glared at Jodee. Jodee pretended not to notice and checked the time on her watch. "Oops, Karen, we better get going. Come on." She started walking. Karen followed, but not before scowling at Tony and Trudy.

"Wow." Trudy backed up, realizing she still had her hands on Tony's chest. Tony dropped his hands from her waist. "Oh, great, we looked like we were holding on to each other."

Trudy gave a nervous giggle. Tony burst out laughing.

"Maybe we *were* giving the wrong idea." He put his arm around her shoulder and started walking down the hall. "Come on, little Momma. Dadda will help you to class."

16

The smell of liquor and cigarette smoke permeated every corner of the chilly house. It went unnoticed by Jodee, sitting lost in her thoughts on the bed holding her cat close, a folded note lying next to her on the thin blanket. A chance of a lifetime had opened up for her.

Steve had picked her up from school, along with Brenda and Trudy, to explain about a meeting he had earlier with her dad. Steve had received permission for Jodee to come and live with the Sanders. And then the most wonderful news—he had met with her mother. Because of some stupid legal stuff, they couldn't see each other yet, but there was a note.

Her glance fell around the stark walls and threadbare curtains in her room. *This is my space.* She gave her cat a squeeze until it fussed at her. *This is my cat. What's wrong with me? I have horrible, lonely memories here and I've been dying to see my mom, only I can't open the letter. Or pack.*

Outside, parked in her driveway, were members of a family who were willing to open their home to her so she could have a loving place to stay. *I should be happy. Why am I so sad?*

What was she going to do without her cat? He was her best friend. Her dad probably wouldn't feed the cat. Who was going to feed her dad? Who would wash his clothes? She had been preparing her dad his meals ever since her mother left.

Jodee wiped the tears from her face. She needed to get packed. The Sanders had her go in alone, in case she'd need a few moments to herself. They were right; she needed it. She grabbed her overnight bag and went to the bathroom to get her shampoo and hairdryer. The light on the portable phone was flashing. She stopped to check the messages. There was one from Karen. Jodee felt bad for her.

Jodee decided to give a quick call to let Karen know she was going to be staying at Brenda's house for a while and to give her their phone number.

"Hi, Karen!" Jodee exclaimed.

"What are you doing?" Karen sounded irritated.

"I'm at home but...it's such a long story. Listen—I'm going to be staying over at the Sanders' house for a while." Jodee found it very hard to say.

"What! At Do-gooder's? What for? What's going on?" Karen yelled.

Jodee struggled to keep herself composed. The more she thought of leaving, the more upset she got. "Something's been going on between me and my dad. I'll explain tomorrow," Jodee managed to say.

"What! What happened? And why did you call her and not me? I'm your best friend, you know."

"Actually, it's hard to explain. Here's Brenda's phone number and address. I'll tell you the rest tomorrow. I have to go." Jodee wanted off the phone. She couldn't believe how upset she was feeling.

"I may call, but I doubt it. You're making the wrong choice. I might think about talking to you later." Karen hung up the phone.

Jodee was slow to hang up the phone. Karen was so mad at her, but even worse was the truth of her own reality intruding on her thoughts. Something she hated thinking about and usually tried to avoid but was unable to right now. Her dad didn't love her. He was letting her go. He'd never cared. She was going to live with someone else to protect her from her own father.

She closed her eyes tight. She'd always wanted him to love her, hold her, and talk to her. Instead he beat and yelled at her, and now he'd agreed to let her live somewhere else.

The pain hurt so deep in her heart. She slid to the floor sobbing, wanting to scream. She wanted her parents to love and be with her. *I don't want my parents to be out of my life. Why does Dad want to beat me? Why can't he love me? I'm his daughter.*

She felt a gentle hand on her shoulder, then another and another. The whispered words of comfort sang a song to her heart as Brenda, Lorinda, and Steve prayed.

* * *

Karen covered her face with her hands and groaned. She was so angry. *How had Miss Do-gooder done that? What on earth happened that Jodee would have to stay over at her house?* Karen shook her head. *I don't get it.* Last week Jodee and Karen were best friends, hanging out together and making fun of Miss Do-gooder. Now Jodee was talking about God and staying with Miss Do-gooder.

Karen was so frustrated she couldn't stand it. She grabbed a cigarette, opened her bedroom window, and climbed out on the ledge. Her mom didn't want Karen smoking in the house. Karen figured she was respecting her mother's wishes by hanging out of her bedroom window. It was ironic to Karen how her mom would get mad at her for smoking, yet she didn't care about what else went on in her house. Karen had never heard her mom say anything to her stepdad or stepbrothers about their behavior. Karen threw her cigarette. Too late, she realized she hadn't put it out before she threw it down. "Who cares? Let it burn the house down."

Karen crawled back in the room and sprawled across her bed to think of a plan. She had lost her best friend. Jodee was now a geek. Karen fought the tears. She'd learned a long time ago that crying got her nowhere. Nowhere at all. But anger helped. It helped a lot.

Well, if she's going to be a geek, she's going to get the geek treatment. Too bad!

Karen really liked Jodee. She didn't really know her very well, but she liked her. She wondered what could have happened that would cause Jodee to have to live somewhere else. It had to be worse than what Karen went through. But then, no one knew about Karen. Everyone thought she had a great family and went on a lot of vacations. Oh, well.

She heard a car pull into the driveway. Karen's heart started racing. She looked wildly around her room for her overnight bag in case her stepdad or brothers had come home before her mom. She checked her pockets for money as she went to the window to look.

It was her stepdad's car. Karen grabbed her bag and crawled out the window. She walked down the roof, carefully checking to see if he was outside. She didn't see him. Grabbing a branch, she climbed onto the tree that was close to the house.

"What are you doing, Karen?"

Chills went up her spine as she turned and saw him poking his head out of her window. Anger blazed as she realized he'd gone directly to her room.

"None of your business," Karen called back over her shoulder.

"What will your mom think if she heard you were sneaking out like this? Or all of the other nights that you sneak out?" he asked.

Karen stared at him. She knew her mom would listen to him, and she'd be in trouble. She knew in her heart that this man would win.

Suddenly, she smiled. Not anymore. He would never win again. She was not coming back. She might come back to get her stuff during the day, but other than that, he'd never see her again. Her mom wouldn't care, and even if she did care, so what? Her mom didn't take care of her. Her mom had abandoned her. It was time that Karen took care of herself.

Karen swiftly made her way down the tree. She could hear him calling her. Her pulse raced. *Would he follow?* She glanced over her shoulder. He was still in the window.

She smiled. She felt safe now. She'd never have to see him or smell his rotten breath ever again. She was gone.

Her heart stirred a little when she thought of her mom, but she reasoned to herself, *What good does my mom do except have a purse I can steal money from?* Karen was glad she'd made sure she had money in her pocket. She was going to need it.

She decided she was going to the place she'd found to sleep at night. The kids just hung out together and slept in secret places.

She would find a job, a place of her own, and would never go back.

Good-bye, Mom. Good-bye, Jodee. Sorry I couldn't tell you good-bye, but I do believe you left me first, without saying good-bye to me.

* * *

Lorinda finished hanging up Jodee's clothes in what would now be Jodee's closet. Lorinda sighed, feeling bad as she looked at the clothing. It was so worn. She hoped Jodee would allow her to give her some new things. Maybe Brenda could pass on some of her clothes.

Lorinda thought back on finding Jodee sitting in the hallway of her home, sobbing. It had broken her heart. She instantly understood it would be hard for Jodee to leave her home. Lorinda had had a hard time growing up—not as hard as Jodee's—so she understood about desiring a parent's love.

Lorinda prayed for wisdom and understanding and that she wouldn't cause Jodee to think she was trying to replace her mother. Lorinda wanted Jodee to know she would always be there for her, but Jodee's mother was important. Lorinda hoped they could come together soon.

Steve had told her about the restraining order against Jodee's mother and that he thought they needed to respect it. With a sigh, she decided to leave it all in God's hands and deal with what God had put in front of her.

She heard Brenda talking excitedly to Jodee in her room. She needed to focus on helping Jodee to feel comfortable. She laid out Jodee's blanket that she'd brought with her from her own house. Lorinda had told Jodee they had plenty of blankets, but Jodee had wanted to bring this blanket with her. It was the last blanket her mom had given her. Lorinda held it tightly to her. The pain Jodee's mom must feel, not able to be near or hold her child.

Jodee had placed a picture of her mom, holding her as a small child, on the dresser. Lorinda studied the face. Clutching the picture to her chest, and closing her eyes to fight against the tears, she prayed," Oh, Lord, may this child be blessed and feel your love. May we be a safe place in the world. And heavenly Father, thank You for this opportunity. May we love her as You, Lord, want this child to be loved. In Jesus' precious name I pray, amen."

* * *

After unpacking her bag and storing it in the closet, Cassie plopped on her bed. So many changes had happened in just a few days right before her eyes. It was as though her family wasn't her family anymore. She stretched out on the bed, flinging her arm over her face. *What has happened? All three of them are now Bible thumpers, and Randy is going to be a dad.* Her sister was probably wondering about their quick departure, but Cassie wasn't ready to explain.

Cassie had to get some sort of control over the situation. The faint laughter of Randy and Katey drifted into her room from down the hallway. She smiled at first, then quirked her head a bit, shocked. "Those two haven't laughed together in years. Ever since Randy got interested in girls, Katey has been the only girl he wasn't interested in at all." She shook her head. "Strange. Oh, well, it probably won't last."

She got off her bed and went over to her assortment of books. She wanted to show Katey that there were lots of different beliefs in the world. Everyone had their own idea about the Bible, and everyone thought their way was the only way. But she didn't recall any of these books referring her to read the Bible like the three of them had been doing the last couple of days.

She wanted her children to have open minds. Grabbing a book that explained about being a goddess and about angels, she went in search of Katey.

* * *

"Good night, Katey," Randy called at her bedroom door.

Katey sat up in bed. "Randy?"

"Sorry. Did I shock you by saying good night?" Randy laughed.

"Well, sort of. But, actually, I was waiting for you to walk by. I need to talk to you."

Randy entered the room and sat on the side of her bed. "Just for a minute, okay? Mom and Dad might get upset if I keep you awake. We have to get up for school in the morning."

"I know," Katey said sadly.

"Hey!" Randy tweaked her nose. "You should be happy. When have I ever sat on the side of your bed before you go to sleep, so you and I could talk about whatever you wanted to talk about?"

"I know."

"Hey, kiddo, what's the matter?"

"Randy, if Mom dies tonight, will she go to hell?"

Randy took a sharp breath. "Katey! Why are you thinking like that?"

"Mom doesn't believe in Jesus. She brought me a whole bunch of books about things that are scary. The books don't like Jesus."

Oh, the poor kid! What should I say? "Katey, I really don't know what to tell you, except maybe we should pray about it. I don't know enough to tell you an answer that will make you feel better. But if we pray, God will give us an answer, and if it's an answer we don't like, I think God will help us deal with it."

"Randy, I'm scared for Mom."

Randy hugged her while he prayed for them. Katey even added to the prayer. When they finished, Katey crawled under her covers, and Randy tucked her in. He kissed her on the forehead. He liked this feeling of closeness he had with her now. "Good night, Katey. Sleep tight," he said as he walked to the door.

"I love you, Randy, good night."

Randy grinned, then went to his room and knelt by his bed. His heart hurt for his mom. He'd always been able to talk with her, so maybe he should go to her now. She always was a good listener.

He found her alone, curled up in her bed, reading a book. He knocked quietly on her open bedroom door, smiling when she looked up at him. She beckoned him with a wave, and he perched on her bed.

She seemed to wear a different expression than normal. He couldn't quite place what it was, but it made him feel uncomfortable. *Maybe I shouldn't have come to talk to her tonight.* He started to get up, then changed his mind. He knew it would bother him all night if he didn't talk to her now.

"Yes, Randy?"

"I wanted to talk to you about Katey."

"Is Katey all right? I just talked to her," she asked, a little alarmed.

"No, she's not."

"What's wrong with her?" His mom started to get out of bed.

Randy reached his arm out to stop her. "Mom, she's not sick. She's sleeping."

"Then why did you say she wasn't all right? That scared me," she snapped as she crawled back under her covers.

"I'm sorry, Mom. Listen, Katey is really upset about the stuff you read to her tonight…," he started to explain.

"What do you mean *upset?* Upset about what?"

"Well, these last couple of days I know you've seen Katey and me reading the Bible—"

"Oh, that," his mother interrupted, waving her hand as if brushing his words away. "It's just a book filling your heads with silly ideas."

"Mom, why do you think our heads are being filled with silly ideas? What kind of silly ideas are you talking about?"

His mom pushed herself up on the pillows. "Religious stuff. You're filling your heads with a bunch of religious garbage. There are lots of books that tell about religions. Look over on that bookshelf. There's a bunch of different beliefs. It doesn't really matter. So you've been reading the Bible…it isn't different than any other book."

God, he prayed, *what do I do? What do I say? This is my mom!* As if he had to explain to God who she was. But he didn't know what else to say.

"Randy, listen," his mom said in the understanding tone she usually used with him, "I know you've made a big mistake, and you're scared. You normally don't get along with your dad, and you're probably very afraid of his reaction. If reading the Bible and acting like you've changed in a religious way is helping you through all of this, okay, I'll support you. But don't drag Katey into this. Or try to convince me that you've changed because you've started to read a book. I know you, Randy. If I wasn't so mad at you, I'd probably stand right beside you and read the Bible just to help you. But this isn't a game. You messed up in a big way. There are consequences for your actions that aren't going to be wiped away because you've suddenly changed and are reading a book called the Bible."

"Ouch. That hurt, Mom." He couldn't believe this lady who had stood by him and whom he could always rely on would talk to him this way.

"Mom," he said in a quiet, firm voice, "I'm sorry I've hurt you. I know this family is going to feel the repercussions for my mistake, and so is Trudy's. But I'm not playing games. Believe me, I'm not! I didn't pick up the Bible to play games with anyone. I picked it up because of something Tony, who is a friend of Trudy's, said about God loving me. I didn't even know where my Bible was until the other night, for crying out loud. I prayed to God with Tony for the first time and asked Jesus into my heart. This is real for me!

"The weird thing is, the next day I wanted to read the Bible and find out more about God. The Bible actually talks to my heart. It tells the story of how God sent His Son, Jesus to die for my sins. Mine! I couldn't believe it! Who would die for me? For the rotten stuff I did. That meant He even died for what I did to Trudy and how I hurt you."

His mom stared at the blankets on the bed.

Now he knew he had to tell her the whole story—the truth about what was in the Bible. "Jesus was up on the cross, and the Bible says He asked the Father to forgive them because they didn't know what they were doing. After all that had happened to Him, He asked for their forgiveness. I was so mad that they treated Him like that. The stories I've read about Him were incredible. He was kind, compassionate, and healed people. One time He saw a mom sad because she was at her son's funeral, and he brought her son back to life again. Those are the kind of things we're learning in the Bible. Not silly ideas or religious garbage, but of God's love and His promises for the whole world. I don't deserve it, but I believe in it. So can you, Mom. It says you only have to believe, and you will be saved."

Randy ran out of words. *Wow, did I say that?*

His mom just sat there, staring down at her hands on the blanket.

"Mom?" Randy leaned toward her to try to see her face. When she finally glanced up at him, his heart sank before she even spoke. He wasn't sure what he saw in her eyes, but it didn't look good.

"That's nice, Randy. You'll make a good preacher someday." She smiled and patted his hand. "It's a book, Randy. If you find comfort in it, great. But please don't push it on Katey. She's very impressionable, and she looks up to you. She'll do anything to make you happy."

"What?" Randy couldn't believe it. "Mom, didn't you hear anything that I said?"

"I heard you. It's the same religious jumbo I've heard before. Now, it's late. You have to go to school in the morning. Give me a kiss and get to bed." She kissed his cheek.

Randy was so dazed he barely managed a "Good night." When he got to his room, he knelt beside his bed. He had no words to pray, only tears to cry.

* * *

Randy woke with a start. He was lying on the floor next to his bed. The house was dark and quiet. The clock read 11:30. Shaking off his sleepiness, he went to brush his teeth before he climbed into bed. He could hear his parents' muffled voices while he was in the bathroom. "Hmm. They don't sound too happy," he mumbled to himself as he stepped out of the bathroom.

"Well!" His mom's voice rang through the hallway.

Randy stopped in his tracks. *Mom and Dad are fighting?* He didn't want to eavesdrop, so he started to hurry to his room.

"Are you going to put that book away or not?"

Randy stopped. *That book? They're arguing about a book?* He knew deep in his heart what book she meant before he heard the next words.

"What, my Bible? You're this upset about the Bible?" Al asked.

"Don't you get it? This is a ploy to get your attention off of the issue of Trudy being pregnant."

"No, honey, it's not. Please come sit with me, and let me show you what's going on with the three of us. Come join me," Al said softly.

"NO!" It was almost a shout.

Randy started to feel guilty for listening but couldn't move.

"Our son's girlfriend is pregnant. He starts to act like he's a Bible thumper, and you fall for it. In fact, you start thumping the Bible yourself. He's made the worst mistake ever, and there are absolutely no consequences for him. I need you right now, but you're so busy falling for whatever Randy is doing that you've left me here alone. Don't you realize what I'm going to go through? How do you think I'm going to tell my family that our son got his girlfriend pregnant? You know I've never added up to my family, and now here we go. I can hear it now: *Look at poor Cassie, blah, blah, blah.*"

Randy felt horrible. He didn't know her family treated her like that.

"I'm sorry, honey. I'm sorry you feel alone. I know I've told you this before, and you probably don't want to hear it again, but Katey, Randy, and I are your family. We love you. You always add up to us." Randy could hear the creak of the bed and his dad's feet shuffling on the carpet. "You don't have to prove anything to anyone, Cassie. Nobody is perfect. Besides, how could you have stopped what happened between Randy and Trudy? He made the mistake, not you."

"That's not how my family will look at it. I will have failed again."

Randy couldn't listen to another word. It sounded like his mom was crying. He made his way to his room and threw himself back on his bed.

"Wow, Lord, have I ever made a mess of things." Randy lay in the dark, angry at himself. Sleep finally overtook him sometime during the night.

* * *

The ring of the doorbell echoed through the house, and Brenda ran to answer it. "Hey, Trudy!" Trudy looked over her shoulder, waving at someone. "Who are you waving at?" He appeared before Brenda got an answer.

Tony. Brenda's heart skipped a beat.

"We both were at physical therapy, and I asked Tony if he was interested in giving me a ride home. We got to talking and thought a few hours at The Cave would be fun. Do you and Jodee want to join us?" Trudy explained as she entered the house.

"Uh, well, sure I would. Not sure about Jodee, though. She's just getting settled. It's been a difficult couple of hours," Brenda answered. "Let's go ask her." Brenda led the way into the family room where she had left Jodee curled up on the couch watching a movie. "Hey, Jodee, would you like to go to The Cave with Trudy and Tony and me?"

Jodee turned her gaze from the screen she was intently watching. "Oh, hey, what are you two doing?"

"We just finished at the physical therapist's office. Want to go?" Trudy repeated. Jodee's expression was a clear giveaway she wanted to stay right where she was planted.

"You don't have to go, Jodee. As a matter of fact, I'll stay home with you." Brenda said.

"No, you go, Brenda. I mean, if it's okay I stay here without you, that is," Jodee said in uncharacteristic shyness.

"You live here now, Jodee. This is your home as well as mine or my brother Jonathon's." Brenda gave her an encouraging smile.

"Then I'd like to finish watching this movie and go to bed early. I'm really enjoying this."

"She seems fine. Come with us, Brenda," Tony interjected.

"Okay, I'll see you in the morning, Jodee. Have a good night's sleep." Brenda motioned for Trudy and Tony to follow her.

* * *

Jodee could hear the three of them talking in the other room to Lorinda, and then the door shut. Lorinda peeked in the family room. "Doing okay, kiddo?" Jodee nodded. "Well, I'm pretty tired, so I'm going up to bed. Steve's in his office upstairs working. Feel free to invade the refrigerator if you get hungry. Good night, honey." Lorinda gave her a wave.

"Good night," Jodee called back. Picking up the remote control, she tried to remember the directions Brenda had given her earlier. Little did Brenda know this was the first time she'd ever been able to wrap up in a blanket and watch a movie without worrying about her dad coming home drunk and swinging his fists. Generally she was doing chores and then homework. This was incredible. She got the movie back to where she had been watching it before Trudy and Tony had showed up.

Snuggling deeper into the blanket, she felt something poke at her back. The letter. *Why don't I read it? I've been waiting for years to see my mom, and now she writes me a letter and I haven't read it?* Jodee tried to focus on the movie again. She couldn't. Hands shaking, she reached under the blanket for the note. With a short prayer, she slowly unfolded the note.

My dearest daughter Jodee,
I've waited for years to have the opportunity to explain why I left without you. I have just a few minutes before I need to pass this over to Mr. Sanders. I doubt this note will answer all of your questions.

Jodee held the letter close to her chest before reading further.

It was a cold, rainy night. When I found myself locked out of the house, with no keys, I stood outside your window, wondering how I could get back in to take you with me. I started to take the screen off to climb in, but your dad appeared at the window. I decided to wait until morning. Fortunately, when he arrived home earlier that evening, he didn't lock the doors to the car, so that's where I slept.

The next morning, when he left, he had you in his arms. I begged and pleaded for him to let me have you. After dragging me out of the car, he drove off and didn't come back for days. I was so scared something had happened to you. I was able to find a spare key in the car and sat in your room, holding one of your blankets just to be able to smell you.

Somehow he convinced his brother and parents to help him, and there is a restraining order out on me. I was accused of abandoning my child. He won.

But I knew someday I'd see you again. I have sneaked into the house often to leave you food and money. Sometimes I throw caution to the wind and stand in your room and watch you sleep when I know your dad is probably out for the night.

I love you, Jodee, and I wait for the day to be able to be with you again. I have a good job that will support us both if you want to live with me.

Forever loving you,
Mom

Tears poured down Jodee's face. Sobs rose in her throat. Anger welled inside her. *Why did my dad have to be so cruel? Why did he keep us apart when he didn't love either one of us? I don't want to hate him, but...why did my dad's parents help him? I haven't seen them since I was little. What did they care?*

Jodee stood with determination. Steve had mentioned her mother's maiden name. He was surprised when she admitted not knowing it. Her dad wouldn't answer any questions about her mother. Jodee had never found anything except a few pictures of her around the house.

Picking up the phone book, she found her mother's maiden name, but there were no Annettes. So she started with the *A*'s, one by one to find her mom.

On about the fourth A, the voice on the other end triggered a sweet memory from when she was little. It hadn't changed. No words came from her lips at first. Then, "Mom? It's Jodee."

A sob was her mom's reply.

"I just finished reading your letter, and I've been waiting for you to come get me since I was five years old. I love you, Mom."

"Jodee! My girl. I love you. I miss you." Annette was practically screaming.

"Mom, I don't want to wait. I want to see you now," Jodee cried.

"I do too, darling, I do too. I can't even explain how much I want to see you. But if we don't do it right, we'll only have further trouble. We've waited this long, so let's let Mr. Sanders help us."

"No one can stop me from calling you. I'll call again," Jodee said firmly.

"I'll look forward to it. And Jodee?"

"Yes, Momma."

"Good night, sweetheart. I love you."

"Good night, Mom. I love you back." Jodee hung up the phone. With slow steps she climbed the stairs to her new nice, clean, warm bed. For the first time in ten years, her mom had told her good night.

* * *

"Hey, Tony, why don't you drop me off first?" Trudy draped her arms around Tony's and Brenda's shoulders as they walked out of The Cave to his car. They'd spent the last couple of hours laughing and talking about everything that had happened the past week. Trudy and Tony were blown away with what Brenda shared about Jodee and were happy Jodee had a safe place to stay. The three of them had had fun together, but it was late, and Trudy was exhausted.

"Okay, if you insist, ma'am. Anything to make you happy," Tony answered. Trudy climbed in the back seat, leaving Brenda to sit in the front.

Brenda was uncertain about the arrangement.

"When he drops me off, you'll have to climb in the front anyway," Trudy explained, following it with a yawn. "I'm so tired."

"Do you think it has to do with the baby?" Brenda asked.

Tony looked at her with surprise.

"Best friends don't have to worry about what they say. We can just blurt it out."

"Yeah, I don't know. I have no idea what to expect. When I think about it, it's kind of scary," Trudy admitted.

"I bet!" Tony agreed.

"When is your doctor appointment?" Brenda asked. "I'd like to go with you to all of your appointments."

"That would be great. I haven't made an appointment yet. Things have been a bit crazy. I wonder if Randy will come with us, too."

"I hope so," Brenda answered.

"I bet he will. Hey, I'd really like to hang out with him now that he's back. Maybe the four of us can go do some things." He lifted a questioning brow at Brenda and received a startled look back.

"I guess," Brenda answered quietly.

"What? You don't want to hang with us? We could go on double dates," Trudy offered from the back.

Brenda stared straight ahead, obviously uncomfortable.

Tony touched her hand. "It's okay, Brenda. You don't have to go. It'd be fun, though," he said in a quiet, gentle voice.

Brenda only gave him a half smile. Silence hung in the air the rest of the drive to Trudy's. The silence seemed to get even louder after they dropped her off at her house.

"Do you mind if I turn on the radio?" Brenda asked.

Tony shrugged while staring straight at the road ahead. It seemed like forever before they pulled into her driveway.

"Tonight was fun. Thanks, Tony. I'll see you tomorrow?"

He nodded with no other reply. Brenda felt awkward and was quick to get out of the car.

"Brenda," Tony called from his rolled-down car window, "could I ask you something?"

Brenda walked back to the car.

"Uh, I just want to get this straight. Do you or don't you want to join me, and hang out with Randy and Trudy?"

She could feel her face turning red in the driveway light.

"Oh, hey, I'm sorry. I don't mean to make you uncomfortable."

"It's not that." Brenda looked him in the eye and blew a big breath out in the direction of her bangs. "Okay, I'll be honest. I didn't know what you meant. I assumed as friends, since we've never been more than that, but didn't know. I don't want to put myself in a position where either of us have the wrong idea about the other one, and we get our hopes up, only to get hurt."

Tony gave her a big smile. "I have no intention of hurting you. I appreciate your honesty. That's one of the many things I like about you."

"Well, I've watched some couples hang out, and it looks like they're dating and they aren't, but usually only one person in the relationship knows that piece of information. I don't want to get hurt in that way."

"So, not to put you on the spot or anything, but how would you feel about dating me?"

"Tony, you brought this up. Now I'm asking you: What are your intentions? Friendship or dating?"

"Okay, you're right. I've never done this before. To be honest, I like you and would like to spend time getting to know you better. I think it would be great to progress to being a couple and starting to date, but we don't know each other all that well." Tony looked down at his lap for a minute, then up with an endearing, shy smile.

Brenda cocked her head to the side. "Great! I can do that. I'd really like that." Heading for the house, she turned to wave in his direction.

Once she opened the door, she waved once more at him before he drove off.

17

Trudy was in a bad mood. She tried to sneak by Jodee, Brenda, and Tony at lunch, but they called her over to the table. She all but dropped her tray down.

Brenda and Jodee raised their eyebrows. "Uh, Trudy, what's up?" Brenda asked.

"I'm really in a bad mood. I just want to be alone."

"Haven't seen Randy?" Jodee asked simply, glancing around the lunchroom.

"No! I thought he'd be here today. He doesn't have any minutes on his phone, and I don't want to call his house in case his mom or dad answers. How embarrassing would that be?" Trudy grumbled.

"I'll call," Tony offered.

Trudy instantly sparked up, shooting Tony a look of admiration.

Tony chuckled and dialed Randy's house. "Hey, is this Randy? I have someone here to talk to you."

Trudy waved both of her hands excitedly, and gave a silent scream of excitement when Tony handed the phone over to her. "Randy?"

"Tru? Hey, I was planning on being there today so I could see you."

Trudy gave a thumbs-up in everyone's direction. They all laughed.

"We overslept and thought it was ridiculous to go to school for a couple of hours. I'm watching Katey for my mom while she's at work, but she should be home in time for me to pick you up after school. Would that be okay?"

"Yes, that would be great," Trudy said as calmly as possible.

"Got your cell with you? I'll have minutes as soon as my mom lets me know. I'll text you to let you know if she's back or not, okay?"

"Okay. I'll wait for your text. Bye." Trudy got up and ran around the table, giving Tony a hug before handing him his phone. "Thank you, buddy." Then she squeezed in beside him and asked Brenda to push her lunch tray down to her.

* * *

Trudy got the text that Randy would be there to pick her up, but not until about twenty minutes after school was out. That gave her plenty of time to touch up her hair and makeup. She dragged Brenda along to the bathroom with her after Brenda let Jodee know where they would be.

"Do you believe it, Brenda? I get to see Randy today. Please pray for us. I'm not sure how our talk will go, but…"

Brenda smiled at her in the mirror. "Don't worry, we'll pray for you."

"We, as in you and Jodee?"

Brenda kind of squirmed.

"We, as in whom?" Trudy confronted her in a teasing way. "Do you mean you and Tony, we?"

Brenda's face colored a bright crimson.

"Are you serious? When were you going to tell me?"

"Wait. It's not serious. We're just getting to know each other and then maybe…" Brenda kicked her toe against the bathroom counter.

Trudy grabbed Brenda's hands and tried to jump up and down excitedly. "Eew, wait, that doesn't work, it hurts my neck." Trudy gave her a big squeeze instead. "You both are so wonderful it can't help but work out. Oh, today is a good day."

Brenda just shook her head.

"Are you guys done in here? Can I interrupt?" Jodee asked as she entered the restroom.

"Sure." Trudy turned and added a coat of lip gloss, then dropped the container back in her purse. "All done." She gave them a bright smile.

"Well, it seems strange to say, since just a week ago I tried to sabotage you, but I hope it works out for you, Trudy." Jodee smiled.

"Thanks!" Trudy led them out the bathroom door to wait outside.

"It's kind of strange. Karen wasn't at school today, and when I called her house, no one answered. I wonder if her family went out of town, and she was too angry to tell me?" Jodee commented as they walked outside, reaching in her purse for a pair of sunglasses.

"That's such a bummer about how Karen is taking all that's going on in your life, Jodee," Trudy replied.

"I probably would've done the same thing." Jodee shrugged.

"Well, there's Randy pulling into the parking lot," Brenda pointed out.

Trudy bit at her lip.

"Hey, you're going to be okay. Call and let me know all about it. I'll be waiting," Brenda called over her shoulder, walking with Jodee to her car.

"Okay, bye you two, thanks." Torn between excitement and nervousness, Trudy started walking toward the direction of Randy's car. She hadn't seen him for a week. Not since she was supposed to have the abortion. How should

191

she greet him? *I don't feel comfortable hugging him or giving him a kiss. I mean, I don't even know if we are still together.*

Then she thought back to their phone conversation earlier and how he'd sounded. She smiled, deciding she didn't care for the moment how he greeted her. She was excited to finally see him after a whole week. It seemed so much longer though, since so much had happened.

* * *

"I hope everything works out for the two of them." Jodee watched Trudy wave and Randy jump out of his car to run around it and open the door for her.

"I hope so, too. All we can do is pray." Jodee rode in silence. "Are you worried about Karen?"

Jodee nodded, then turned to look out the window. Brenda noticed her hand brush at her eye.

"Is something else bothering you?"

It took a minute before Jodee turned back in Brenda's direction. Her cheeks were wet with tears.

"Jodee! What's going on?"

"I called my mom last night," Jodee admitted.

"What! Why didn't you tell me?"

"I didn't want you to have to lie to your parents," Jodee explained.

"Oh, well, thanks, but is it wrong for you to call your mom? I thought it was the other way around, She can't help it if you call her," Brenda said.

"I think that's how it works, but just in case, I didn't want anyone to tell me I couldn't talk to her. I keep hearing her voice. I waited so long to be with her, and now that I've talked to her it makes it even harder."

Brenda only nodded. She didn't know what to say.

"I don't understand why my dad is so cruel. Why can't he be like your dad? Why can't he love his family?"

"I don't have answers for you, Jodee, but I can imagine the alcohol is the cause of his anger. I happen to have an uncle who was an alcoholic. Mean. He lost everything and everyone in his life. I wasn't allowed to be around him at the time, but my mom told me about how he used to be. Now he's a different person." Brenda gave a half shrug. "If I didn't know the story, I'd never know he used to be like that. I think he's so cool."

"I wish that would happen to my dad. Do you think it could?"

"I don't know. God works in everyone's life, but it looks different for each person. I would hope, though, and pray."

"I guess I should be grateful for everything that's happened this last week. And be happy that I can really hope for the day I get to be with my mom."

"That's a good way to look at it, Jodee, a really good way."

* * *

The car ride had been filled with Randy hearing about the changes that had happened in Jodee's life. Even Trudy, who experienced it, was blown away while she told the story. Then Randy shared what happened in his family. Tremendous things had been happening around them all week.

Now they stood looking out at the lake they'd been at the week before. They had finished sharing about everything and everyone. Now it was time for their story. *What is our story, God?* she wondered.

Randy leaned against the picnic table close by Trudy. She looked over at him, and he smiled at her. He was so gorgeous she felt as if her knees could not support her. She grinned back and reached to give him a hug. Her heart danced as he hugged her in return.

Then Randy released his hold and looked down at her. "So, we have quite a bit to talk about, I mean, about us."

She gave a nod.

"For starters, will you forgive me?"

"Yes, I forgive you," she said, then stopped. "But for what exactly?"

Randy threw his head back and laughed. She laughed along nervously.

"For one thing, that I wasn't more responsible about *not* getting you pregnant. You weren't experienced, and I was, so I should have made sure this didn't happen."

Trudy felt deflated, and he must have noticed.

"Maybe that came out wrong, but I don't know how else to say it."

He didn't have to remind me he was experienced. Does he still want the abortion? I was hoping he'd help me with the baby.

"I can't believe I made love to you to begin with. I mean, you're a good girl. You went against everything you believe in. I'm really sorry, Trudy." Then he gazed right into her face. "Will you forgive me for what I've done and then for asking—no, telling—you to have an abortion?"

Wow! "Randy, I should be asking you for forgiveness. I knew better than to have sex with you, and I did it anyway. That was my choice. We both...will you forgive me?" Trudy asked.

Randy nodded and gave her that incredible smile again.

She pushed on, no matter that her knees barely held her up. "Randy, you need to know, right up front, that no matter what happens between you and me today, I will never walk away from my faith ever again."

"Good. That's what I want to hear. If you and I work out and stay together, I want to know your faith will come first, before me."

Trudy cocked her head. "Really?"

"Really."

"When you prayed with Tony, you got it, didn't you?"

Randy nodded.

Tears sprang to Trudy's eyes. *I prayed for us to get back together, and this is way more than I had hoped for.*

"I don't ever want to be the reason again for you to compromise anything in your relationship with Jesus. I want to be with you. I always have, even when I stormed off the other day. But first, God has my heart and then you."

The most beautiful words I've ever heard.

She stepped closer and took his hands in hers…confident now, in a way she'd never been before with Randy, trusting what Jesus meant to him and that he valued her faith. They gazed into each other's eyes.

Randy cleared his throat. "I know we have a baby to think about, and I honestly want and think the baby deserves our best. If you let me, I'll go to every appointment, but before we make any quick decisions regarding the two of us, I'd like the opportunity for us to get to know each other in a different way."

Trudy took a step back. "Meaning?"

He pulled her back to him. "Meaning, as a couple who follow Jesus together , if you'll have me back, that is."

Trudy didn't have to answer with her words. She knew her eyes spoke all he needed to know.

He pulled away from her, still holding her hand. "Okay, on that note, if you are going to look at me like that, you need to do it from over there." He met her eyes. "I'm serious. The only way I want to have a relationship is to love you the way God would want me to."

A laugh sprung from Trudy's lips. With a little skip in her step, she gazed at the sky. "Thank You," she whispered.

Then, with a shove at Randy, she took off running in total abandonment, for the first time in over a week, screaming and laughing with Randy chasing after her.

Dear Reader,

IF, AFTER READING THIS STORY, you desire to say a prayer like Randy and Jodee decided to do in the story, but you're not sure how, use these words:

Father in Heaven,
I believe that Jesus is Your only Son and that He died for all of my sins. I confess I am a sinner and need a Savior in order to live eternally with You and to have a relationship with You. I ask to be cleansed from my sins and that you would come live in me. From this day on, I will follow You.
    In Jesus' name, amen.

If you prayed this prayer, or one like it, you are now a Christian. It's time to get a Bible and start reading. Also find a Bible teaching church and get to know other believers, especially those who've had a relationship with God for a while.

If you are pregnant and not sure what to do, call a local Pregnancy Resource Center or an Options 360, depending on where you're located. Or go to a local Bible teaching church and talk to a women's leader. Don't stop looking for someone to help you. There are many options available for you besides abortion. Abortion may seem the answer today, but the repercussions that come with abortion are many.

If you've experienced abortion and feel guilt, shame, detachment, or any other negative emotion from it, I personally lead healing groups for women who have experienced trauma from abortion. These groups are located all over the country. You can check with a local Pregnancy Resource Center, Options 360, your local Bible teaching church, check out my blog, or email me confidentially at **lindajreinhardt@gmail.com** to share your story. I'd love to help you find a group nearby.

If you are feeling suicidal, or hurting yourself in any way, please seek help immediately. Call **1-800-273-TALK (8255),** and you'll be connected to a counselor at a crisis center in your area anytime, 24/7. You are too valuable to me and to God, and He has a role just for you to play on this planet.

No matter what side of abortion you are on, I pray you'll receive hope in the knowledge of how much the Creator of you, and every baby in the world, loves each one of us.

LINDA J. REINHARDT

Silenced Song

LINDA J. REINHARDT

What do you do when all is swept away?
When life goes topsy-turvy in an instant?

Trudy and Randy's wedding day has finally arrived. In spite of what has happened in the past, their dreams for their future are big and filled with the hope of following God together. But then, in a moment, everything changes.

Trudy's friend, Jodee, is so grateful to finally live in safety with clean sheets, plentiful food, and the love of the Sanders' family. But she misses her dad—as abusive as he's been all her life—and longs for the day she can be reunited with her mom, who was forced to leave when she was five years old. Is it possible for her dad to change? For her parents to find happiness again?

Walk down the road with the Sister Blue Threads
and find hope, healing, and joy for your own journey.

See her on Facebook and at www.lindajreinhardt.blogspot.com
www.sisterbluethread.blogspot.com
www.oaktara.com

About the Author

Raised in beautiful Washington State, since age eight, LINDA J. REINHARDT has always enjoyed writing a poem, song, or story. She's contributed to church newsletters, a puppet ministry curriculum, and wrote/directed a Christmas play and Women's Bible Study play, and has written for Girlfriend 2 Girlfriend online magazine. Linda wrote a song performed at her wedding, which has now become a lullaby to her daughter before bed. She is now a speaker for StoneCroft Ministries and has also lead writers' workshops.

On the top of the list of favorite pastimes is spending time with family, especially husband, Ben, and miracle daughter, Sarrah.

Besides the Sister Blue Thread series, Linda has coauthored, with Sharon Bernash Smith and Rosanne Croft, the historical novel *Like a Bird Wanders*, Book One in The McLeod Family Saga, as well as the Christmas classics, *Once Upon a Christmas* and *Always Home for Christmas*, and coauthored with Sharon Bernash Smith another Christmas classic, *Starry, Starry, Christmas Night*.

Linda is a stay-at-home mom. Her favorite activity is spending time with her best friend and husband and her miracle daughter. She also enjoys sitting over a cup of coffee with her sister or a friend, sharing the details of her heart. Passionate about ministering to post-abortive women, Linda is active in leading small group Bible studies: HEART (Healing and Encouragement for Abortion Related Trauma), Time to Heal, and Life Groups. As an avid believer in the power of prayer, she has met for the last nine years with a prayer group dedicated to supporting family and friends.

You may write the author at *lindajreinhardt@gmail.com*.

See her on Facebook and at www.lindajreinhardt.blogspot.com
www.sisterbluethread.blogspot.com
www.oaktara.com